The Arbor House Library of Contemporary Americana is devoted to distinguished works of fiction and nonfiction, many of which have long been out of print. Included are a number of novels, highly praised and warmly received at the time of publication, that have secured a permanent place for themselves in the literature of twentieth century America.

GREAT CIRCLE

GREAT CIRCLE

by Conrad Aiken

Introduction by Graham Greene

ARBOR HOUSE • NEW YORK

 Published in the United States of America by Arbor House Publishing Company and in Canada by Fitzhenry & Whiteside, Ltd.

Manufactured in the United States of America

10 9 8 7 6 5 4 3 2 1

Library of Congress Cataloging in Publication Data

Aiken, Conrad, 1889-1973.
Great Circle.

(The Arbor House library of contemporary Americana)
I. Title. II. Series.
PS3501.I5G7 1985 813'.52 84-28386
ISBN 0-87795-706-1

FOR
Creighton Hill

INTRODUCTION*

by Graham Greene

The method of the novelist and the poet is more similar than is generally allowed; the same form of criticism is often applicable to both. Henry James found it possible to criticize *The Ring and the Book* as a novel, and it would be impossible to treat *A La Recherche du Temps Perdu* or *The Waves* without reference to their poetic content. So the best explanation of Mr. Aiken's subtle and important novel will be found in Mr. Eliot's essay "The Metaphysical Poets":

> . . . it appears likely that poets in our civilization, as it exists at present, must be difficult. Our civilization comprehends great variety and complexity, and this variety and complexity, playing upon a refined sensibility, must produce various and complex results. The poet must become more and more comprehensive, more allusive, more indirect, in order to force, to dislocate if necessary, language into his meaning. . . . Hence we get something which looks very much like the conceit—we get, in fact, a method curiously similar to that of the "metaphysical poets."

---

*From the *Spectator*, October 20, 1933.

As Mr. Eliot found that the way to revitalize contemporary poetry, which was dying of the romantic tradition, was to go back to earlier and unexhausted influences, so Mr. Aiken, aware of the equally blind alley into which the novel had been led (it is still possible to hear reviewers chirping in praise of the latest stillborn novel, "the true Dickensian touch"), has chosen, instead of the verbal experiments of Mr. Joyce, to cast back to the first metaphysical poets, the Jacobean dramatists.

The manner of this novel is all-important. The story is deliberately simplified. In the first section, Andrew Cather, the jealous husband, is returning home to catch his wife in the act of adultery. The second section is a series of mental pictures of childhood and reveals the influence (the boy's discovery of his mother's infidelity) that has helped to make Cather's marriage unsatisfying. In the third section, Cather, with conscious self-dramatization, unburdens himself to a psychoanalyst and works back to the early causes of his misery; and in the last section, he surrenders to the past and finds some sort of release. The four sections that complete the character might be described as thought, memory, speech, and action.

Subjective as this book is, a great gulf separates it from the horde of introspective novels that have enabled their authors to soliloquize on the particular slings and arrows offending them. These are novels of escape: delicious daydreams in which the writer is enabled to utter all his complaints and bafflements aloud, to tell any listening deity exactly where his scheme has failed. But Andrew Cather is not a mask for the author; nor is his wife's adultery a mere symbol of maladjustment. These people live as vividly as the characters of Jacobean drama, and their jealousy and guilt have the same rankness. One remembers Leontes: "It is a bawdy planet," the technical exactitude of his jealous images:

> . . . Is whispering nothing?
> Is leaning cheek to cheek? Is meeting noses?
> Kissing with inside lip?

It is this nicety of expression and intensity of feeling in his choice of images that Mr. Aiken has borrowed from the Jacobeans: "And my God, the quarrels, the late night wrangles, the three-day silences, the weepings in dark rooms face downward on dishevelled beds, the blows struck in sudden fury, the livid eyes of hate over the morning grapefruit." Or, to show again Mr. Aiken's cunning choice of imagery: "the caught breath, the changed voice, the ill-chosen word, the overdone welcome, and then the hairpins on the pillow." It is possible sometimes to name his influences. Cyril Tourneur was surely in mind when he wrote, "taught her the animal pleasures and with them gave her the great gift of horror"; and a disciple of Webster wrote this passage:

> Have you ever looked at a map of the brain? It's like those imaginary maps of Mars. Full of Arabia Desertas. Canals, seas, mountains, glaciers, extinct volcanos, or ulcers. The pockmarked moonface of the mind. And all that strange congregation of scars, that record of wounds and fissures, is what speaks and acts.

But it would be unfair to a very original novel to give the impression that it is a pastiche of the past. The mind it describes is contemporary; the solution of the problem set is contemporary; the images used are contemporary. Mr. Aiken no more imitates the Jacobeans than Dickens imitated Fielding. But finding it impossible to describe a modern consciousness by working in the accepted tradition, which has only been modified since the Victorians, and not willing to break with the past entirely as Joyce has done, he has linked the novel to the poetic tradition. This is to beat a new road; one man cannot do it, and it is to be hoped that Mr. Aiken will find fellow workers.

GREAT CIRCLE

I

WHY be in such a hurry, old fool? What good is hurry going to do you? Wrap yourself in a thick gauze of delay and confusion, like the spider; hang there, like the spider, aware of time only as the rock is aware of time; let your days be as leisurely and profound as months, serene as the blue spaces of sky between clouds; your flies will come to you in due season. Must you always be running desperately from minute to minute? Have you such an appetite for action? Have you such a passion for decisions? Must you always be snatching your hat from its peg in Shepard Hall, Shepard Street, Cambridge, Mass., and rushing out to an encounter with some one, with any one, with every one? Must you forever be listening for the telephone to ring, or the doorbell; hoping that it will be Floyd, with news of a wild party; or Celia, who wants you to dance with her at the Brunswick; or Bert, drunk, with a new poem which he is frantic to read to you; or a total stranger with the keys to hell? By all means accept the invitation to hell, should it come. It will not take you far—from Cambridge to hell is only a step; or at most a hop, skip, and jump. But now you are evading—you are dodging the issue. You do not really desire to drink with Floyd at a wild party, nor to hear Bert's poem, nor to dance hieratically with Celia in the Egyptian room; you do not even desire to go to hell with a total stranger, for, after all, Cambridge is hell enough. What you really desire is the simple finality of action, or of decision; you have yet to learn the most elementary facts about life. And what, my dear Andrew Cather, are the elementary facts of life? . . . Why, you poor idiot, you know them perfectly well, or you ought to, at thirty-eight. Permit yourself to be sifted by time, slowly,—be passive,—wait. Learn to rot gently, like the earth: it is only a natural rot that is creative. The least violence, the least hurry, the least eagerness for action or decision, the least forcing of the issue——!

Damn—blast—putrefaction.

The tendency of his thought becoming unbearable, he jumped up, snatched his ticket from the window-sill beside the Pullman chair, and bolted toward the smoking-car. A pale girl reading a magazine listlessly, her knees crossed under green satin: she looked up at him with wan evocation. She was bored, she wanted to talk to some one, her reading of the magazine was only a pretence. Too bad, darling—but I'm afraid it can't be easily enough managed. The conductor, in a chair at the end of the car, counting tickets and making notes with a pencil. The green curtains over the men's room awry, and a fleeting vision of a sad salesman, cigar in hand, who stared uncomprehendingly at the sliding Rhode Island landscape. His suitcase, cracked at one seam, stood on the black-leather settee. Poor devil—on his way back to Boston, from Bridgeport, defeated; the other salesmen had been before him. He was cursing the trees, the hills, the wind, the infrequent drops of rain that grazed the windows, leaving chains of fine beads; he was cursing them without seeing them. . . . Then the corridor between cars, swaying violently, knocking and bumping, with the little iron stepping-stone which was always to be avoided by the wary foot: it creaked and sidled. He stepped over it, smiling, and entered the smoking-car. The familiar smell of soot and tobacco-smoke, of stuffy plush and foul spittoons—garboons!—arched his nostrils: he felt more masculine, and more at home, as he chose a chair in which was a newspaper.

The Premier of France was ill. The boxing

commission of New York had disqualified Zylenski. Prices were lower on the big board, owing to the usual week-end profit-taking. The President had received a committee of boy scouts: photograph of a weary handshake. Miss Dolores Vargas, new star of the talkies, was said by her friends to be engaged to a prominent Chicago banker: photograph of Dolores waving a handkerchief from the rear platform of a train. The Maroons had beaten the Bruins in overtime. The boll-weevil was moving north, a drought in the east Sierras was causing serious alarm about the water-supply in Nevada, Oswald Morphy, well-known author, was dead, Klenkor would remove corns and bunions quickly and painlessly in two or three applications. . . . And the murderer of Jennie Despard, Providence school-teacher, had not yet been apprehended. An automobile salesman was missing from his home in Putnam, and while the police authorities declined to state that they connected this in any way with the murder, they admitted that they were anxious to ascertain his whereabouts. Mark Friedman. A married man with two children: his wife was prostrated. Best of luck to you, Mark: you'll need it. And she probably deserved it, too—though was it entirely necessary to do it with a hammer? Still, there is no accounting for tastes. The poor man might have been in a hurry.

Hurry—hurry—hurry—everything was hurrying. The train was hurrying. The world was hurrying. The landscape was hurrying. The wheels rushed blindly over the rails, over the joints, over the switches: rat-te-tat-te-tattle-te-tat-te-tump-te-tattle-te-tee. The locomotive-driver, or the fireman (it was probably the fireman), was obsessed with the panic of speed, and blew prolongedly and repeatedly on the whistle. Scarcely a minute was left unpunctuated by the moan of the whistle. Horses in twilight-brown pastures threw up their tails and galloped away for a moment, turning alarmed heads. Birds darted in clouds, zig-zag, off wires, swooped, circled, glided to rest again. The whole world, it seemed, was to be made conscious of the important hurry of the train. For wasn't this train, this Knickerbocker Limited, like everything else a consummation of æons of evolution? Wasn't it the categorical imperative? It was achieving its terrific destiny. Like the daisy in the field, or the honeysuckle, or the hummingbird, or the fungus, it was pushing its way blindly and terribly to its end. Nothing could stop it. Nothing? . . . And here was himself also,

Andrew Cather, hurrying from point to point on the earth's surface, describing his swift little arc: and all these things were a part of him, a symbol for him. Here was this eternal rush, of which the external speed was merely an index, a portent, of the internal panic. Panic! God forbid. Was it anything so bad as panic? Must one always be taking things so seriously? Must this fever in his brain be forever urging him to a passion for consummations?

Calm yourself, old fool. Survey this row of dead faces opposite you: these hard business men, these watchers of ticker-tape, these casters of balances, these signers of important letters and foreclosers of mortgages. Do they allow themselves to be rushed into decisions? Do they walk at midnight, hatless, in a rain, plopping through puddles, because of a secret anguish in the heart? When their offices are closed for the day, and the stenographers are gone, and everything is quiet, do they stretch themselves on the floor in paroxysms of weeping? Absurd. They have no hearts. Or if they have, they have learned the secret of the granite: they are silent, they wait, they fall instinctively into the slow rhythm of the stars, everything at last comes to them. But you, you poor idiot, you simulacrum of a soul

—good God, what a fool you are. Here you go, outstripping with speed of mind the speed of this train. You are already in Cambridge, you are already noiselessly letting yourself into your flat in Shepard Street, you are already standing, just inside the door, and listening to hear if your excellent wife Bertha is at home. Not a sound—not a whisper—not the creak of a board. You cast a furtive look at the chairs in the hall: what is it that you are expecting, or even almost hoping, to see? A hat? A man's hat? No, you avert your eyes from the thought. You had not really expected this. But you are curious, just the same, and that is why you are here, three days before she had expected you. It is like a melodrama. But that has nothing to do with it. If life chooses to imitate a cheap melodrama, why then it is obvious enough that you have to behave like a character in a melodrama—a ridiculous hero with a permanent expression of long-suffering, or a villain with violent mustaches. And so you are acting the part: you are stealthy, you walk swiftly and softly on the balls of your feet, you half hold your breath as you approach the sitting-room, you crane your neck at an unnatural angle in your endeavour to reassure yourself that there is indeed no one there. . . . But supposing there *should* be some one? Ah. This is what you really want. You really want to find some one there. Do not deny it—do not pretend. You are deliberately seeking a catastrophe—you are yourself in the act of creating a disaster. You want to see your life violated, broken in two, your precious secrecy exposed in a yellow light of pure horror. Could you not have avoided this? Could you not have ignored Fred's letter? My dear Andy: it's none of my business, perhaps, and probably you'll be the last to thank me; that's always what happens, but I wouldn't be doing my duty to you as a friend if I didn't write to tell you— Oh, Christ. Why read it again? Why remember it? Why act upon it? Why not get off at Providence and return to New York, precisely as if it were a return to sanity? It was growing dark, they were crossing a river, a row of lights sped across rain-sodden ice, a lamp was lifted in a farmhouse window. *Whoooo—whooooo*—the demon fireman blew his whistle again, prolongedly, nostalgically, into the gathering gloom, rain began pattering again on the train-roof and grazingly along the windows, came and went in flaws of needles. My dear Andy, it's none of my business. My dear Andy, it's none of my business. But whose business was it, then? Was it

Tom's? Was it Bertha's? Was it God's? Perhaps it was nothing at all. Perhaps they were merely playing duets. Side by side on the long mahogany bench, leaning together, leaning apart, Tom the bass and Bertha the treble, the Haydn Surprise, the Drum-roll Symphony, his foot on the pedal, her hand on the page. Shall we take that again? We'll start at G in the second bar. Haydn duet, hide and do it. The clock was ticking, the curtains were drawn. Shepard Street was outside in the rain, everything was cosy, everything was peaceful, New York was far away, merest of whispers in the southwest, and Andy—what was Andy? A ghost behind the music, a shadow beside the hearth, an echo in the corridor. He was an old raincoat in the cupboard, a towel in the bathroom, a napkin ring in the sideboard, a name on the letter-box. He was a handful of bills on the hall table, a catalogue of second-hand books, a pair of rusty skates in an old trunk. And the cocktail shaker on the Japanese tray, the shaker that leaked, Tom holding it muffled in a handkerchief, shaking it over the hearth while he laughed—come on, Andy, let's have another round—the night is young—let's get well oiled and go and see Dynamite Gus—come on, Bertha; come on, Andy—I'll pay for the taxi—we'll have some arak at the Greek's, and ringside seats at the Garden. Have you read the *Childermass?* Let's experiment with the Kieseritzky gambit, or the fianchetto. The new record of the "Love of the Three Oranges." Let's walk to Fresh Pond in the rain, visit the pumping-station, or drop a tear on the tomb of Henry James. Plymouth for the weekend. Chocorua. A game of poker at the new bookshop. Come on, Bertha, come on, Andy, I'm back from a faculty meeting and I want to raise hell. Tea at 3.30. Meeting at 4. The committee appointed to prepare a minute on the life and services of the late John Jacob Morrison, Professor of English, *Emeritus,* will present the minute to the faculty. Recommendations from the administrative board for changes in the Regulations for Students in Harvard College, of which the most important is that section 14 be amended as follows. Let's discuss methods of suicide. Potassium cyanide. Tell Bertha you're spending the night with me, and we'll take Louise and Molly to Concord. Treason! Treason! The treason spoke innocently through the Haydn, rose softly and guilelessly under the fingers of Tom, under the onyx signet ring, under his long brown hands, the wrists held high and arched, under the wedding ring on Bertha's fourth finger, on whose inner surface was a fine incised inscription. Treason chimed with the chiming clock, a present from Tom, wreathed itself in a water-colour of nasturtiums, shone softly on the opened score from a shaded lamp. Where is Andy? Andy's in New York, said the bass. Come on, Bertha——

This must stop, this turmoil must stop. The Maroons had beaten the Bruins in overtime. The Prince of Wales had been thrown by his horse. Beautiful Blonde Sues Millionaire Scion for Heart Balm. American Womanhood Purest in World, says Bishop. Tax Scandal Shocks Senate. Rain will be followed by snow. Unseasonable warmth soon to end. Blizzards in far West, Denver under three feet of snow, villages in Rockies cut off from the world. Krazy Kat Is On His Way. Says you? Says me. Utilities Lower on Curb. Love Baron Leaves Hollywood. Oh, yeah?

—You can't teach 'em a thing.

—You can teach 'em, but they won't learn.

—They don't *want* to learn.

—Believe me, I'm through.

—God! and those hotels.

—Never again for me, no sir.

—Say, porter, what about a cigar.

Pack of cards, informative bid, clubs, diamonds, pass. Amherst Quintet Invades Crimson Territory Tonight. Lapp Life Studied in Racial Investigation. The Lapps are a nervous class of people and would be termed neurasthenics . . . where a stick was whacked against the side of a tent, the inhabitants fainted from fright . . .

God's Providence is our inheritance. One hour to Boston. Once more the train gathered speed, fled through dwindling suburbs into the night, whistled for crossings, devoured immense spaces of darkness, clattered past interminable strings of freight-cars on a siding, swooped over bridges, lurched, steadied, whistled again and again. Small stations whirled past, dimly lighted, their wooden platforms glistening with rain, their names telescoped with speed. Hurry—hurry—hurry—everything was hurrying, the world was hurrying, the night was hurrying. The bells for a crossing chattered madly ahead, rose to a higher note, fell away behind to a sad minor murmur, were lost. He closed his eyes. The back of his hand rested against the cold glass of the window, vibrating; smoke stung his nostrils; long lights flew beside him in bright parallels; this was Andrew Cather. Calm yourself, you idiot—pull yourself together—you must regain control. Think of New York, the stars in the Grand Central Station, the girl who dropped her ticket at the gate, blushing as she stooped to pick it up, looking over her shoulder. Think of the fern-fringed fountain in the lunchroom at the hotel, old Rodman scratching his beard with a pencil while he figured the cost of the textbook, the marble clock, the rows of brass keys behind the desk. Mr. Cather, please—Number 218—Mr. Cather, please. Fred's letter. My dear Andy, it's none of my business. It's none of my business. Think of the blocks of ice in the urinals, the disinfected sweetness of the telephone booths, the silent corridors of plush, the stealthy chambermaids with jingling keyrings. Drive down Broadway at night, as if flying into the heart of a vast fiery opal. Take the express and change to a local at 14th Street. Climb the dirty stairs to the elevated, reading all the enamelled advertisements, clacking through the heavy turnstile with a nickel.

—What I mean is——

—Oh, sure——

—. . . kind of a turbine principle——

—. . . on the level, yes——

Wah-wah-wah-wah—the voices all rose at once against the clamour of the train through a deep cutting. It's none of my business—Oh, of course not. But it was a mere disinterested love of music, that was all. Companionship. Years and years of it. Just like a brother. Come on, Andy—come on, Bertha—we're going to Revere Beach, we'll have a drunken battle with marshmallows on the boardwalk, we'll find the monkey in the cage, we'll raise a little polite hell. He waved the gin-bottle over his head, gave a whoop, clutched Bertha, and began dancing along the hall. Bertha screeched, slapped her hands against his chest, pulled his ears. A harmless lark, they had so many tastes in common, like brother and sister. Why, for years Tom and Bertha hadn't missed a night at the Sanders Theatre concerts. No indeed. How they loved Haydn! How they adored Bach! What about a little Brandenburg tonight? and a little ravioli to begin with? what about the North End? what about the fortune teller? Bertha's eyes were on Tom while the dark lady studied her palm. What was the look in her eyes which had so struck him at the time? Nothing. Sense of change, sense of time, the flowing away of all things, cloud-shadows on falling leaves. Who was Bertha? Bertha, to begin with, then Bertha plus one, Bertha plus two, Bertha plus three: never the same again. The sudden kiss in Craigie Street, the laugh, the shock, the readjustment to terrific wonder, the wedding, the honeymoon, and then the amazing flight of years and places, the dance of rooms, the dance of apartments, the dance of houses, the chorus of changing voices and faces. And now, after ten years, it was Bertha plus four, Bertha with Tom, Bertha with music, her arms grown heavier at the shoulders, her clothes more careless, fond of cocktail parties and dances, golf at Belmont, lunch with the Sewing Circle. Well, by God, if it was true—! Treason. Horror. He jumped to his feet, flung down the paper on the seat, and hurried forward. Pocahontas. The passengers were beginning to be restless, old ladies were waking up, the porter was gathering the bags from their reluctant owners and carrying them to the vestibule. Swaying, he touched the green velvet back of a chair, then another, then a third. A long row of lights fled past the windows, illuminated houses rushed at them and rushed away again, a cement wall converged on them perilously, whipped a series of swift column-shadows at them, and was gone. Cordaville? One of the Newtons? Auburndale? The houses closed in on them, their path was being narrowed, one deserted station succeeded another. He sat down, put his feet on his suitcase, closed his eyes, and listened to the delicate sound of the rain on the roof and windows, which could be heard as a secret accompaniment to the train's violent storming of suburb after suburb. The Harvard Club, first—cocktails and dinner at the Harvard Club, a little leisure, a little peace, time to pull himself together, to muster the phrases, the attitudes. What attitudes? A genial bursting in, gay homecoming, followed by instant surprise? Bewilderment? An entrance quiet and suspicious? Announced beforehand by the bell from below? Unannounced? Suppose they were at the piano. Ah yes. Then the easy comradely smile. But why are you home so soon? Why, indeed. But suppose, on the other hand—! And the phrases. Hello, darling—are you there, darling? Or perhaps it had better be in the plural. Idiot! What you need is a few drinks at the club—that will put you right, don't worry, wait. Relax. Believe in God and the sanctity of marriage, not to mention the holiness of friendship. Have faith in Massachusetts and the Pilgrim Fathers. How do you do, Tom; hello, Bertha—what a fortunate coincidence to find you together—did Gieseking play on Thursday? Is there any ice in the ice-box? Wonderfully mild weather for the time of year, isn't it? But the papers say the rain will turn to snow before morning. Don't stop playing—do go on—shall I turn the pages for you—or the sheets? Have I come to the right place? Is this Shepard Hall, Shepard Street, Cambridge, Massachusetts? Or was it two other fellows? Excuse me for intruding. I must have made a mistake. Haven't we met before somewhere?—your face is very familiar—too damned familiar, if you ask me—and now let's all join hands and have a good laugh together. But on the other hand—? No, no, no, no, no. Not. Never. Couldn't. Not that! This is no place for old-fashioned melodrama, we don't do such things in Cambridge, no indeed. There are no beds in Cambridge—how could we be so vulgar? My dear Tom, it's none of my business, I'll be going, just dropped in to see how you two lovebirds were getting on; hope everything is going swimmingly, that's fine, O. K., see you in hell one of these days, good-bye, good luck, God bless you, send in the bill. We aim to please. By the great love I bore you—Christ. Bores me, the sum.

With long thrusts, with smooth and powerful lunges of speed, they overtook another train, measured bright window against bright window, drew abreast of statuesque lethargic passenger after passenger, newspapers, hats, hands lifted or falling, swaying coats, listless inquiring eyes, men, women, girls, a final clack, and gone. The porter bent deprecatingly with his whisk, he rose and followed him, fishing in his pocket for a quarter, feeling for the right size, the milled edge.

—You all gettin' off Back Bay, boss?

—Yes, I'll take my bag myself.

—All right, boss.

The pale girl in green satin passed him, humming, holding her thin arms away from her thin swaying body for balance, the white hands a little lifted, self-conscious. Too bad, darling—where have you been all my life? If only you had introduced yourself more efficiently, perhaps at the ticket gate, or last night, or last year, things might have been very different. We'd now be like an old married couple. What secrets left? None. Do you perspire freely? Snore? Chew gum? Sing in your bath? Do you scratch the mole on your left clavicle every night till it bleeds? Cascara or castor oil? And exactly how good a liar are you? Liars need good memories. Yes, indeed. Don't forget how you were caught in that little fib about Mehitabel Mockingbird and the dead pansy, or that other one about Methuselah and his sponge-bag. Ah ha! We know all about it. And my God, the quarrels, the late night wrangles, the three-day silences, the weepings in dark rooms face downward on dishevelled beds, the blows struck in sudden fury, the livid eyes of hate over the morning grapefruit! And lying beside each other for sleepless hours at night, the hands clenched, the eyes wide open but unseeing, eyeless at Gaza, while the digestion of each in turn interrupts the dramatic silence with obscene squeals and snickers. Love? after all that? My dear woman, pull yourself together. Go your way, take your little smells and snoops to another station, send your laundry to the North Pole, order a sandalwood coffin at Woolworth's. . . . Marriage. In Cambridge there shall be neither giving nor taking in marriage, but all shall be as one sex, and that shall be without which is without, only the dead moon will dare to maculate the red macula. My dear Andy——

He put on his hat, his heart was beating, he felt a curious constriction in his throat, as if speaking would be difficult, his voice somehow misplaced. Think, you idiot! Think—don't feel. Be calm. Cast a sure and slow balance of the figures in the situation, weigh the years one with another, measure each room, each wall, against the last. Why, to be sure, the sitting-room in the Shepard Hall apartment was smaller, much smaller, than the lounge at the Harvard Club, and there was no bar beneath it, nor was there a bison's head above the fireplace, nor a pair of brass shells from the Somme. There were no palm trees in it, as in the lobby of the Touraine, not even a news-stand behind which one could take shelter: and as for the natatorium, why, the poor fool of an architect had left that out entirely. Just the same, they were getting on swimmingly. Come on, Andy, come on, Bertha, come on in, the water's fine. Let's walk down to the Square and get a cup of coffee; let's go down and skate on the Common; let's see what there is at the movies and make loud remarks about the hero. But it was all so innocent, so natural and boylike, so good-natured, so ringed about with brassy and wholesome laughter, how could one suspect anything wrong? . . . Patience. Run the eye slowly along the edge of the chair back, note the reflected lamp in the dark lustrousness of the window-pane, and another station passing; listen to the mournful rain-quenched cry of the whistle, cut off abruptly by a bridge, released again, silent. The train began shuddering and slowing, shuddering and slowing, lurched, glided, lurched again, and then quietly, evenly, with rhythmic soft hisses of steam which fogged the windows, no longer like a train, but like a ship on even keel in quiet waters, slid past slowing lights, and stopped with a last prolonged profound sigh.

—Back Bay . . . Back Bay.

—Back Bay.

—Back Bay.

Let Rome in Tiber melt, and the wide arch of the rang'd empire fall. Here is my—station. A taxi, please. And now the solid rain-drenched antipathy of Boston, the buildings in Copley Square all aloof and black, Trinity Church withdrawn and cowled in rain like a weeping nun, the Library staring down from an immense height with Florentine hauteur—what was this change, this difference, this withdrawal of friendliness? It was a new and hostile city. The people were foreigners, the wet streets were menacing, the bare trees brooded like skeletons over Commonwealth Avenue. We knew you, Andy. We know you not. We knew you, Andy. We know you not. Was this the guy that went to New York with bells on and now returns with horns? Give him a hand, boys, give the little fellow a great big hand. Drop a twig on him or a dead leaf, or maybe a brick. That's the guy—that little feller in the Armstrong taxi, with the text of a textbook on Spanish literature in his suitcase. *Tu pupila es azul. Y quando lloras*— What was that dirty crack? No more of that. Cold shoulder him, boys—it's nothing but *El Diablo Mundo*. The very spittin' image with number eight shoes, a Harvard Coop hat, and deformed toenails. Cut him dead. What he's got he deserves. He was askin' for it. Give him the snake's eye, Fairfield Street, Gloucester Street, Hereford Street, Massachusetts Avenue—! He's made his bed, let his friend lie in it. Wot's de flower-bed between friends? Begonia. Look how nervous he is. He's sticking his finger down his collar for no good reason. Not a thought to his navel. Say, if he had to pay the taxi by the heartbeat! Call the taxicologist, and we'll have him stuffed. To the Peabody Museum with him, *quam celerrime,* we'll show him up. Give him a birthday present. Ha! For Christ and the Church.

Horror preceded him into the Harvard Club, but evaded him among these friendly walls and stained-plaster Corinthian columns. Even here the familiar, the warm, the assuring, eyed him aslant, sneered when he turned his back. My dear Andy, it's none of our business, but—! And what should stare him in the face but a row of telephone booths, five of them numbered, the sixth a pay-station. A Greek Chorus. Stationary chorus. Call her up,

Andy—give the poor girl a chance. Our ears are in Shepard Street. Warn her! Tell her you're coming home after dinner! Tell her to ask Tom in for a drink! Make it easy for her, leave it all in darkness, in subterfuge, in evasion, in the hell of the forever unknown. Hello, darling! Is that you, chuck? This is Andy. Yes, Andy—your premature Andy, back from the bright lights, back from the unearthly paradise, wizened little Tithonus returned from false heaven. But we won't go into that, no, we'll talk of something else. I meant nothing by it. Just my foolish little joke, that was all. Make the bed up, hang clean towels in the bathroom, run to the corner fruitstore for another can of grapefruit juice, and start the cocktails. . . . No, impossible. This must not be evaded—whatever the issue, the situation must first of all be faced. No warnings, no signal, not even an inquiry at Tom's apartment to find out if he were absent—in a melodrama one must above all be melodramatic. If later one prefers to turn it into a farce——

And who should be standing at the bar, eating little-neck clams as usual, but Jitter Peabody, that ruined scion of a noble race, half-shot too as always, leaning with supercilious languor against the bar, his long horse-face flushed with gin, his drooping mustache dripping clam-juice on to his weak chin.

—Hello, One-eye!

—Mr. Peabody, I presume?

—You do presume.

—I suppose you wouldn't join me in a little mild elbow-lifting? The better the deed, the better the day.

—No, I've sworn off till I finish these sea-fruits.

—Tom, you might take this flask, and empty it, and make as much old-fashioned out of it as it'll make. And you might get me a dozen of these little pink little-necks. And two glasses.

—Good evening, Mr. Cather—yes, sir. That'll go quite a little ways.

—What've you been doing, Jitter?

—None of your damned business.

—That's the *second* time I've heard that today. Only the other fellow was politer.

—That must have been in New York—couldn't have been in Boston.

—How did you guess it?

—I was in the train with you.

—The hell you say! Why the hell didn't you tell me?

—I saw you, but I was asleep at the time. Only just waked up.

—Ah, I see. So you were in New York on business.

—Shhhhhh. Very private. I went down on the midnight and came back this afternoon.

—Alone?

—Legally speaking. I'd have stayed, but my fiancée expects me to dinner.

—Thanks, Tom. Come on, Jitter. I'm thirsty and heartbroken.

—What *you* need—! You damned walking textbook.

—We won't go into that.

—No, you wouldn't.

—Abstinence makes the heart grow fonder.

This turmoil must stop, and Jitter would help to stop it. Time out. Time out for a little peace, a little leisure, a little cool unhurried reflection, for a calm re-shuffling of the pack of marked cards which is the mind. In the presence of a person so disorganized, it was easier oneself to become righteously or recognizably organized: one felt again vividly the numbered inches between the hat and the shoe. Think, you idiot! Think, don't feel! Your brain depends upon it, the brief roman candle's parabola of your sanity. Follow green arrow for shuttle train to Grand Central. Follow red arrow for trail to bottom of Grand Canyon. If one had been cornuted, was a chiropodist the thing? Or must one be chiropracted? Kindly remove the imaginary, but all too palpable, horns. A present from my best friend. Kind of him, but so inconvenient when one wears a hat, unless one is a horse. Let us order a striped calico bonnet, with holes for the ears.

—And so, Jitter, you've been spying on the Vincent Club again.

—Who told you?

—I won't have any soup—I'll begin with the fish.

—So will I.

—But just why you should have gone to all that trouble, to see Boston's Best Bosomless Beacon Street and Back Bay Beauties clad only in their canvas shifts, I can't imagine.

—My dear One-eye, that's only the half of it.

—What was the other half—the better, I hope.

—You're vulgar. You always were. . . .

A telephone was ringing. Bertha? University O!O!O! Put the salt neatly on the edge of your plate, my boy. Or fling it over your shoulder. An old Spanish custom, to avert the evil eye. The glass eye was the root of all evil. Green glass eyes on a plush tray—are you washed in the blood of the Lamb? *Tu pupila es azul.* And when you cry, you cry with two eye-sockets, but one eye. How much had this affected Bertha? And that heartless nickname! Jesus. It was no wonder. She had probably heard of him as One-eye Cather long before she had met him. With sympathy? Pathos? Horror? Or more likely a mixture of pity and disgust. Poor fellow—he can't judge distances. Have you heard how he lost it? Such a shame.

—Drink up, Jitter—there's another round.

—Say, what's come over you? . . . anyway.

—Well, what do you mean by that?

Fool. You will now be accused of unnecessary sobriety.

—Aren't you drinking a little too much for one of your habits?

—Don't make me laugh.

Jitter pulled his mustaches mournfully, slouched back in his chair, narrowed his long low-lidded eyes.

—You always *were* a failure.

—Says you?

—Even your talk is a fake.

—One puts the fake in one's windows.

—Make it singular.

—Window.

—Well, to hell with you anyway.

—Keep the change.

But there was no clock in this room. Time, in this room, was not recognized, was excluded, relegated to the more conscious upper floors, where there was no bar. Singular foresight, for which perhaps one ought to be grateful. Where were they now? Dining at the Commander? At the Greek's? Oysters, followed by broiled live lobster, or chicken *pilaf*, or chicken livers *en brochette?* Sitting opposite each other, with their feet together on the table-rung, or side by side in the leather seat in a booth? And where were his hands in that case? The little hard nodule of her garter-clasp, felt through the skirt. Unprotesting. . . . Or in the kitchen at Shepard Hall, side by side beside the stove, a dishcloth hung over his arm, Tom the waiter and Bertha the cook—scrambled eggs or shrimp *soufflé*.

—What's wrong with you, anyway? Jitter was saying. I don't think I ever quite made you out. I don't think I ever really liked you, even at school. Something fishy about you. Too damned secretive. God knows you can talk the hair off a dog's back; you can talk all right, but, Christ, what a life you lead. Now look at me, you think I'm a drunken rotter, and so I am, and I don't give a damn, I've done everything from digging ditches to laying rails or busting bronchos, I can't keep a job, every one thinks I'm just a good-for-nothing shite. That's all right, the point is I'm intelligent and I live my life the way I *want* to live it, family and conventions can go to hell. I'm honest. But you, One-eye, I think you're *yellow*—you're even afraid of a whore! Good God, I'll never forget that night when you spent the night at my place and sat there shivering in a blanket when I brought that bitch in at two in the morning to talk to you. Anybody'd have thought you were trying to talk so some God-damned duchess. And that wife of yours—where in the name of God did you ever pick *her* up! Just the sort of damned Brattle Street lemon you *would* pick out . . .

—Thanks for the battalion of compliments. No defence. I'm both yellow and secretive—that's the fate, my boy, of the self-conscious. Also manic depressive. Advance one day, retreat the next.

Jitter's drunken gaze, slit-eyed, roved about the room indifferently, as if delighting in nothing it saw, least of all in his vis-à-vis. His collar was dirty, his necktie was skewed to one side, his skeleton fingers were yellow with cigarette smoke. When he talked, it was as if to himself—his diction beautiful, clear, caressing, but the voice monotonous and whining, low-pitched, as if the effort, for one so picturesquely exhausted, were almost insupportable.

—Oh don't talk to me about psychology. I know all that stuff—I've lived it all—what do you know about it? You read books and think you know a lot, but I'd like to see you break a horse, or a woman, for that matter. I know you can sling words better than I can, but where the hell has it ever got you? Here you are writing rotten little textbooks and tutoring for a living and going to your damned little teas—what kind of a life is that.

But there was no clock in this room, this room which had once been the billiard-room, this room where so many evenings had been spent in playing cowboy pool with Tom, and which now, decorated with paris-green Audubon prints of precise birds in fantastic landscapes, had become grill-room and bar. There was no clock, the time seemed as vague as Jitter's wandering melancholy monologue, full of changes and pauses, ticking and then resting, but with this difference, that after every rest, every pause, it resumed its course more heavily, more menacingly, more swiftly, the tick becoming louder and more insistent, the bloodstream in the artery threatening with every beat of the pulse to breach its walls. It was as if, also, this stream more and more persistently and *meanly* were choosing and following an inimical direction, like a snake with its eyes on the heart, which nothing could deflect or dissuade. Pressingly and insinuatingly it encroached; forgotten or ignored for a moment, when next looked at it would be a little nearer, a little more vivid, a little brighter, a little more alert. To be in a hurry, but not to be able to hurry—the familiar nightmare sensation, of course, that appalling slow-motion, languid agony, with which one tries to escape the vague claw of the unknown. On the train it had been better, for there one had at least had the satisfaction of being immersed in speed, of rushing forward from one place to another; but even in the train he had felt at moments an almost overwhelming desire to get out and *run,* as if this more primitive effort might somehow be more effective. Hurry—hurry—hurry—the world was hurrying, the night was hurrying, and nevertheless here was this exasperating slow counterpoint of conversation, this idiotic talk, this exchange of profoundly uncandid candours, each lying laboriously and laconically to the other. And so odd to be perfectly indifferent to Jitter's drunken and intentionally injurious remarks! What would Jitter make of that? An added yellowness, no doubt. Yes, and then no, he said, no, and then yes, finding that Jitter had reached a point at which replies were immaterial to him. He was talking about the actress to whom he was engaged, describing her, reporting fragments of her vaudeville slang, what she had done in Paris, how they managed to sleep together on the steamer. My dear Andy, it's none of my business—but suppose it all turned out to be nothing, a delusion? No. It wasn't a delusion. There had been that look of Bertha's at the fortune-teller's, that strange, deep, secret look, that appeal as to the person most intimately known and liked. And the episode at the breakfast-table, when, breaking a lifelong habit of Cantabrigian modesty, not to say prudishness, Bertha had come to the table in her pyjamas, very self-conscious and flushed and so obviously pleased by Tom's surprise. Was this the way all things ended? Was it inevitable? If not Tom, would it have been another? And precisely how much did it matter? Damn. Blast. Putrefaction. A deep wound opened in his heart. A gulf fell through him, dividing all things, he held hard to the edge of the oak table, trembling.

—She sounds very gay.

—What do I care what you think she sounds like?

—Oh, I don't give a damn about her.

—She wouldn't about you.

—That doesn't worry me, either. I've got enough cancers of my own. My dear Jitter, I'm lousy with them. I'm falling to pieces . . .

—And I'm supposed to be dining with her.

—Good beginning.

—It will probably end like the others. What the hell.

Smiling cynically, mysteriously, he rose without reply to this obviously quite-true prediction, and walked rapidly past the bar, across the hall, and into the locker-room which smelt of sour male sweat. This is what we smell like. Would a woman enjoy this quintessence? He took the jug and tin funnel from his locker, refilled his silver flask, and then stood for a moment with his forehead against the reticulated ironwork. Time. Nine o'clock. If a taxi to Harvard Square, driving slowly, and then on foot across the Common—the air would clear his head, prepare him for the scene—give him the necessary poise.

But would it be late enough? Would they have—? Yes, at this stage, they would. Their time was still precious.

—Harvard Square, please—and make it slow.

—Slow, yes, sir, and which way would you like to go?

—Across the Harvard Bridge, and along Memorial Drive.

—Yes, sir.

A surprise: the bridge was jammed with cars: something must have happened. From curb to curb they were packed, their black tops glistening with rain. Newcomers, joining the slowly moving mass, honked, hooted, skirled their klaxons, yipped and snarled; but farther on, half way across the bridge, with its double row of lights, beautifully arched into the night, a string of brilliantly lit street-cars marooned among them, the mass of sedans and taxis seemed to be motionless and silent.

The driver slid back a glass panel.

—This looks like a long job. Will I go the other way?

—No, go ahead, plenty of time.

The motor humming, the clutch engaging and disengaging, they crept forward, weaving a slow passageway among the creeping vehicles. All faces were turned forward, intent, curious, artificially bright over dashboard lights, like illuminated death-masks. A hand, holding a cigar, hung out of a window, was held sparkling for a moment in the beam of a searchlight, waved lazily, and withdrew. People sitting upright in back seats, hatted and cloaked, motionless as waxwork specimens, their hands on the window ledges or crossed on their knees. And as they advanced, as they crossed the drawbridge, passed the first of the street-cars, the silence deepened, grew ominous, began to speak a meaning into which all this procession was irresistibly drawn. They were moving into the orbit of something more powerful than themselves—their own purposes, aims, directions, ideas, were suffering a fascinated change—they could no longer go at what speed they liked, or where they liked, but moved, like the lemmings, to the dark sea of their unknown desire. Ahead, to the left, the lights of Riverbank Court, high up, lightly shrouded through the fine rain, appeared to be looking downward at something, as if the dark focus of all this attention were somewhere below them.

—Smash-up, looks like, said the driver.

—It does.

And why not, in the name of God? We

specialize in smash-ups. If there's anything we dearly love, it's a nice little smash-up. We serve them hourly. And what more appropriate than this bridge, where Longfellow had once octosyllabically sentimentalized, and he himself, Andrew Cather, One-eye Cather, had won a bet of twenty-five cents by walking from Cambridge to Boston on the outside of the railing? X marks the spot. And here, too, the driver of the ice-wagon, deep in thought on a summer's day, had suddenly been catapulted off his high perch, over this same railing, twenty feet down with his cigarette still in his mouth, and drowned. Perfect example of the inscrutability of fate. Because the driver of the car behind the ice-wagon had got dust in his eye—! But now the stream of cars was moving a little more quickly—the string of bright street-cars had drawn ahead and crossed Memorial Drive—the policeman in his little tower could be seen frantically waving a white-gloved hand—and as at last the taxi swung to the left he saw the dark police-boat on the dark rain-stilled water, with a solitary lantern in the bow, and two dark figures leaning waterward over the stern. Ah! they were dragging. Somebody was down there, somebody who this morning had had an egg for breakfast, and a cup of coffee, was down there, aimlessly drifting, his mouth wide open and his hands clenched.

—Draw up where you can, and we'll have a look at this.

—Yes, sir.

On foot, they dodged through the creeping parade of cars and joined the silent crowd at the water's edge, three policemen stood on the float. The police-boat, which had gone slowly upstream and turned, was now slowly coming back, and it could be seen that the two men in the stern held ropes.

—Who was it?

—An old man.

—They ain't sure.

—Somebody saw him step off the float at six o'clock. They been dragging three hours.

—Well, *he* don't have to worry about his income tax.

The crowd was hushed, all the faces stared downward at the water. The boat turned once more, moved out a little toward midstream, became invisible save for the lantern. The *put-put* of the exhaust came slowly and intermittently through the night.

—It'll take them all night. Let's get going.

—Hell of a job for a night like this.

In the taxi again, he lit a cigarette, and noticed that his hands were trembling. Good

God, was this a symbol, a kind of warning? Cling to life, you poor bastard—have your eggs and coffee for breakfast—and be damned glad you're alive. Is it you down there, with your mouth open? Have you lost your felt hat? Has your watch stopped? Are you cold? What did you do with your money, and the incriminating letter in your pocket? Did you tell the Chinese laundry that they needn't bother to finish ironing your blue shirt? Did you write to Deirdre in Pawtucket and tell her you wouldn't be home for the week-end? Did you did you did you did you? And if not, why not? And what did you want to die for anyway? Was it love or was it money? Speculation leads to peculation. The rain quickened on the taxi roof, he reached under his raincoat for the flask, unscrewed the silver stopper, and took a drink, a burning little gush of raw juniper-tasting gin, another, a third. No use trying to be sober. The scene would require reckless hilarity, a certain amount of blindness and denseness. Cheerfulness. No good being too sensitive. Let the imagination loose, let it run, let it fly. Give it a couple of alcoholic wings. What ho, Bertha, what ho, Tom, I'm home again with a boxing-glove. I had a dozen little-necks with Jitter Peabody, and a flock of cocktails, and then, only pausing for three hours on the Harvard Bridge, I drowned myself, hat in hand. I am still there, lodged in the deep water against one of the piers, bowing, hat in hand, my mouth open in the act of saying Good evening, Madam. Do you see the water that drips from my shoes? The Charles River, my dears: I am newly come from the dead. This is my bright little *doppelgänger,* my alter ego, who stands before you and screeches with laughter at finding you thus together. Did you both brush your teeth before you went to bed, like good little children? Papa spank. Naughty naughty. You should never, *never* go to bed without first brushing the teeth. There's a new toothbrush with black bristles, I especially recommend it for smartness, particularly in cases of mourning. So tactful. Like that story of the young woman in the Paris drug-store—*Ah oui, Madame, quelle delicatesse!* Madame is a widow! You remember? Tom? Bertha? So run along now and do it and after that I'll tell you both a nice little bedtime story and you can go to bed again, with visions of sugar-plums dancing in your little heads, and in the morning I'll be Santa Claus and bring you your breakfast in bed. Madam will have a nice little grapefruit? Or a pruin? A few wild oats and cream? My dear Andy——

And this was that street. Yes, that street. Where, a month ago, after the first rumour, after the first quarrel, the first quarrel about the first rumour, he had walked blindly in the snow, under that very arc-lamp, along this path, past the power-station, the power-station where years and years ago there had been a little tank swarming with turtles and alligators and gold fish. Here was the agony in the garden, the public garden. Why must one do such things? Why must one be hurt? Why need one so helplessly surrender? Better have a drink, old fellow. A few minutes more and the taxi will have reached Harvard Square, and there'll be no chance, unless you prefer to tilt your flask in the rain-dark Common. He lifted and tipped the silver flask, the fiery trickle sluiced his tongue, ran down under his tongue against his teeth, burned the gums, burned the uvula, streaked the throat with flame. A month ago—he had been dead, and then alive again, and was now again dying. It was here that the first forsythia bushes would light their little yellow lights a few weeks hence, here that the young couples would lie on the scented grass in the early summer, the children playing at the water's edge, where now were broken slabs of scabby ice. Crowds after the football games. Crews practising in the spring, the coxswains barking through megaphones, the canoes, the motor-launches. And here once with Bertha—under the birch trees beyond the Newell boat-house—at midnight, looking across the velvet darkness of the river towards the lights— "No—" she had said—"no —no—no." And "Yes—" he had answered, "yes—yes—yes." The bells, the pleas of water, the slow sleepy seethe of new leaves, the beginning of the world, the quiet beginning. Oh, God, that do'st with tooth-picks take the world apart and gladly break the mechanism of the spring for school-boy glee in such a thing!

—Turn *right* here—up Plympton Street.

—Yes, sir, I always *do* miss that turn.

He leaned forward, staring, watched the flight of buildings, wet poles and trees, an empty yard with a forlorn and ruined car standing in gleaming mud, broken palings of a white fence, Mount Auburn Street, the Lampoon building. Here with a snowshoe once. The polychrome marble of the basement floor. The green lampshade full of Mib's homemade punch. Dooley, with a roller-towel round his neck, "pully-hauling down the bay." And the midnight operas, with Tom at the piano, the screams of bumwad, bumwad, Heeney's Palace of Pleasure, falling down the thickly carpeted stairs, out of the shower-bath, with a cake of soap in his hand——

Bumwad, bumwad, bumwad, bumwad. The first step towards Haydn, and a more refined appreciation of music. Oh, yes! Oh, yes, indeed.

—All right—stop here.

Enter, to grow in wisdom.

A dollar, ten cents for the tip.

And now to take the rain on the chin, and the world on the heart. The solar knockout. Through the Yard? Through the Square? But Tao is round and square by turns, and perfectly indifferent to its participant particles: what does it matter: salute the cheerful lights of the Square: walk under them: bathe in the lamp-lit perpendiculars of the rain: count the drug-stores: the restaurants: the dealers in athletic goods: the skates in the windows: the fur-lined gloves and neckties. In that lighted room up there, as a freshman, I carved my initials on the window-sill, meanwhile saying over and over to myself, *"tu pupila es azul, y quando lloras—"* I who had never wept, to whom tears were unknown, whose little griefs were the merest trifling creak of growing wood. Christ. How things change. And here, all of a sudden, it was almost half-past nine, a hundred years later, and gray hairs beginning to show above his ears, rain falling on a row of yellow taxis beside the subway entrance, and now a deep swirling bell striking the half hour, half-past nine, half-past God, and only a ten minutes' walk between him and a new destiny with a new dragon shape and new dragon eyes. Be calm, old fellow. Look at it carefully and quizzically, from a distance, measure it with a calculating eye, count the hackles and spines on its back, offer it a tin of condensed milk. Perhaps it will be friendly. Perhaps it will curl up before you like a pet cat, and go to sleep. Why worry? Will a mere disaster kill you? Is love so damned essential? Or pride?

But you should have called her up on the telephone. You should have called her up. It isn't fair. You aren't giving the poor girl a chance. Girl? Don't make us laugh. Yes, just the same, you know it's true, you should have called her up. Why not do it now. Here at the drug-store. What difference does it make? Even over the telephone, if she's guilty, she'll know you know she's guilty. Say you'll be home in five minutes: that wouldn't give her time to put things to rights. All the little telltale things: the caught breath, the changed voice, the ill-chosen word, the overdone welcome, and then the hairpins on the pillow.

He stood at the counter, put his wet hand on the edge of nickel, looked down at the rows of cigars in cedar boxes, the gaudy paper covers with lithochromes of Cuban beauties, flags, palm trees. The row of telephone-booths were just beyond, at the back, beside the little tables and chairs of twisted copper. He saw them with the corner of his right eye. Come on Andy, be a good guy and call her up. Give them a chance. But whose funeral *was* this? It wasn't Bertha that was going to suffer—it wasn't Tom—it was himself. This was nothing but cowardice, cowardice, cowardice masquerading as consideration. The thing must be cut off instantly, with a knife. Fsst: and done. Antiseptic. A pure and beautiful therapeutic murder, severance of connections now no longer real or useful, in order that each of them, released, might continue to grow. Of course. Why hadn't he thought of that before? Just the same ——

—Yes, sir.

—A package of Camels.

Just the same——

His eyes were full of rain. Unreasonable. Church Street, where the lilacs used to be, and were no more, and the gray wooden steeple of the Unitarian Church, pointing upwards toward the low bright illuminated clouds full of Cantabrigian and Bostonian rain. And the old gymnasium there, amongst the stables, and the huge book on physiology which they had all read in secret. Sex! Good jumping Jesus, to think of the nuisance, and nothing but nuisance, that sex had been. And after all this time, after a hundred years, at half-past nine, or half-past God, this final climax. This banal climax.

At the corner of the old graveyard, beside the milestone, he paused in the rain, hung hesitating, watched the brightly lighted Belmont bus splash through a wide sheet of water. Garden Street, or through the Common? Common or Garden? What on earth did it matter? Better take the shorter way, and get the thing over. Past the cannons, which he used to straddle. Past the baseball-field, where he used to strike out every time he came to bat. And the Civil War monument, about which the French architect had said, *"Ah! Il est sorti!"* This is your life here, here are all the days and nights, the sunlit afternoons, the school mornings, the bird-hunting expeditions to the Botanical Gardens or the Observatory, here was the dancing-school, misery of miseries, where later too, in freshman year, were the Coffee Parties, the Cheap and Hungries, all your past life here lies about you, *cauchemar* of echoes and whispers, here palpably still vibrating in the rain and darkness. Take hold of them. Resume them. Immerse yourself in them. Pull yourself, as it were, together. You are only a football-field in the frost, the hard frozen turf, the raw knuckles, the mud on the cleats, the baseball-glove rubbed with olive oil, the baseball with scarred skin. You are only a drawing of a bowl of nasturtiums, the flowers drawn faintly and delicately, with tenderest self-love, the leaves heavily and boldly outlined, black-leaded, the veins deliberately varicosed. Here you are still bringing across the dance-floor a glass cup of lemon sherbet to your darling Bertha, who waits for you in a varnished folding chair, with a white shawl drawn across her young shoulders, the violets pinned to her waist, her eyes still looking up at you shyly as you approach, as you continue forever approaching, like an eternal variable which never reaches its ultimate in God. Shall we sit this one out? Shall we go down to the steps for a breath of air? It's so hot in there. You know, I'm so afraid I bore you. Bore me! You couldn't bore a hole in a wall. I saw you yesterday on Brattle Street. Did you really—why didn't you come and speak to me? I saw you walking with a girl by Fresh Pond. Oh, yes, we went to see the pumping-station. And the algæ. The algæ? The algæ. You know, Miss Wentworth is so interested in lichens and algæ. Well, it seems a harmless taste, doesn't it? Would you rather have had chocolate ice-cream—I ought to have come and asked you, but there was such a crowd packed round the table that I thought I'd better get what I could. Tom wants the next dance—I think I'd better let him have it. It would look better. Here he is, coming now, laughing as usual, with that long athlete's lunge of a step, his beautiful slippers turned inward in studious imitation of the Indian walk. Another variable approaching another limit—and now—no no no no no no. But it couldn't be. No. This is not that time, that year, this is later, another world, another place, another pause between star-ruins, there is no connection, no logic. You are here alone in the cold rain, under the lighted windows of the new apartment-house, under those very windows where a fortnight ago the man and girl were found shot in a suicide pact. Two dead in Love Nest. You tear open the package of cigarettes, breaking the blue stamp with your forefinger, pinch the edge of a cigarette between two finger-nails, draw it forth, light it on the corner of Concord Avenue and Follen Street. This is you, Andrew Cather: you have changed: you are no longer there, in that dance-hall, nor there at Arlington Heights looking for star-flower and False Solomon's Seal and anemone, nor do you still wait patiently for hours in the Botanical Gardens with a pair of opera-glasses, hoping to see the scarlet tanager or the grosbeak. These have nothing to do with you. This is dead. You are dead. You are at most a shadow of those events, they no longer concern you: cut yourself off from them: give up forever that pale Narcissus who everywhere wants to walk beside you: beat him down, away, break him as you would break a false mirror, walk freely away from the shining fragments, which still would whisper to you their intriguing lies. This is you, this being whose steps stagger just slightly with alcohol, whose hands just now again trembled as you again lit your cigarette, in whose hip-pocket the flask of gin is beginning perceptibly to grow warm: taste it and see. Why this desperate and eleventh-hour attempt to recapitulate? You are engaged in a victory, an exodus, not a recapitulation. Cut them off with a word. Blow them out of the window, out of the world, out of bed, with a word. One ringing word like Roland's horn, winding among the wind-worn Pyrenees.

Bores me. The sum.

The immediate engulfed him once more,

the fine rain saluted him, a gust of cold wind lifted the tail of his coat, and here was Montrose Hall. Tom. Enter, to grow in wisdom. He entered, slipped on the marble floor, the worn wet heel slipping metallically, and slid toward the row of brass letter-boxes and the double row of bell-pushes: Diana of the Ephesians. Thomas Lowell Crapo. To ring or not to ring. He leaned his forefinger against the button and pressed prolongedly, at the same time lifting down the receiver and listening: he could hear the faint buzz in Tom's apartment. Why must one hold one's breath? Was life as exciting as all that? He breathed quickly, held his breath again, again listened to the far-off cicada trill. Is there an adulterous human in that room, sitting perhaps by the window with a book on his knee, or maybe a married woman? Is Troilus at home? Taking a bath? No answer. The room is dark, the cockroaches are scuttling in the pantry, the melting ice drips in the ice-chest, the little gold clock ticks patiently by itself on the yellow table. Tom is abroad. Tom has gone forth. He is probably at the Faculty Club, or gone to a burlesque show, or a prizefight. He has gone to the Square to see Greta Garbo. He is playing the grand piano at the Signet to an admiring audience of sophomores and a pederastic philologist. He is walking back from the Square with two doughnuts and a cup of coffee in his belly. He hums the waltz from the "Rosenkavalier," feeling the chords tensing his long fingers. He is dining with his aunt in Sparks Street. He is doing all these things simultaneously—Why? precisely to avoid doing anything else: safeguarding the world against a catastrophic suspicion: he runs from star to star protesting his innocence: he is a good fellow, a faithful friend. His pockets are full of spider-wasps and colloids. He has tied a knot in his handkerchief to remind him of an innocent appointment. Come on, Bertha, come on, Andy, we'll drive down to Duxbury and have a lobster and some steamed clams. Clam broth. A drive out to the Long Beach, the Gurnett. Dead fish on the sand. The sea . . .

Christ, no.

He released the bell, turned, went out, was re-immersed in rain, walking rapidly and uncertainly, his eyes downward, watching the uncertain thrust of his mud-tipped shoes. Blood was in his face, his neck and throat felt swollen and vague, everything was dimmed and rushed and whirling. Garden Street. In this street once—you broke a watch-chain, wrote a valentine, threw snowballs at the feathered trees. In this street once. The red bricks glistened darkly, became near and important and highly organized, rich-patterned symbol of the complicated world. Speed must replace thought. Action must replace idea. You are now an automaton. Thank God, your revolver is at the bottom of the trunk: by the time you dug it out the impulse would have become ridiculous. Hurry—hurry—hurry—everything was hurrying. The world was hurrying. The rain was hurrying. The water in the gutter was hurrying. Be a child, why not, step into the gutter and walk along in the rushing water: it will conceal your spoor, you will leave no traces for the detectives to follow, and besides it will be such fun. Go on, I dare you. Wet feet? You have been drowned, and are wet all over. But these bricks, now, these dead leaves, now, these limpid braids of brown water, this elaborate pattern of the earth's floor, this curious wall of star-surface on which you walk like a fly—admire it, Andrew, be bewildered by it, let it confuse you in such a way as will be cosmically useful to you in the coming scene. But what if there *were* no scene? It will be useful anyway. It is your insulation. It is holding you off from your agony. The unimportant has become important in order that the important may become unimportant. Found it marble and left it brick. Bumwad, bumwad, bumwad.

Shepard Street.

The turning-point.

A letter-box.

Arc-light.

Dripping forsythia bushes.

Turn right along board walk for fifth act of "Uncle Tom's Cabin." Real blood-hounds. See Eliza crossing the ice. See little Eva go to heaven.

He walked with dizzy carefulness, tried in vain to place his feet on the dark cracks of the board walk, gave it up, and began to smile. It was probably not Tom at all. Or maybe it would be a party. Bert with a new poem. Celia with a new frock. Floyd with a new dance-record. Why, for goodness sake, if it isn't old Andy! But where are your things, Andy! Where's your bag! What's happened! Explain yourself! How come you're back so soon! Welcome home and have a drink. But what about your bag? What indeed. Left it at the Harvard Club by mistake, after too many cocktails—as you can see. Yes indeed. Telephone for it: they'll send it out in a taxi. All very simple.

Shepard Hall.

He stood, stared, the wind whipping his

coat, held up his hand to shelter his eyes from the rain, regarded aslant and unseeing the large wet words of carved stone in the wild lamplight. In this house once. The little red table being taken up the stone stairs. The bed-spring being juggled into the shaky old elevator. Old Mr. Macumber sitting on the steps in the summer evening to listen to the whirring of nighthawks. The bare floors, before the rugs had come. The bare walls, before the pictures had been hung. Old newspapers on the floor of the bathroom. The white enamel doors of the ice-chest open, showing the lining of dull and stinking tin. Stale smells of former occupation: the history of the world. In this house once—but that was long ago. Prehistoric. Before the flood. Before Christ. Before Tom. Retreat, you idiot. Go back to the Harvard Club. Get your bag and hire a taxi and drive to Duxbury. Duxbury? Why Duxbury? Go to Concord. Go to Montreal. Anywhere. Let the rain and wind decide it for you: they are already shaking you to a decision: urging you towards Garden Street: obey them. This house has ghosts. Its walls are made of nasturtiums and Haydn, its ceilings are a gossamer of lost words and cries, forgotten embraces and tendernesses, rebukes, reproaches, and quick words of anger.

Rain ran bubbling from right to left along the granite steps. This house has tears. This house has hates. It has arms, hands, and eyes, it listens to you with a conscious expression which is neither pity nor contempt: it knows you without remembering you. Bid it farewell.

He entered the rococo marble hall, ignored the elevator, feeling as he did so a sharp cessation of breath, and automatically thrust his hand into brass letter-box number sixty-four. No letters. Of course not. Bertha would have removed them, as he perfectly well knew. Dishonest device to gain time. What for? Terror. Abject terror. His knees were trembling, blood was singing in the side of his neck, his wet hand still hung tremulously in the cold metal box. Remove it: bring it back to you, inform it that it is still yours. But the bell—what about the bell? Six rings, or seven, or the mystic nine? Something to alarm them and put them on their guard? He rang the bell twice, prolongedly, as at Tom's, smiled suddenly at his own instant decision not to listen at the receiver, unsteadily entered the elevator, and ascended. At the third-floor gate a woman was waiting, holding an umbrella. On the fourth floor a rubbish box of canvas. On the sixth floor—exit to grow in wisdom.

He let himself out, trembling horribly, smiling, feeling like an idiot, paused insanely with one finger uplifted, took out his key, crossed the oilcloth floor on which were muddy footprints, and let himself in, closing the door with a bang. Good God—are you going to faint? Are you so weak? Lean your back against the door, and regard Tom's hat and stick on the chair, the fur-lined gloves, too, and the wet galoshes. Observe also that there is no light in the sitting-room, but a dim light coming from the crack of the bathroom door. All very cosy. All very quiet. Christ. Rain flew across the Shepard Street window.

—Hello! . . . Hello, darlings! Lochinvar is home again.

He swept the gloves, hat, and stick on to the floor: the yellow stick clattered. In their place he flung down his own soaked hat and coat.

—View halloo! Tallyho!

The light in the corridor was switched on, and Bertha's hand and face were motionless, frozen, inclining forward from the bedroom door. The mouth was relaxed, the eyes concentrated, with fright.

—It's a melodrama, Berty. Will you come forward singly or in pairs?

—Andy!

—Andrew One-eye Cather himself!

The surprised face disappeared, taking with it the white plump hand. The bedroom door creaked very slightly.

—Take your time about dressing: I'll wriggle some cocktails. . . . Wriggle is the word.

He stumbled into the sitting-room, turned on the light, stood in the centre of the Kerman rug under the hideous brass chandelier, and stared out through the black window. Rain. All the way from Boston to New York. Rain devouring New England. Wonders of the Invisible World! And there were the God-damned nasturtiums too—the nasturtium quid —and the damned little gilt clock, ticking subtly and complacently to itself, for all the world as if it were Tom's own pulse. Break it. Dash it to smithereens on the red-brick hearth. Step on it, kid—let time be out of joint. But where were they? What were they doing? What were they saying? He listened. Nothing. Not a sound. If they were saying anything, it was in a whisper—a frightened whisper—they were pulling themselves together—wondering what line he would take —pulling on their stockings and shoes—perhaps not daring to look at each other. The room gave a streaming lurch, and to steady himself he put his hand on the corner of the yellow-grained mantelpiece. A Spanish grammar. He plucked the red book out of its place on the shelf, opened it at random, then flung it on to the couch. What about another little drink. Or the cocktails.

In the kitchen, unthinking, he assembled on the table a can of grapefruit juice, a lemon, a small sharp knife, the sugar-bowl, the cocktail shaker, and began chipping the ice in the ice-box. A cockroach ran out and fell to the floor. Then Bertha's voice spoke oddly behind him.

—Andy.

He missed his stroke, his hand slipped along the smooth cold surface of ice, then he resumed his chipping, the chunks of ice clunking into the grooved pan.

—I'm sorry, Andy.

—Gosh, is that all. I said this was a melodrama, didn't I?

He flung the ice-pick point forward so that it stuck, quivering, into the wooden drainboard of the sink. Then he began gathering up the broken ice between his two palms and dumping it in the shaker.

—I think we'd better talk reasonably about it.

—Sure. Go ahead. Step right up with a

wagonload of reasons. This is going to be fun, by God. Go fetch Tom and tell him to have a drink.

—Look at me, Andy!

—Why the bloody hell should I? But I will, if it'll do you any good.

He put the cap on the shaker and started shaking, then turned and looked at her, smiling. She had on the Mandarin jacket, a band of black velvet was round her copper-coloured hair, her eyes were deep, dark, tear-bright. She leaned against one side of the door.

—I see you, Berty! There you are—the known unknown at last.

—*That* ought to be something.

—Oh, it is, believe me. Hell, I forgot to put in the grapefruit juice. And the lemons.

He found the can-opener, opened the can, breathing heavily, poured the contents into the shaker, sliced three slices of lemon, then shook black squirts of angostura over the floating ice. Five, six, seven, eight. He felt dizzy, and held an ice-cold palm against his forehead. Whoof. The world must be slipping sideways. Better grab on to something. Perhaps Bertha. The prop of your old age. Perhaps the rung of a sideways chair. A dish-cloth.

—I don't see what good it's going to do

you to get any drunker than you are already. For six months——

—For God's sake, don't talk to me about six months! Go on, get out of here, sit down and I'll bring the glasses. . . . Oh, *there* you are!

He tilted his head to one side, elaborately, and grinned at Tom.

—Hello, Andy.

—Nice little surprise you planned for me. Have a drink.

Bertha turned abruptly on her heel, went into the sitting-room, and sank on to the couch. She sat upright with her hands beside her, staring at nothing. Tom followed her awkwardly. As if to avoid the appearance of approaching her, he went to the farther side of the room and stood for a moment by the black piano, frowning. Then he took a step or two back towards the kitchen.

—I don't think I'll *have* a drink, if you don't mind.

—Oh, sure, come on, might as well do it amiably, say the hard things amiably——

He put the shaker and glasses on the red table, and waved his arm over them.

—Go on—make yourself at home. Everything that's mine is yours. Don't try to smile, though, till you've got your face under better control.

—Look here, Andy, old man—I think I'd better go. You two had better talk it over first—don't you think so, Bertha.

—Yes.

—Nope. Nothing doing. This is now a *famille à trois*. Family conference. Every one to be represented. Though I must say you don't either of you seem to have much to say. Strikes me the scene is a little disappointing. Oughtn't you to say you were waiting for a street-car? Or came back for your umbrella? Did you lose your motor-bike? You know, something like that. But of course the thing isn't really a surprise to any of us, is it—we've all seen it coming for such a long time—months and months—Jesus, I've got to laugh.

He laughed, pushing his shoulders against the mantel, while Tom, his face white and strained, handed a cocktail to Bertha. She took it mechanically, without looking at it, and as mechanically drank it.

—Why did you come back tonight, she said.

—Why? Because a little bird told me.

—I don't think it was very sporting of you.

—Neither do I. But what can you do. I've never faced a situation quite like this, my dear, and you must forgive me if my technique is a little crude. As I remarked to begin with, it's a melodrama; and in a melodrama, you've got to behave like actors in a melodrama, haven't you? Suppose I'd telephoned from the club. Everything spoiled, postponed, all of us left in doubt and suspense and agony, nothing settled. What the hell was the use of that? I thought of it, believe me—looked at the telephones—but, no, I decided it must be cut off with a knife. Psst—and done. . . . Here's how.

Tom had perched himself on the arm of the big chair, and was tapping his glass with a finger-nail.

—You're perfectly right, he murmured—Perfectly right. Of course I don't need to say how sorry——

—Oh, no. We needn't go into that. We all know how sorry. One of those awkward complexes, *nicht wahr,* in which delight and sorrow are so painfully and inextricably mixed. I'll give you credit for the sorrow, which I know must be real. Of course. Naturally. You like me—I like you—we're old friends, aren't we—knew each other before we knew Bertha—grew up together—how couldn't you feel sorry? Same here. I feel sorry, too, though it may surprise you. Sorry for you and Bertha and myself in about equal portions. Yes. A sort of *weltschmerz*. Perhaps a little sorrier for myself than for either of you, which is selfish of me, but you'll forgive me. I suppose, as a matter of fact, I ought to kill you? I even thought of it. I thought of it at the corner of Garden and Shepard Street: had a vision of my revolver lying brightly at the bottom of my steamer-trunk. But that would be ridiculous.

He walked over to Bertha, lifted her chin with his hand so that her eyes were raised toward his own, looked idly into them for an instant, saw that they were now hard and tearless, and turned toward Tom with a conscious brightening of expression.

—Besides, you've got on one of your most beautiful waistcoats, and the handsomest tweed suit in Cambridge, and I couldn't bear to spoil them. And if I missed—good God. You'd kill me with one hand. In self-defense. And I'd rather go mad than die. Oh, much. . . . Jesus.

—Thank you, said Tom—I appreciate your æsthetic tact.

—Don't mention, old fellow—there's nothing I wouldn't do for you. Step right up and help yourself. . . . But as I was saying. What was I saying?

He frowned into his glass, then covered it with his hand. Tired. His wits were gone. He was saying things badly, saying the wrong things, off the track somehow. Something else must be found, some other direction, something deeper, more to the point, more plangent and poignant. Profound abstractions, self-sacrifice, nobility, a great constellation of bright and beautiful stars. A vast bouquet of planets in a purple sky.

—Why don't you say something, Berty? God knows you usually have enough——

—What is there to say. It's done.

—I suppose you didn't think of consulting me about it.

—Yes, I did. But it came too vaguely, and then too suddenly——

—He swept you off your feet.

—Oh, for the love of mud, Andy!

Tom stood up, very straight and angry.

—I wonder if you quite realize your own part in this situation, Andy. For six months you've left me practically alone. You've been drunk night after night. If Tom behaved decently to me, did a little something to make things happier for me—if I could get a little enjoyment out of life——

—I see. Yes, indeed. Tom as the good Samaritan. The neglected wife. But I suppose it hasn't occurred to you that it was partly just because I saw this business beginning that I withdrew myself?

—Oh, no! You can't get away with that. Oh, no. It had begun before that, and you know it.

Silence. This wasn't right at all. He stared at the carpet. He felt their eyes fixed upon him, and for the moment wasn't quite sure that he could look at them. A deep pain opened somewhere within him, a deep sadness, an enormous sense of lostness and futility. It was all no use. Impossible to explain. What on earth could one do with words? Memories? Ideas? A trifling little barter of facts? He walked to the table, refilled his glass, went to the window beside the couch and looked out, looked down into the rain-dark street, where the twin lights of Shepard Hall entrance illuminated the board walk, sodden with water. Perhaps it was himself, after all, who was wrong. Was it wholly impossible? Ten years. The dance of places, the dance of rooms, the dance of houses. Bertha plus one, Bertha plus two, Bertha plus three, Bertha plus four. Bertha at the Coffee Party, at the skating-rink, on the toboggan at Oakley, on the river at Concord, the Sudbury, the Assabet, walking in spring along the granite lip of the Frog Pond—and now Bertha here, Bertha belonging no longer only to himself, if indeed she belonged at all. Where was it all gone? Where was it now? It was nowhere. It was gone forever. Nothing could now ever be the same in the world, never again. This was no longer his Berty, that was not Tom—two new persons sat in the room with him, two strangers who looked at him with hostility and misunderstanding, whose minds and memories were now allied against his own. He was outnumbered, outmanœuvred, outwitted. What was the use. Better get completely drunk, and let it all go to hell. Speak out his bitterness and be damned to them. Yes. Be damned to them. Let them go to hell and stay there.

—All right, Tom, I suppose you're right—you'd better go home and leave this to Berty and me. Go on, get out. Put on your damned little galoshes and gloves and carry your pretty little malacca. But first I'd just like to call you, to your white face, a worm: a curious and very handsome worm. Don't you think so?

He lifted his glass in a toast and drank it off. He had come quite close to Tom, and they were looking with an extraordinary amiability into each other's eyes. Protractedly. Exchanging what? He felt his gaze move subtly from one to the other of Tom's two eyes, was for a moment conscious of Tom's ancient embarrassment at having to look at a glass eye, and felt it now as a peculiar but too fortuitous advantage. He was pleased at the thought.

—Good night, Bertha, Tom said.

—Wait a minute. There's one more thing. I suppose you'll want to marry her, and make an honest woman of her? It'll be a divorce, of course?

—Andy! Is that quite necessary?

Bertha flung the words at him crookedly as she flung off the black velvet band from her hair, which she tossed angrily to the right.

—Perhaps not—perhaps not. . . . Go on, Tom—get out.

From the doorway, he watched Tom pulling on the galoshes, straining and flushing. This was fun. Awkward moment for Tom.

—Sorry your hat and stick are on the floor.

—It doesn't matter, old man.

—I suppose you'll be going to Sanders on Thursday?

—Probably.

—Well, sleep well!

—Good night, Andy. Come in and see me when you feel like talking about it.

—Yes, indeed!

He patted Tom delightfully on the shoulder of his raincoat, smiled, and softly shut the door. A beautifully managed exit. Couldn't have been better. And the idea of Tom's sleeping. Good God. Who would sleep after this? Who? Himself only, for only himself would have the sense to get thoroughly and completely and obliviously drunk. Yes. Drunk. He was drunk already. He was beginning to feel gay. Rubbed his hands on his forehead and then together and stepped quite nimbly into the sitting-room, where Bertha, her back turned, was looking at the books on the mantelpiece.

—Well, darling, now we can discuss this quite amicably and privately. Isn't it nice? Now we can really go into it, without self-consciousness.

—I think you're behaving revoltingly.

—Revoltingly! What the hell do you mean. I'm behaving like a perfect gentleman.

—You know what I mean.

—I'm damned if I do. But I'll be delighted to hear. Have a drink?

—I think you might at least have kept sober, and not introduced, or tried to introduce, this element of disgusting farce.

—God, you make me laugh. Your usual total lack of perception. Blind as a bat. I suppose I ought to have sent some flowers first, in a taxi, with a little message? Congratulations and facilitations. The bridal chamber was decorated with roses and syringes. Typical of you not to see that the only way, the only way, of handling such a scene is humorously! Good jumping Jesus. It's that, among other things, that's always been wrong with us. Your heavy-handedness: this fatuous Brattle Street dignity: all these God-damned poetic hypocrisies. I suppose we ought to be tragic about it, and behave like people in a novel, or an Ibsen play. Ought I to have apologized for having come into my own flat and then cried about it? Tragic! Who's it tragic for, if not for me, supposing I wanted to give in to it? What the hell have I come back to? To a stinking void. To a part of myself that's dead. Well, all right. That's my funeral. Not yours, and not Tom's. If I want to make a joke of it, for the moment, so as to avoid cheap sentimental dramatics, the sort you act in at Brattle Hall, you might at least have the intelligence to see why I do it, and that it's my own business. I get drunk because I don't want to be wholly conscious. Because, I admit it, I'm partly a coward, and don't want to know, or to have you and Tom know, exactly how many volts of pain I'm carrying. Do you want me to cry? Do you want me to comfort you? Or do you expect just a calm rational discussion of the ethics and æsthetics of sexual fidelity?

—There's no use discussing anything, if you're going to be merely abusive.

—There you go. If I state facts, I'm abusive.

—I think you might at least have tried to see my point of view. I've been starved——

—Yes, for Christ's sake drag *that* up again, starved for love! You don't know what love is. You're a thirteen-year-old romantic, a bleached little Cantabrigian Madame Bovary. I want *love,* she cries, and pulls on a pair of tarpaulin knickers.

—Shut up!

She turned suddenly and glared at him, her mouth dreadfully relaxed, the tears starting quickly from her eyes. He was looking at her quite coldly, with the familiar hatred, the familiar deep ferocity and need to injure. She was beginning to suffer. Pursue the advantage. Grind it in, beat her down. Give her the works. Analyze the whole marriage, drag it all up by the roots, reveal her to herself for once and all, all the piecemeal horrors laid out like entrails on a bloody platter. Bumwad, bumwad, bumwad, bumwad. The whole prolonged obscene and fæcal grapple in steadily deepening darkness, year after year of it, the burden upon his consciousness becoming hourly more foul and more frightful. The history of a bath-room. Dirty water. Dirty clothes. Dirty habits. The upright soul indifferent to filth. Jesus, angel of grief, come down to me: give us a speech as pure as ocean. A tumbler of neat gin, fiery strangulation, a cough, tears on his marble eye which might be misinterpreted, a sudden impulse to make them real. The awful contraction of the belly which precedes weeping. A new red edge provided for anger.

—All right—I'll play the piano. . . . No, I won't, either.

He played two bars of a Bach gavotte, then stopped.

—Isn't it ridiculous. Why do we make such a fuss about it? Especially as we all flatter ourselves that we saw it coming. Or did we? I must confess though——

—What.

Bertha's face was averted, her voice flat.

—I hadn't really expected you to go through with it. I thought Brattle Street would be too much for you.

—I see. You thought as usual that I wasn't quite human.

—Not at all. Don't be in a hurry. I thought you were too damned moral. Or loyal.

—Loyal to what, exactly? I'd like to know.

—Oh, me, for instance.

—Yes! After you'd flaunted Molly——

—Don't be more of a fool than you have to be.

—Besides, if you admit withdrawing from me, what difference does it make. You know our marriage hasn't been a marriage for almost a year——

Of course. There was that. There was that, which he had forgotten. But how explain it to her? There was no explaining it. The problem of rhythm: the inevitable succession of approaches and retreats: love, indifference, hate—then over again, love, indifference, hate. Disgust, then renewed curiosity. Exploration, then renewed retreat. Soiled clothes, then sunlight, a concert, a few drinks, an evening of witty conversation, psychological discussion—and all of a sudden the divine recapitulation. Would this have occurred again? Had he really wanted it, or hoped for it, to occur again? Or had he at the bottom of his heart desired this precise consummation, this disaster? The sacrifice of everything. And in that case, why make a fuss about it: how could it hurt him? How, indeed. Step up, ladies and gents, and see the unwoundable pig.

—Oh, God, what's the use.

—I meant to tell you that I thought I was

falling in love with him. And that he was in love with me. He meant to tell you too.

—How long have these discussions been going on?

—I meant to tell you before anything happened. But you see——

—I suppose you want me to believe that tonight is the first time?

—No.

—Well, by God, *that* opens up a nice vista into the past, doesn't it.

To ask or not to ask. To pry or not to pry. He stared at the carpet, pushed a cigarette end with the toe of his muddy shoe, felt the blind agony beginning to contract his whole body. One night, or two. One week, or three. Before he left for New York, or after. In Tom's flat, or here. To think this was sickness, madness, disruption. Drunken and maudlin disruption. What was Bertha, then, that even now he should suffer? This pale oval of female face, with the speckled gray eyes and the always too-innocent mouth? A mere face. A mere idea. A mere history, now finished. Or *was* it finished?

He picked up his glass and crossed to the table. Bewilderment. The empty glass in his right hand meaningless.

—Yes, a *lovely* little vista into the past. The

past suddenly becomes the present, doesn't it? And a damned pretty future.

—Well, you've always preached psychological freedom and honesty——

—Christ!

—Why not practise it?

—I can safely leave that to you!

—That's not fair!

—That's the coolest defense of whoredom——

A curious singing began in his right ear. He put down his glass very hard on the red table, which was unexpectedly near, then walked quickly, with Bertha's glare still fixed upon him, across the corridor to the bathroom. The door closed, he stared at his reflection in the greenish mirror. White as a sheet. First stage of drunkenness. Boy, you ain't seen the half of it. This is going to be a souse in a million. He watched himself swaying, rested his hands on the marble basin, and saw his face beginning to cry. The mouth curled itself grotesquely, like a child's, like the wound in a tragic mask, his eyes closed themselves to slits, the white face began absurdly jiggling up and down, in time with the rapid soundless convulsions of his chest. He turned on the two taps in the basin, to drown out the extraordinary noise Andrew

Cather had begun to make. A sound like a swift departure of wings, pigeon's wings, whe-whe-whe-whe-whe-whe-whe-whe — then a shudder of breath quickly indrawn, and another hissing flight of wingbeats, and a long oooooooooooooo—subsiding to caught calm, as the tears fell into the steaming water. Grates me. Is this the face that launched a thousand quips? Is that you, One-eye Cather? Wash your bloody, drivelling little map. If, the last time your mother spanked you, when you were seven, you refused to cry, why cry now? What is there to cry about? Is it manly to cry? Disgusting. Step up, ladies and gents, and see the weeping pig: the pig with wings, the pig with a glass eye. Look at the little red veins in his nose, heritage of six months' drunkenness, the whiteness of the white of his left eye, the redness of the white of the right. Wash your face with cold water, as you have often seen Bertha do after a midnight quarrel. Observe yourself from a great distance, as if you were an ant crawling over the toe of your shoe. Isn't he a funny little thing? Does he know where he's going? Has he a god? Does he distinguish right from wrong? Has he sexual appetites, loves, hates, despairs? Has he an ideal? A secret richness of soul, tenderness of heart, susceptibility to injury? Have you lost your wife, your friend, or is it only an egg? *Tu pupila es azul; y quando lloras*—the world is a lost egg. A mislaid egg. It will hatch, out of season, in a universe of intemperate weather, an absolute zero, and the god it contains will be born dead.

You are not angry: you don't want to be angry: you are hurt.

His face washed, the temples cold and transparent over the brain, he returned to the sitting-room. It was now Bertha's turn to cry. She lay huddled at one end of the couch, her back turned, her cheek on a green pillow, a handkerchief held over her eyes. One of her pianissimos, a soft whispering sound, persistent, uninterruptible, the kind that could go on for hours, for all night. She looked small and pathetic, but also absurd. He felt a profound detachment and irony towards her, watched the slight shaking of her body, the irregular lift and fall of the blue mandarin jacket on her left shoulder, the movement of the blue elbow, noted the heaviness of the upper arm: she was getting old.

—I'm not angry, Berty: I don't want to be angry: I'm hurt.

The rain answered him. Hurt? The word seemed singularly inadequate. But words in a scene were always inadequate: it was always like this: these midnight quarrels were always the same: ridiculous phrases followed by ridiculous silences, sudden shifts from fury to pathos, from the heroic to the absurd, and at last a bedside reconciliation dictated by sheer fatigue. But not tonight, not this time. No. Good God, no.

—Are you going to say anything?

No answer. His hands in his pockets, he walked into the kitchen, looked at the table, the empty tin, the tin-opener, the half lemon, the sugar-bowl, the spots of gin and water on the varnished wood. Still life. A cockroach signalled at him with alert antennæ from the edge of the kitchen sink. The ice in the ice-chest settled itself with a grating slump, metallic. Domestic interior: the persistent order that underlies all disorder, the useful tyranny of the inanimate. Say good-bye to it, old fool—this is the beginning of the end. All is over. No more ice-chests, shared cockroaches, fruit-knives, gin-rings to be mopped up with handkerchiefs. To hell with it. No more mosquitos on the window-screens in the summer evenings, to be squashed with one finger against rusty wire. The last day of the calendar, the calendar with the sacred cow. Out with it: this is the terminus. Let Rome in Tiber melt——

—Perhaps you're right. Yes, I believe you may be right. What's the use? How can we summarize everything in a few well-chosen words. Your life, and my life, our life together. *Non si puo.* . . . Just the same, I don't see what you're crying about—you've got what you want, haven't you?

He looked at her quizzically: she was quieter, but he could still see her left shoulder now and then spasmodically lifted, hear the sharp intake of breath. He picked up the red Spanish grammar from the other end of the couch, seated himself where the book had lain, being very careful not to touch the slippered feet which were so close to his knee.

—Impossible to find the right words, isn't it. Just as well read at random out of a book. For example. It is lightning, and I fear that it will rain. Is she unhappy? She appears to be so, but I cannot believe that she is so. He is sorry that he is ill, and I am sorry that he is ill. Use the subjunctive after expressions of doubting or fearing, joy or sorrow, or necessity. *Mientras dure la vida*—as long as life lasts. *Ella está enamorada: y si lo está, que mal hay en ello?* No harm at all.

The rain answered him. No harm at all.

—Or how about this. This seems to settle

everything. It seems to me; it seems to you (fam. sing.); it seems to him; it seems to us; it seems to you (fam. pl.); it seems to them, I go to bed; you go to bed (fam. sing.); he goes to bed; we go to bed; you go to bed (fam. pl.); they go to bed. All life in a nutshell, by God. We hate each other; they (masc. and fem.) hate each other. We embrace and kiss each other. . . . Cardinals and ordinals. We shall reach the city of Waltham before night comes on. Let us take leave of the wounded man: he slept well yesterday, and he is not moaning tonight. This is a Spanish proverb: "Although the monkey dressed in silk, she remained a monkey!" It is snowing or raining all the time in this town: we hope that the weather is better in yours. . . .

No answer to his lifted eyebrow: he began to feel angry again.

—I like the "fam. sing.," don't you? He has a toothache, and is shedding a lot of tears. If you do not prefer to lend them the pens, do not lend them the pens.

The sound of Bertha's weeping became louder: she made a sudden convulsive gesture with her lifted elbow, turned her face farther away into the pillow, and said:

—Will you stop it, please?

—Certainly, if you like.

—I believe you have—I believe you have—no heart at all.

—Step right up, ladies and gents, and see the pig without a heart. . . . To drink is to live. An old Spanish proverb. Have a drink, Andy, old fellow. Yes, I will, thank you.

He sat still, staring, let the opened book slide to the floor, then rose and stood before her, jingling the silver in his pocket.

—Well, what do you suggest?

—Nothing. . . . Whatever you like.

—I see. You want me to make the decisions. Is that it?

No answer.

—By God, I could kill you when you take refuge in weeping and silence. It's a damned dirty way of evading your responsibilities, if you ask me! I'm going back to the club. I don't know where I'll go from there. Anywhere. I'll let you know——

He lurched into the hall, struggled into his wet coat, put his hat on, returned to the couch, where Bertha still lay motionless, squeezed her elbow once between finger and thumb, saying, "I'm off," and a moment later found himself running along the slippery board walk towards Garden Street. In this street once. He got into a yellow taxi, which started moving before he had quite seated himself: he found himself on his back, and for a few seconds lay inert, uncertain whether he wanted to laugh or cry. Lights. The expensive hum of a Packard. Bertha at the opera, in the borrowed car. Mrs. Skinner, the old buzzard, sat behind them. "They were just finding each other," she said. Just finding each other. Oh, yeah? And now they were just losing each other. One as easy as the other—now you see them and now you don't. Close the eyes. Let the chin come to rest, where it will, on mother's breast. Let us frolic on the hills at Arlington, under the shadow of the water-tower. Wild barberry. Black-eyed Susan. Does some one see us. Is some one coming. Beams multiply in a scaffolding, the scantlings cant, the lashed ladder topples, falls, veers, descends dizzily down the booming well. She has bats in her belfry. Long sounds, long lines of sound, long lights on backs of sounds, rode like the *Valkyrie,* whooping through the tunnel. Let fall your chin on mother's breast. No, you mustn't here, this is too public, some one might see us, don't, Andy, you're too dreadful. The taxi ticking, Mr. Rodman said: I said: Mr. Rodman said: *tu pupila es azul.* Paid the bill. Saw the spittoons, garboons. The ice in the urinals, too, and the brass keys on the rack. Who's on the rack? Beams multiply in a scaffolding, the scantlings cant, cross-levers, struts and stays, footholds and handholds, giant's jackstraws, you are lost among them, come down, oh, maid, from yonder height, get out from under before it all falls, it will fall, is falling, fam. sing. and all, go on and hoot your way into hell. Who was hooting? The dead man under the bridge, fumbling in darkness along slimy piles, bowing to the tide, felt hat in hand. Good evening, madam. Have they found me yet? Has my watch stopped ticking? What brick was it that spoke that about ticking? It was the train, over the joints, over the rails. In Rome too as the Romans too.

The silence——

—A dollar and a quarter. *And* ten.

—Thank you, sir.

—Don't mention.

That probably surprised him.

The club was empty and still, opened before him spaciously and with marble echoes, followed him downstairs with subdued lights and sounds, with portraits of philosophers and a bison's head, with shells from the Somme and a Chinese dragon on scarlet silk. The chessmen too. The Hoboken gambit? I'll pawn my queen. The bar closed for the night, but water would do. A lily-cup of waxed paper, cold water on greased skin.

At the locker, he refilled the silver flask, took a long burning drink, filled again, then placed six lily-cups in a white row on the table in the bomb-proof, two of them filled with water: supplies for the night. Within reach of his hand, as he lay on the red divan. Better have a night-cap. Jitter might have been here, often was. You know, Andy, I think there's something yellow about you. Close the eyes, to shut out swimming. Rest the chin on papa's hairy chest. Not very comfortable. Screwed his head from left to right against the hard leather. Sleep drunkenly, tomato juice in morning, cold clam-juice, ice-water, cold shower set you right. Wake up, Andy, it's time to get up: you have an appointment to tutor at eleven. That little Jew. Weisskopf. The long swift darkness swept over from left to right, here and there a streaked star, a dark pouring sound, the subdued roar of all blood. Bumwad, bumwad, bumwad, bumwad. Oh, bumwad. Now nausea plucking at the corners of the arid mouth, the twitch of sickness, the race between sickness and unconsciousness, the interstellar skid. The hands nerveless and placeless, now on the belly, now at the side, now hanging towards the floor, touching the cold leather, stubbornly conscious, waiting for something, afraid of sleep. Wake up, Andy, it's time to get up. That was a footstep, near, menacing.

—Mr. Cather, sir.

—Hello.

An attendant, deprecatory.

—Pardon me, sir, Mr. Cather, but would you like to be found here?

—Found and left.

—Yes, sir.

The long darkness swept superbly from left to right, the blood began its universal pouring over the small tossed body of the world, hurled it and whirled it, swung it obliquely through a screaming abyss, hoisted it again to a toppling pinnacle. Good evening, madam. This is my drowned hat that I am eating. We signed the contract. I am successful. When he saw the sparrow in the road, he got off his horse. It had a broken wing, the bones were sticking out. Of course, what did I tell you. More calmly now. More darkly now. Smoothly, on even keel, into the dark station, the tunnel, the banked lights stately and still on stone columns, birds of brightness, cold and light. I saw you before you saw me, yes, I did. Why didn't you tell me, and, besides. I was walking there.

In pure light came the remote flight, the little flight of a flock, coming nearer and larger and brighter, the flight of little winged bones, winging through heaven, little wrist-bones and delicate ankle-bones and even figulas and femurs and scapulas, and each with as neat a pair of wings as you'd see on a bleeding sparrow, and every one of them on its way to a star, far off; or was it God himself? He watched them with one eye, while he picked up the skeleton and began to eat it; first the feet, then working slowly up the legs; and dry going it was, what with no sauce, no mustard, no Worcestershire, and the bones getting bitterer as he crawled right up through the pelvis, devouring all, and crunched the ribs. The spine tasted like the Dead Sea, like ashes in the mouth, getting worse as he crawled nearer to the skull; and the skull itself was a black mouthful of charcoal, which he spat out. And in mid-space then he saw behemoth in the act of biting off the conning-tower of an interstellar submarine, one of these ether-going craft with one eye, a little way off to the southwest of a pink star, which was wearing white drawers, like a woman. And in a canoe then, in a canoe, a birchbark canoe, up the marsh channel, above the red bridge, in amongst the hosts of seething reeds in the hot salt sun-light—the bright drops on the paddles, the bare arms freckled and wet—is this the way to the Gurnett?—Oh, no, that's the other way—you'll have to turn round—yes, it's the other way. The other way, to the Gurnett.

The other way, a long way.

And when he came, they gave him an oval reception.

II

(———particularly the smell of the pine-wood walls, soaked in sea-fog, but pine-smelling also in the strong sea sunlight, smooth to the touch, golden-eyed with knot-holes, and the wind singing through the rusty wire screens, fine-meshed and dusty, or clogged brightly with drops of dew, or drops of rain, or drops of fog—the morning outlook seaward, over the humped grass beyond the puddled tennis-court, over the wild sea-grass windblown, beyond the new house of bright shingles, where the new boy and girl lived, and then across the bay to Clark's Island, and the long yellow outer beach, with its deserted and mysterious shacks of houses, and then the Gurnett—the small white twin light-houses of the Gurnett—I was looking out of the window at this, at all of this, feeling the cool east wind from Provincetown, but with no mirage to show precisely where Provincetown lay, and the voices came then over the low partition between the bedrooms. I was dressing, and as I put on my khaki shirt I looked at the fly-trap, which I had made out of fragments of window-screen wire, to see if my flies were all still alive after the night. What would they be saying now. The voices were low and secret, early morning voices, Uncle Tom and Aunt Norah. I removed the screw in the wall beside the wash-stand and peeped through into the maids' room, saw a pink chemise very close to me, so close that I was frightened, and walked softly away, back to the window. Did Molly know I was there, that I was watching her day after day? I had seen them putting on their bathing-suits. Afterwards, when I met them on the porch, they were embarrassed, tried to pull down the short skirts over their knees, ran down the road giggling and looking back. Molly's skin was very white, Margaret's was brown.

—But why should he come like this, Tom? It isn't like him not to let Doris, or any one, know. Perhaps you'd better go to Boston and see him. Do you think there's anything wrong.

—The whole thing is very queer. Do you think he suspects. Do you think we ought to say something to Doris.

—I think you'd better go to town and see him. Before anything worse happens. He ought not to come here, if that's what he's thinking of doing. I'm sure he suspects. It would hurt him too much to see it. It would be better if you talked to him.

—We'd better put off the picnic till next week. Too bad to disappoint the kids again, but it can't be helped. It was queer to begin with that he let Doris come here alone, with the children, when he could perfectly well have come, too—his business was only an excuse. I think they had already quarrelled about it.

They were talking about Father and Mother, and I went close to the partition, to listen, holding my breath; but the voices stopped, the door opened, and I heard Uncle Tom going down the stairs, and Aunt Norah pouring water out of the pitcher into the wash-bowl. No picnic at the Gurnett this week—the third time it had been postponed. Porper would probably cry when I told him, but instead Susan and I could take him down to the front beach and build villages out of shells, and show him the dead seal. In that little cleared place between the banks of eel-grass, flat and sandy at low tide, where the horseshoe crabs were. The new boy and girl, too, Warren and Gay, except that Gay was always crying, as when we had taken her to the log cabin in the pine woods and tried to make her undress. Had she told her mother and father about that, the little sneak.

———particularly the morning walk to the

village, along the Point Road, past all the houses and windmills, the wild cherry trees and crab-apples, to get the morning mail. The wooden windmills were the best, with their wings of fine white-painted slats, and the great wooden tanks at the top, and the strong girders of white-painted wood, and of these I couldn't decide whether I preferred Daisy or Sunbeam. Of the metal ones, there were five Comets and three Aermotors, and our own Vulcan, the only three-legged one on the Point. They were all going busily in the east wind. The Tuppers had a special little shingled tower, with a red railing around the top, where Frank Tupper went with a telescope to watch the yacht-races in the bay, but this I passed quickly, looking at the house and garden out of the tail of my eye, to see if Gwendolyn was there. Had she got the box of candy I had left on her porch for her, with the heart on it, and our initials. Would she laugh at me. Did I dare go in the afternoon to the drill of the Company at the Camp. Would she have told Frank about it, and would Frank say anything. When we were playing cross-tag I had caught her by her pig-tail, and she had looked at me in a very queer way, half angry and half pleased, and then had refused to play any more. What was this about Father and Mother. Was it because she went sailing all the time with Uncle David, just like last year, and walks to the beach always at night after Porper and Susan had gone to bed. The stage passed me, coming from the morning train, the one named Priscilla, painted a bright yellow, with red wheels, and toothless Smiley driving the horses and saying "Giddup, giddup" out of the side of his mouth, spitting tobacco juice. I would be in plenty of time for the mail, in fact I would have time to go to the drug-store and have a chocolate milk-shake at the marble fountain, which always smelled of vanilla. If it rained in the afternoon, we would play Gonko in the playhouse, and perhaps make some new racquets out of shingles. If it didn't rain, I would go for a row in the dory, through the long bridge and up into the marsh channel towards Brant Rock and Marshfield, for the tide would be low, and I could explore the channels. If I got stuck, I could pretend to be just clam-digging, the way Uncle Tom always said the yachtsmen pretended to do when they got stuck on the mudflats in the bay. They always took pails and shovels with them in case they got stuck, and then rolled up their trousers and went digging, as if that was what they had come for. Or perhaps

Uncle David would invite us out in his cabin motor-boat, late in the afternoon, with Mother, and Uncle Tom, and Aunt Norah, and that would be fun, except that I didn't like Uncle David. I heard Molly saying to Margaret in their room when they were going to bed that he was always drunk. Did that mean falling down. I had never seen him fall down. But I had seen bottles under the bunk in the cabin of the motor-boat several times and he had bottles in his room downstairs, on the table under the row of dried and mounted seaweeds, which Uncle Tom and I had put there the year before.

———and beyond the golf-links, where I always left the bicycle-path, paved with broken clam-shells, to walk along the edge of the course, among the bayberry bushes and cherry trees, hoping for lost golf-balls, prodding in the poison-ivy with a stick, beyond this the boarding-house kept by old Mrs. Soule, where we had stayed last year and the year before, with the hen-houses at the back, and the little sandy-rutted road which led down to the cove and the stone dyke where beech-plums grew. The floors were painted gray, with white speckles, the whole house had a marine smell like a ship, conch-shells lined the path and stood against the doors, and on the lawn, among the croquet wickets, I had found four-leaved clovers. Molly Soule always sat alone in the swing, large-eyed, pallid, her thin little hands around the ropes, looking sadly at us, because we never played with her. Nobody ever played with her, because her name was the same as her mother's, and she had no father. She was always hanging about and watching us from a little distance, and would run away and cry if we said anything to her, especially the Sanford boy, who asked her so many times what her name was. This was where I played baseball with Father in the evening, or ran races with him from one telephone pole to another. Was it true that he was coming again this year. Why was it that this year we were staying with Uncle Tom, and Aunt Norah, and Uncle David, instead of at the Soules'. Though it was nice, particularly as Uncle Tom knew so much about the wild flowers, and had that nice little tin cylinder to bring back the flowers in, the one he had brought all the way from Switzerland a long while ago. It hung over his shoulder on a strap, and we had found swamp-pink in the marsh near Pembroke woods, and arrowhead, and ghost-flower. Jewel-weed, on the way to the Standish Monument, pickerel weed, and button-bush. If only he could go more often

—we already had more than fifty kinds, pressed in the blank-book, it would be easy to get a hundred before the summer was over. Why was he so thin, and his knees so funny, and he always wore that funny yachting-cap with the green vizor, his ears sticking out at the sides, walking in his bathing-suit over the humped grass to the Point with the row-locks jingling in his hand. I said to him that I thought I was getting fatter. He gave that nice little chuckle and said, No danger, Andy. Why was it he and Uncle David had never learned to swim properly——

———when we got to the oak woods we decided after all to go to the pine woods instead, because the oak woods were smaller and closer together, there were no logs to build with, and no room anyway; so we took Warren and Gay with us and we sat in the houses of logs while it rained, and only a few drops of rain came through the roofs, which we had made out of pine boughs. Susan was in one house with Warren, and Gay was in the other with me. I asked if we should take our clothes off and go to bed, pretending it was night, but she said no and began to cry. Warren and Susan had taken off theirs. Warren didn't mind, but Gay said she wanted to go home, and I was afraid she would tell her mother.

So I told her about the villages we made of shells on the beach, and the dead seal.

—It's swarming with maggots.

—What are maggots.

—Little white worms, millions of them, and it smells so bad that you can smell it all the way up to the house when the wind is right.

—Do you go bathing every day, we go every day, and we have a sailboat at the Point.

—I have a dory of my own, and my uncle has a motorboat which he takes us out in. It has a real cabin with doors that lock.

The smell was so bad that we couldn't get very near to the seal without feeling sick, but I showed her the maggots. Then Mother came down the hill walking very slowly, with Porper holding her hand. She was carrying a red silk parasol over her head.

—Porper wants to see the village. Show him how you build houses, Andy and Susan, I want to read my book. Are these your little friends? What are your names, children? Oh, you're the little girl and boy who have just moved in next door, aren't you.

We made houses out of rows of quartz pebbles in the sand, in between the beds of eel-grass. First they all had to buy their land from me with shells for money: scallop shells were five dollars, clam shells were one dollar, toe-nail shells were fifty cents. Mother had made a pile of dried eel-grass to lean against, and was reading a book under her parasol. Warren sold quartz pebbles to us for building material. Susan kept the bakery shop where we bought bread and cakes, Gay was the grocer. I built a house for Porper, and showed him how to go in and out of the imaginary door, and where the bedroom was, and how to go along the streets without stepping into the other houses by mistake. The tide was way out, all the mud-flats in the bay were showing, and a little way out two men with a dory were digging clams.

—Shall we dig some clams for supper, Mother.

—Not today, Andy.

—When are we going to the Long Beach for a clam-bake, and to see the Gurnett. Tomorrow?

—Not till next week, I'm afraid. Now don't bother Mother, she's reading. And she may take a nap, she's very tired and sleepy, so don't disturb her.

Susan took off Porper's sneakers so that he could go wading.

—There you are, lamb. Don't mind about the clam-bake, we'll have it next week, and you'll see the ocean and all the dead fishes.

—What dead fishes.

—And here are some more scallop-shells for you, and a horseshoe crab.

Warren and I walked along the beach toward the Point, and I showed him the hunting-box, all covered deep in dried seaweed. We got into it and lay down for a while. It smelt very nice. There was an old beer-bottle in the corner, with sand and water in it, and we took it out and threw stones at it until it was broken. Take that. And that. And that. And that for your old man.

When we went back, Uncle David had come, and was standing in front of Mother, with his hands in his duck trousers. He was looking down at her and laughing. The parasol had fallen on the sand, she was lying back with her hands under her head.

—Say that again.

—Why not?

—Well, say it.

They laughed together, and then he turned his head toward us and said, Hi, there: what mischief have you fellows been up to?

—Andy, why don't you take your little friends down to the Point and show them your dory. I'm sure they'd like to see it. Wouldn't you?

———at the Company Camp, on the edge

of the other oak woods, in the late afternoon, with the long yellow sunset light coming over the stunted trees, Frank Tupper drilled us in a row, Sanford and myself and Gwendolyn and the two Peters girls, Warren sitting on the grass and watching us, because he hadn't yet been elected. Present arms. Shoulder arms. Port arms. Ground arms. Parade rest. The wooden cannon was dragged out of the hut and loaded with a blank cartridge for the sunset salute. The Peters' windmill, a Sunbeam, was pumping, and water was spattering down from the overflow pipe to the cement base. Frank looked at his watch, looked importantly at the sky, at the oak woods, behind which the sun might or might not have set, then gave the order to fire. Bang. The sun had set, and the cloud of blue smoke floated quickly away. Gwendolyn hadn't said a word to me. What had she done with the box of candy. Had she shown it to any one. Was it she, or some one else, who had first found it there on the porch. Did she throw it away. Had she laughed. Was she angry. She stood next to me as we saluted the flag, which Frank was hauling down for the night, the folds winding themselves about his shoulders, but she was careful not to touch me. Did I dare to look at her. No. She was stronger than I, taller, but in the wrestling match I had got her down and held her down, with my hands hard on her shoulders. At the picnic in Pembroke woods, she and I had gone off by ourselves to look for firewood, and had gathered wood in a separate heap before taking it back to the others, but all the while we hadn't said a word. Why was that. Was she as shy as I was, or was she annoyed with me. What was their house like, inside. I had never been into it. They had a bathing-hut of their own, in the Cove, and a long narrow pier which led out across the eel-grass to deep water, with a float at the end, where their green canoe was hauled up. It was near the place where Molly and Margaret went to bathe. Once I had followed them down the road, to watch them bathe there, but when I got to the beach I saw Frank and Gwendolyn there on the float, so I had slunk away.

—Moved and seconded that Warren Walker be made a private in this Company. All those in favour say aye.

—Aye.

———in the evening, after helping the cat, Juniper, to catch grass-hoppers among the hummocks of wild grass, swishing his tail against my leg, and purring, Uncle Tom and Uncle David and Aunt Norah and Mother having all gone to a dance at the McGills', and Porper in bed, singing to himself in Mother's room upstairs, and Susan swinging in a hammock on the porch, with one leg out so that she could push herself to and fro, I walked across the tennis-court and watched the moon rise over the Long Beach. The tennis-court needed hoeing again. And it needed new lines of whitewash. There were lights in the Walker house, and Mr. Walker went from the house to the barn with a pail in his hand. Then we sat at the dining-table under the swinging lamp and played jackstraws.

—I heard Uncle Tom and Aunt Norah talking about Father and Mother.

—You shouldn't have listened.

—I couldn't help it. They were talking while I was dressing.

—What did they say.

—What do you want to know for, if you think I shouldn't have listened.

—Oh, well, you don't have to tell me, do you.

—They said they had quarrelled.

—Who had quarrelled.

—Father and Mother.

—I don't believe it.

—You don't have to. And they said something about Father coming down to Duxbury.

—Andy! He's coming for the clam-bake! Is that it?

—How should I know. That's all I heard, nitwit.

—Well, I'll bet that's what it is.

—Anyway, the clam-bake's been put off again, hang it. We'll never get to that Gurnett. I think I'll go by myself. I'm sick and tired of waiting for them to get ready—first it's one fool thing and then another.

—Well, go ahead, why don't you. You could row there, couldn't you?

—Row there! Seven miles there and seven miles back? I guess not. What about the tides. Or what about a thunder-storm. How'd you like to get caught in a thunder-storm in a dory, twit! If I go, I'll walk.

—Well, you rowed to Clark's Island, didn't you?

———particularly also the sense of timelessness, the telescoping of day with day, of place with place, evening with evening, and morning with morning. The thunder-storms always coming from the southwest or west, the sky darkening first to cold gray, then to livid purple behind the Standish Monument, the wind rising to a scream across the black bay, the lightning stabbing unceasingly at the far, small figure of Miles Standish. Then the little house lashed wildly by the horizontal rain, the rush to shut the screens and doors and windows, the doors that would hardly shut against the wind, and the leaks everywhere, through walls and roof, pails and tins set out to receive the rapid pinging and clunking of drops, the struggle to get the hammocks in from the porch, take down the tennis net. Andy! Did you get the net in? The bows and arrows? Where are the racquets? Susan—Susan—where is Susan? Always the same thing. Or, at night, the splendid spectacle of the lightning across the bay, the storm advancing rapidly towards the open sea, and presently the lights of Plymouth far off across the water, like a long row of winking jewels, reappearing once more, and the lights of the Standish House, bright through the rain-washed evening air, as if nothing at all had happened.

Uncle David stared at them through the spyglass, from the wet porch.

—They must have turned the power off.

—Why do they turn the power off, Uncle David.

—Oh, I don't know—to prevent a short circuit, or something.

—But they don't turn them off in Boston.

—Well, Plymouth isn't Boston.

—There they come again.

—Yes, now they've turned them on. Take a look, Tom? Here, Doris, take a look.

They all looked in turns through the little telescope, the same one through which they regarded the moon-mountains, sweeping it along the row of distant twinkling lights and the beards of reflected light in the water, Susan and myself coming last. Nothing to see, why bother? It was always Uncle David who went out first to see whether the Plymouth lights had yet been turned on. Or what trees had been hit, or whether a haystack or barn had been set afire. Uncle David this, and Uncle David that. Was it because Uncle David was rich. Or because he had nothing to do. He was always there, he was always in everything, pushing about with his red moustache and blue eyes, as if the world belonged to him. It was Uncle David who made us hoe the tennis-court, and mark the lines, and who beat everybody except Father at tennis. This year, he was forever playing Mother, sometimes before breakfast, when the rest of us weren't up yet, at seven o'clock. Several times I was waked up by hearing them, and got out of bed and went to the window to watch them, keeping back from the window so as not to be seen. Mother dressed in white, with her hair in a pigtail down her back, like a girl, and laughing a lot, and saying, David, how could you. Once she turned her ankle, running out into the field after a ball, and then Uncle David picked her up and carried her round the corner to the front of the house. It was because of those hummocks of wild grass, those hard tufts—it was easy to turn your ankle. But when I asked her about it at breakfast she looked surprised, and said it was nothing. Nothing at all.

—But, darling Andy, how did you happen to see? How did you happen to be up so early?

—I heard you playing, Mother.

—David, that was very naughty of us—we mustn't do it again—we woke them up.

—Oh, I think the little rascal was up on his own account—weren't you, Andy. He was probably catching flies for that cage of his.

—No I wasn't, either. I heard you playing, and then I got up to see who it was.

—It doesn't really matter, though I often think that on these summer mornings, when the light is so early, we might all get up earlier than we do. But, of course, Norah, we won't—I know your habits too well. And the children must get their full sleep.

———and the tiny little brown pond deep down in the cleft behind the Wardman house, only a stone's throw from our windmill, with the black alders around it, and the sumachs, and the frogs, and turtles, the turtles which sidled away into the dirty water when we came, and the high rock at one side. I went down to it in the morning and found a rose-quartz Indian arrowhead in the sand at the edge of it, a perfect one, very small and sharp. It was a beauty. How Uncle Tom would be pleased when he saw it, for it was better than any we had found before, better even than the white quartz one we had found out at the end of the Point, better far than the flint ones. I sat there on the rock by the sumachs, and knew that it was Thursday, for on Thursday afternoons I had to go to the village and have my Latin lesson with Mr. Dearing, in the white house at the water's edge, with his knockabout moored a little way out, in which, perhaps, after the lesson, he would take me for a sail. His house was a nice one, with lots of books and pictures, it was quiet and small like himself, and smelt of lavender. He was like Uncle Tom. Uncle Tom, if Mr. Dearing asks me to go for a sail, can I go. Last time he let me take the tiller, and I learned how to come about. We followed the yacht-race, and beat them, on the same course, too, but outside them at every buoy, which made it longer. The course with the first leg towards Clark's Island and the second towards the Point. You know the one, we've often watched them from the porch. Can I do that. Or can I go by myself to the woods on the other side of Standish Hill, to see if I can find some wild indigo, and press it, and see if it turns black in the book. Or would you like to come with me.

—No Porper, I can't take you to the Horse Monument this afternoon, because Uncle Tom and I are going to the woods to look for wild flowers.

—But I want to see the Horse Monument.

—But you've seen it dozens of times, Porper.

—I want to see it. I want to see where the horse was buried.

—Why don't you take him, Susan?

—Oh, Porper—why do you want to see it. You know what it's like—it's just like any other tombstone, only it's made of bricks, and it's because a horse was buried there, a man's favourite horse, and he put up a monument for it when it died. He was a nice man, wasn't he?

—I want to see the Horse Monument.

—Go on, Susan, and take him. It's your turn. I took him last time.

At Mr. Dearing's, the clock ticked on the white-painted wooden mantelpiece, between the model of a ship and a barometer, the clock ticked Latin, and Mr. Dearing's gentle voice asked me questions, went through my exercise, alternately chastened and sustained me, while through the open window, on the side of the house toward the bay, the soft sound of the waves came, lapping among reeds and eel-grass, and the knocking of a dory against the float. If I turned my head I could see Mr. Dearing's knockabout, with its boom, the mainsail neatly furled, propped up in its shears of wood. Now that declension again. You're a little shaky on that declension. Those ablatives seem to bother you, don't they? And those verbs. You must get them into your head. *Utor, fruor, potior, fungor,* and *vescor.* They have a nice sound, Andy, don't you think? *Utor, fruor, fungor, potior,* and *vescor.*

Uncle Tom had on his white yachting-cap, with the green vizor, and the tin cylinder hung from his shoulder, and as we climbed the sandy road over Standish Hill, I asked him if he had heard the bell ring, the bell of the Unitarian Church. We were passing a clump of sumachs.

—These aren't poison sumachs, are they, Uncle Tom?

—No. But what about that bell?

—I rang it myself, at ten minutes past two.

And I told him how it had happened. The village barber was cutting my hair, and said that he was the church sexton, and that he had to go and wind the clock, and asked me if I'd like to see how he did it, it was just across the road. We unlocked the church and went in, and climbed up two flights of dark stairs in the tower, and then two ladders which went straight up through narrow trap-doors until we got to a shaky landing beside the machinery of the clock, where there were lots of cobwebs and dust. The barber wound a crank, and we could hear the clock ticking very loud. Then he asked me if I would like to strike the bell, and gave me a short rope and told me to pull it: I gave it a pull, and the machinery began grinding to itself, a sort of growling, and then suddenly came the huge ring of sound, shaking the belfry, everything trembled with it, and I thought of the bell-sound travelling all the way to Powder Point, and every one wondering what time it was.

Shad-bush, wild sarsaparilla, St. John's Wort, sand spurrey, wild indigo, and checker-berry. The goldenrods belong to the compos-ite family, there are forty kinds in New

England; but this sort, *solidago sempervirens*, which grows in the salt marshes, or near them—the heaviest, the strongest, the most fragrant—the one that the bees love, and the flies——

——or again to remember the first arrival, the arrival at the end of June after school was over, that first and sweetest deliciousness of escape and renewal, the foresight of so much delight, the largeness and wideness and brightness, the sun everywhere, the sea everywhere, the special salt spaciousness, which one felt even at the little shabby railway station, three miles inland, at the bottom of the hill, where the road turned. Even the weatherboards of the wooden station seemed to be soaked in salt sea-fog, the little cherry trees had about them a special air as of knowing the sea, and the old coach, the Priscilla or the Miles Standish, with Smiley driving it, or Bart Cahoun, waiting for us there with its lean horses, had on its wheels the sand of Powder Point. In the very act of getting down from the train we already participated in the rich seaside summer—our trunks, lying on the platform, on the hot rough pine-planks, shared in the mystery, became something other than the humble boxes into which we had put our bathing-suits and sneakers. The world became dangerously brilliant, ourselves somehow smaller, but more meaningful; in the deep summer stillness, the country stillness, it seemed almost as if already we could hear the sea. Our voices, against the little cherry trees which the coach was passing, their boughs whitely shrouded by tent-caterpillars, and the gray shingled cottages covered with trumpet-vine, and the stone walls and the apple orchards, were different from our Cambridge voices. Even Mother became different, was smaller and more vivid. Would it all be the same again. Would the tide be out or in. Would the golden weathervane still be there. Would the dam under the village bridge be opened or closed. Would it be as nice living at Uncle Tom's as at the Soules'. It was nearer to the end of the Point, nearer the long bridge, nearer the sea——

—Now you must remember, children, it's not quite like staying at the Soules', we are visitors, and Uncle Tom has built a nice playhouse for you, and you must try to play there as much as you can, so that the house can be quiet.

—Can Porper kneel up, Mother, he wants to look out.

—You can keep all your toys there, and on

rainy days it will be very nice for you. It's a nice little house, painted green, down at the foot of the hill, near that rock——

—You mean Plymouth Rock Junior.

—Yes.

—What's Plymouth Rock Junior.

—Oh, Porper, you don't remember, but you'll see.

—Susan, will you keep hold of Porper's hand?

—Is that Plymouth Rock Junior.

—No, that's just a rock in front of the library. That's where Andy goes on Wednesdays to get books, don't you, Andy.

—I'm going to read *Calumet K* again. And *Huckleberry Finn* again.

Would there be any new books. To carry home under my raincoat in the rain, past the house that was always to let, and the bowling alleys, and then along the lagoon to King Cæsar's Road.

—Will Uncle David be there, Mother?

—Yes, I suppose so. He has a new motorboat.

—We must have a picnic on the outer beach soon, Mother, we must have two of them this year, not one like last year.

—Will we have blueberries and cream, and blueberry muffins?

—Yes, yes, now don't bother Mother, Mother's thinking.

—Why are you thinking.

—Andy, for goodness sake take Porper's other hand. Sit still, Porper. Look, do you see the weathervane. It's a rooster made out of gold.

———the particular breadth and suggestion of sea-wonder that began always when the coach turned north at the fork of the road, under the weathervane, and then rounded the lagoon toward King Cæsar's Road, and passing this, rattled along the rutted sand Point Road—we were getting nearer the sea, there was now water on both sides of us, water and marshes, we were going out into the Atlantic Ocean. We were getting nearer to the outer beach, and the long red bridge that led to it, nearer to the Gurnett, with its squat twin light-houses. How soon would the picnic be. There would be steamed clams, and sweet potatoes, and corn, hidden in the nests of hot wet seaweed, on a bed of charred stones. We would gather shells. We would find fragments of driftwood and take them home with us in the little cart which Porper would sit in, with his legs spread out. We would climb the dunes and slide down the slopes of hot loose sand. There would be new breaches in the wall of dunes, where the sea had broken through during the winter, wide flat beds of stones. Where I went wading last year with Gwendolyn, and she held her dress up high, and I saw her garters, the quick exciting flash of silver. We were looking for live horseshoe crabs. I pretended to look for crabs, holding my head down, but was really watching her knees, and she knew that I was watching her, and held her dress higher. Andy, I've found three, and you haven't found one. And look, here's the smallest one yet—! She held it up out of the water by its beak, and it arched itself almost double, small and transparent. I took it in my hand and we looked at it together, and holding up her dress she leaned against me, and I heard her breathing.

———the night when Uncle Tom and Aunt Norah had gone to the Yacht Club to see the fireworks, riding on their bicycles, with the little lamps lighted, the red jewel at one side and the green at the other, and the smell of hot kerosene, we watched the little wobbling arcs of light moving away along the sand-ruts, and I pointed out to Susan the stars in Cassiopeia's Chair, standing on the tennis-court. Mother and Uncle David were talking on the porch, each in a different hammock, slapping at mosquitos and laughing, for they had decided to stay at home and watch the fireworks from the Point. We sat down on the edge of the porch and looked at the Plymouth lights and waited for the fireworks, but they didn't come. Perhaps they would be later. Mother was lying back in her hammock, with her hands under her head and her white elbows lifted and Uncle David was smoking a cigarette. When he drew in his breath, the end of the cigarette glowed and lit up his face, and he was always looking downward at the floor and frowning.

—Susan, darling, how did all that water get there on the floor.

—It was Porper, Mother, he was blowing soap-bubbles before supper.

—Will one of you please clean it up. Andy, will you get a mop or a cloth from the kitchen and wipe it up. You're the porch-cleaner, aren't you.

—Oh, Mother, I'll have to sweep it in the morning anyway——

—But it doesn't look nice. Run along. Perhaps afterwards you and Susan would like to have a game of croquinole together.

—Could we go out for a row in the dory.

—If it's a very short one. You must have Susan back in time for her bedtime.

In the kitchen, I stood by the sink and

looked out of the window at the back, and saw some one carrying a lighted lamp across one of the windows in the Wardman house. Molly and Margaret were talking to a man in the darkness on the back porch, probably the chauffeur from the Tuppers, who was always hanging around them. I didn't either. You did too. I didn't either. You did too. You're crazy to say such a thing you ought to know better than that I never said any such thing to him in my life, not me. I only said I saw them on the beach. I wouldn't say more than that. What were they talking about? I listened, but they must have known I was there, for they lowered their voices, and I couldn't make out anything else, especially as the windmill was pumping, and I could hear the groan of the rod and the regular gush of water into the cistern. I went out into the pantry to get the mop, went down the three wooden steps to the earthen floor, and stood there in the nice smell of potatoes and squashes and green corn and damp smell of earth, watching the indicator on the cistern, the little lead weight jiggling lower and lower against the pine boards as the water raised the float. Last year we had to pump all the water by hand. A hundred strokes without stopping. I rolled up my sleeves, and always felt my muscles when I had finished, to see how hard they were. Why was Mother always trying to get rid of us like this. With Father it was different, he always wanted to do things with us in the holidays. Like last year, when he gave me the camera and took me on walks and showed me how to take pictures, and I got the picture of the beach-plum dyke all crooked, so that it looked like a wave of cobblestones. And I took the Horse Monument, but it was out of focus, or light-struck, or something. But I had fifteen blue-prints that were quite good.

When I got back to the porch Susan was alone.

—Where have they gone.

—Oh, down to the front beach or something.

—They make me sick always going off like that.

—Andy, you shouldn't talk like that.

—Well, they do. I bet they've gone out in the motorboat, that's what they've done, and without inviting us.

—They don't have to invite us every time they go, do they?

—No, but they might invite us sometimes. Come on, we'll go out in the dory, and I don't care if we never get back.

—But we won't see the fireworks, Andy.

—Who wants to see the fireworks, besides we could row around to this side of the Point, couldn't we? Don't be a twit.

We walked down across the humped grass to the Point, in the dark, the blades of the oars clacking together as I carried them over my shoulder, the row-locks jingling in Susan's hand. It was warm and the crickets were chirping. Susan was ahead of me when we got to the bluff, I watched her white dress vanish down the sandy path to the beach, and then I looked out at the water and saw a light in the cabin of Uncle David's motor-boat. It looked far out, because the tide was high, almost up to the foot of the bluff. Susan was already sitting in the stern of the dory, hanging her hands in the water, the ripples were slapping against the sides, and I pulled the anchor out of the bayberry bush and got in. Ought I to tell Susan what I was going to do, or not. If I didn't, she might talk, and spoil everything. If I did, she might not want to, and besides we might see something——

—I tell you what we'll do, we'll pretend we're spies, and row right round them. I'll row round them so close we could touch them, and they won't hear a sound.

—But, Andy——

—Shut up, will you?

I pushed the blade of the oar into the sand and shoved off with two shoves and then began rowing very softly, rowing backwards, so that I could face towards the motorboat. Why was I frightened. What was there to be frightened of. It was only like playing the Indian scouting game. It was only like the guerrilla war in the Pembroke Woods. How could they possibly hear us anyway, with the ripples washing against the Osprey, making that hollow coppery sound that you heard when you were down in the cabin. And they couldn't see us, because the little yellow curtains were drawn across the two cabin portholes. I backed out till we were past the white bow, which looked very high, and then shipped my oars and let the tide take us slowly alongside. We could hear them talking. The tender, which was tied with too short a painter, was bumping against the port side of the stern, and in the cabin there was a thump as if something had been dropped on the floor.

—Come on, Doris, let's have another.

—Oh, no, let's——

—Oh, come on, the night is young.

—I don't like it, David.

—What's wrong with it? Are you getting a conscience or something?

—Oh, no, but if they thought——

—Thought what.

—Oh, you know as well as I do.

—Let them think. Here, try this——

—Please, David——

I gave a push with my hand against the brass corner of the sternplate and we just barely cleared the gunwale of the tender, which was swinging across. They were drinking, Uncle David must be trying to make Mother drunk, that was it, perhaps the thump was a bottle falling on the floor of the cabin. I let the tide carry us a little way toward the bridge, where I could see the high wooden piers of the draw, and then I shipped my oars and began to row.

—We'll go through the draw, and then across to the outer beach. Then we'll walk along the beach to the dunes and watch the fireworks.

—Andy, what were they saying, what was Mother saying.

—I couldn't hear. Was the cabin door open or shut.

—It was shut.

I shot the dory through the draw, where the tide was swift, the deep eddies sucking and chuckling at the foot of the tall piles, and felt my face hot, and I wanted to do something, to go back there, to bank at the side of the Osprey, to shout. But what was the use.

———particularly always, too, the hour after lunch, the hot and peaceful hour, the sleepy hour, when Susan and Porper always had to have naps upstairs, and Mother and Aunt Norah stretched themselves out in hammocks on the porch, and Uncle David went into his room to read, and Uncle Tom wrote letters on the dining-room table, or painted screens on the grass in front of the house, the screens supported on wooden horses. What would we do later. Would we be sent to the playhouse for the whole afternoon, or would we go clam-digging, or take a walk to the cove, or would Sanford come to tell me that there was a baseball game at the Peters'. I went down to the playhouse by myself, it was very hot and smelt of new wood, greenhead flies were on the insides of the screens, and I thought it would be a good chance to see if I could take off the handlebars of Aunt Norah's new Columbia bicycle, so I stood on the table, the one we played Gonko on, and hauled myself up to the top of the wooden partition, and dropped over into the bicycle shed. This business of taking naps after lunch. This hammock business. Mother's hand lying over the edge of the yellow striped hammock, the fringe of long yellow strings rippling in the southwest wind, her book fallen to the verandah floor, the opened pages fluttering. Susan, pretending to take a nap in her room, but really reading. Uncle David pretending to take a nap, but really drinking out of one of those bottles, using the tumbler on the washstand, which always smelt like bay rum. I took the monkey-wrench out of the little cylindrical tool-kit under the saddle and got the handlebars off easily enough, but I was worried for fear I wouldn't get them back on again at the same height and angle, and sweated at the thought that Aunt Norah might notice it. It was a Columbia Chainless, and what I really wanted to do was to open the gear-box and look at the gears, but the nuts were too tight, and I was afraid. Besides, somebody might come—Uncle Tom might take it into his head to come down looking for me, maybe to ask me to go on a wildflower hunt, and I wouldn't have time to get it together again. I climbed back into the playhouse, and then I went outside and crawled under the floor and got some more shingles, with crickets walking on them, and took them into the playhouse to make some new Gonko racquets. We would need some more ping-pong balls. Porper was always losing them or stepping on them. He kept throwing them into the bed of poison-ivy at the foot of the hill, by the stone wall. That was where all the golf-balls used to go when Uncle Tom and Father played golf. I looked at my shin to see if the little blue map of the golf-ball was still there, and it was almost gone.

I walked down the lane as far as the Horse Monument, went back into the pine woods for a minute, near our houses, thinking about Gay, and then about Gwendolyn, and wondered what she would think if she knew I played house in the woods with my sister, like a little sissy. When I got to the hotel I went first out on to the stone wharf, and watched a tug towing a barge across the bay. Some of the maids from the hotel were in bathing-suits, sitting on the stone edge of the wharf, and when they saw me they began laughing. I walked back to the hotel and went along the edge of the golf course, toward the Point Road. There was nobody playing golf, it was too early. Too hot. The sheep were all lying under a tree chewing their cuds. I threw acorns at them and made them get up, and then I was ashamed and went up between the houses and through the small oak woods to the Company Camp. The Peters were there, and Sanford, and Warren, and Frank Tupper, but not

Gwendolyn. They were lying in the grass. What were we going to do. Should we go and play in the hay-loft, dive down through the chute, slide down the rope.

—Andy's got a sweetheart.

—Where's Gwendolyn, Andy?

—Shut up.

Frank Tupper looked at me and then got up and walked to the Company hut. He went in, and in a minute came out again holding up a baseball bat.

—Scrub one, he said.

—Scrub two.

—Three.

—Four.

—Five.

We played baseball till Gwendolyn came, and then we took turns standing under the overflow of the windmill and letting the water splash on our heads. I turned my face up, and let the water spout out of my mouth.

—He thinks he's smart.

—Rats live on no evil star.

—What do you mean by that?

—Just what I say. Rats live on no evil star.

Frank Tupper spat in his baseball glove.

—That's an old one. A palindrome.

—A what?

—It spells the same thing backwards.

Susan came running across the field and fell down and began to cry. I walked home with her, and we sat on Plymouth Rock Junior under the cherry tree, and she said that Mother and Aunt Norah were quarrelling upstairs in Aunt Norah's room, and Uncle Tom and Uncle David had gone off for a walk not saying a word, and Porper was all alone with the maids, sitting in the soap-box sailboat—and Molly with an earache——

———lying awake, too, with the wind singing through the wire screens, and the soft muslin curtains sucking and fluttering against the screens, and the sea-moon shining through them on to the floor and across the foot of my bed, and the crickets chirping like mad, the mosquitoes, too, humming so loudly outside the window that they sounded as if they were in the room. What was that they had said at supper. When Aunt Norah was pouring the cocoa out of the jug. It should have been here this evening. Who was it that got the mail. It was Smiley that brought it. Why didn't Andy go. Well, anyway it didn't come. Mother was humming as she buttered more bread for Porper; Uncle Tom tapped with his fingers on the bare edge of the table as if he were playing a tune on a piano. What letter was it that hadn't come. Was it from

Father. Were they expecting Father. What fun that would be. He would get out the cameras, and he would teach me how to pitch an out-drop. And now the two sets of voices downstairs—Molly and Margaret, at the back of the house, murmuring and giggling secretly, slyly, insinuatingly, and the others on the front porch, a little farther off, more intermittent, now and then more loudly, and Uncle David's deep laugh which always sounded a little angry. Andy's got a sweetheart. What did they mean by that. Had Gwendolyn told everybody about it, or was it perhaps Frank who had first found the box of candy. Perhaps he had found it and had never given it to Gwendolyn. Shame on Andy, shame on Andy. Let them say it. I would row right round Clark's Island, taking all day if necessary, and find my way at low tide through the channels, counting the seals on the mud-flats. I would row to Plymouth. I would borrow Mr. Dearing's knockabout and sail right out past Plymouth Beach into Massachusetts Bay, and watch the Plymouth steamer going past on its way to Boston. I would swim across from the Point to the Long Beach. I would dive off the pier of the draw on the long bridge, twenty feet down into the swift current of the tide. I would strike out Frank Tupper every time he came to bat. And I wouldn't say a word to Gwendolyn, not another word all summer.

They were beginning to sing. It was always Uncle David who started them on that, he had a swelled head about his voice, and always sang when he was hoeing the tennis-court with us. Oh, you beautiful doll, you great big beautiful doll.

Margaret was talking to a man under my back window.

—Quit it.

—I will not.

—I said quit it, will you?

I got quickly out of bed and went to the window to see what they were doing, but I was too late, they had gone round the corner of the house into the shadow, to get out of the moonlight. I waited, listening, but they didn't come back. He must have been kissing her. I would keep awake until they came to bed. Watch them through the hole by the washstand. It would be dark on my side of the wall, I would stand very still in bare feet, get back into bed without a sound, they would never suspect that I was watching them. Should I go to bed now or stay up. Better stay up, and watch the flies in the flytrap with the electric flashlight. I got the flashlight and looked at the flies. They were all asleep, standing upside down under the roof of screen wire, their white bellies turned towards the light. I ought to let them go, Uncle David was beginning to suspect why I kept them. Perhaps I had better give him one of my arrowheads. What mischief have you fellows been up to. Uncle David, I thought you might like to have one of my arrowheads, it's a quartz one.

I went to the side window, beside the tennis court, to hear them singing. They were singing the song that Uncle David had made up. When I slap on the kalsomine I think about those gals o' mine way down in old Kentucky where the moon is shining bright. When I slap on the Reckitts blue I think about the thickets through the mountains of Virginia where I walked with them at night. Walls and ceilings have their feelings the same as you and me. I'm only a paper-hanger, but my heart is pure as mud. When they had finished it, they all laughed in the silly way they always did, the laughter rising and falling, mixing and unmixing, but I could make out Mother's and Uncle David's, particularly at the end, when Mother's went up and Uncle David's went down. The twits. The nitwits. But what about the letter, and why, come to think of it, hadn't I been sent for the evening mail, as usual. Instead, I had been sent to the playhouse with Porper, and when I brought him back, I had to sail him in the soapbox sailboat.

Footsteps were coming up the stairs, candlelight wavered on the rough, pine beams of the unfinished roof; it was Molly and Margaret coming up to bed, and I tiptoed with cold, naked feet on the bare floor and stood by the washstand, hardly breathing, and waited.

———the dust, too, as the stage coach rattled past me and turned up King Cæsar's Road, to go to Powder Point Hall, skewing a little, the rear wheels slewing in the sandy ruts as Smiley touched up the old horses, the whole thing like Buffalo Bill. I looked through the packet of letters again, to make sure that there was none from Father. Harvard University. Jordan Marsh. Acme Cleaning Company. A small blue envelope, addressed in small handwriting, to Mother. Another, in the same handwriting, to Aunt Norah. Both postmarked Plymouth. Nothing that looked as if it might be from Father. By this time the train would be at Kingston. Or maybe at the Cordage. The people in the train would see the back of the Standish Monument, which I had seen only once, when we went to Plymouth to see the Plymouth Rock. We had lunch at that old house with four English elms in front of it, which Captain Something-or-Other had brought back from England in 1750.

I leaned against the wooden fence and looked at the two new knockabouts in the lagoon, exactly alike except that the *Bobkat* was brown, with a silver waterline, and the *Moujik II* was white with a gold waterline. The bowsprits were very short. Mr. McGill, who manufactured oil stoves, owned them both, and one or the other of them came in second in every race at the Yacht Club. Mr. McGill had that new house near Powder Point Hall, with the imitation windmill which had an electric pump inside. That was where the dance had been. Mother had brought back a Japanese lantern and Uncle David had brought home a clown's mask with red holes for the eyes. He put it on at breakfast. What was that thing he had said to Mother, when we were going round Clark's Island in the motor-boat, something about drowning. To drown with thee. They were both holding the wheel, one on one side, and one on the other. Laughing, as I jumped down from the cabin-roof into the cockpit. To drown with thee. It was that Quaker-talk that the old man had talked in Salem, putting his hand on my head. And Mother and Father had been talking it when I went to the top of the stairs that night after the card-party in Cambridge. To drown with thee. What had they meant by that.

I played ducks and drakes, skipping one stone twelve times over the water towards the *Bobkat,* and then went through the bayberry jungle and the grove of wild cherry trees to the edge of the golf-course. Should I try to kiss Gwendolyn or not. Did she expect me to. Was Sanford just trying to get me into trouble when he told me to. When she saw me diving off the end of the dory she laughed, turning her face back towards Dorothy Peters as if she were saying something about me. I swam out a long way into the channel, hoping they would row out toward me, but they didn't. They went along the shore, very slowly, not looking at me again. And disappeared round the end of the Point, still laughing.

There were no golf-balls in the bayberry jungle, though I kicked the grass in the places where I had found them before, so I went along the west side of the golf-course until I got to the bungalows, and then crossed to the road and walked along the sandy bicycle path.

The telephone poles were humming in the southwest wind, a little boy was trying to fly a kite on the lawn of the mystery house, behind the trumpet-vine arbor, but he couldn't run fast enough to get it off the ground. A pretty girl was leaning out of a tiny window in a dormer at the top of the house, watching him. I blushed when she looked at me, and walked on quickly, and was opposite the Soule House, where Molly was sitting in the swing, when Father—I was thinking about the box-kite, meaning to ask Uncle Tom if we could hitch it to the cart and give Porper a ride over the tennis-court——

He came out from behind the lilac bushes and skimmed his panama hat at my head, twirling, so that it almost settled on my head, but fell on the path. He took the back of my neck in his hand and shook me, not saying anything. He was smoking a cigarette. Then he threw the cigarette away and sat down on the lawn where the four-leafed clovers were. His brown cigarette finger was tapping on his knee. He frowned and asked me how Porper and Susan were. I said they were very well, and asked him if he had come to the clam-bake. He wanted to know if Susan had learned to swim. I told him no. Had I played any baseball. Yes. Wild flowers. Yes. Done my Latin with Mr. Dearing. Yes. Was I a member of the Company this year. Yes.

He got up again, and we walked along the little road that led down to the cove and the dyke, past the henyard, where last year the trap used to be set at night for skunks. We had heard shots in the early morning and gone out to see the dead skunk. The road led through sweetgrass, the kind the Indians made into baskets. Every year they came, selling baskets from door to door, old women and old men. We walked as far as the top of the little bluff, overlooking the cove, and stood by a crab-apple tree, talking, and Father asked me how far out into the water I could throw an apple. I threw one, and he smiled, watching it splash at the edge of a mud-flat, and then said, Watch me. He took a short stick out of the grass and stuck an apple on the end of it and then whipped it with a whistling sound over his head: the apple went clear across the cove and thudded into the soft mud at the foot of the eelgrass. I tried it several times and sent one apple half way across, into the middle of the channel.

—That was a good one.

—Where did you learn to do that, Father?

—Your grandfather taught me at Jackson Falls.

—That was where the wildcats were.

—And the moosewood.

He took out his packet of Sweet Caporals and lit another cigarette. We started walking back slowly towards the Soules'.

—Did you come down for the clam-bake, Father? Are we going to have it this week?

—No. I don't know.

He took off his spectacles and polished them with a blue silk handkerchief. He was frowning again.

—I don't know how long I'm staying: I'm staying at the Soules'. I don't want you to say anything about having seen me—understand? I may go back tonight, or I may stay for a week. But I don't want you to say anything about it. I suppose you go for the mail every morning, don't you.

—Yes, usually.

—Come here tomorrow morning to see if I'm still here. And now run along back.

He stood watching me, and I ran the whole length of the narrow bicycle path to show him that I could do it this year without slackening once. When I got to the end, by the cross-roads, I turned round, but he had gone. I was out of breath, but it wasn't because of the running. Did he mean that I couldn't even tell Susan? Probably not, because, of course, the twit would get excited and say something without meaning to. What was it all about. Why was he staying at the Soules' instead of coming to Uncle Tom's. Why was he keeping it a secret. Did he want it to be a surprise, and did Mother know about it or not. Gwendolyn and Dorothy Peters coo-eed from the door of the Silliman barn, but I didn't stop. Let them coo-eee. I took the short cut past the Wardman house and the little brown pond, dropped a twig close to a frog so that he dived into the warm soupy water, and then ran up the slope past the windmill and round to the front porch. Mother was cutting Porper's hair, and laughing, and I didn't dare to look at her when I gave her the letters. Uncle David was mending the tennis net with a reel of white cord.

—Why not use a bowl. Clap it on the young feller's head and then cut round it.

———particularly also the food, the wonderful and perpetual sense of delicious and abundant food, the great jugs of rich cocoa, the great deep dish of blue-misted blueberries, the piles of muffins with their warm fragrance under the fresh napkins, the hot sweet corn wrapped in damp linen, the mountain of steamed clams. Porper beating with his spoon and saying second help, third help, fourth help, fifth help. The floating island pudding with the little white islands of stiff-beaten white of egg, which vanished on the tongue like sea-fog, and the brown column of griddle cakes, Molly laughing as she brought in a new batch. This is the grub that makes the butterfly. Every time we had griddle cakes Uncle David said that. And the procession of covered carts that brought the food every morning, standing at the kitchen door by the corner of the tennis-court—Mr. Crowell's shiny white one with all kinds of meat in it, hanging on hooks, and the red board at the back where he cut it up, which he always scraped with a knife when he had finished; and the little blue fishcart, and the great truck of vegetables and fruit. Aunt Norah always standing with her hands on her wide hips and chaffing with Mr. Crowell or Mr. Peterson. You ought to grow vegetable marrows, they're as easy to grow as squash, and have a much more delicate flavor. Why is it, Mr. Chase, that when we come to live by the sea we never can get fish. Or have to pay through the nose to get it. And those little mackerel—why they're not big enough for the cat, let alone Porper here. Shall we buy Porper a whale?

—What whale.

—Juniper won't need any fishheads or fishtails today, he had a mouse this morning.

—What mouse.

—But he never eats them, Aunt Norah.

Juniper followed me on to the tennis-court, and I caught a grasshopper for him, which spat tobacco juice in my hand. What's the use, what's the use, chew tobacco and swallow the juice. I gave Juniper the grasshopper, and he purred, crunching it, and swished his striped tail against my leg. He ran after me, crying, when I went to the stone wall by the sumach, I bent down the loose strand of barbed wire to stoop through to the other side, and he stood on a lichen-covered stone as I walked away across the field toward the front beach. The silly little cat, always expecting me to take him with me, wherever I went. And now he would probably be sick on the porch, leave a little waffle of grasshopper legs and wings for me to clean up when I came back. Andy, the cat's been sick again. Andy, will you turn on the windmill, the tank's low. Andy, will you get out the targets, we're going to have some archery practice. Andy, will you mix some limewash for the tennis-court. Andy, you shouldn't feed him grasshoppers, you know it always makes him sick. But he likes them, Mother. He likes them, Aunt

Norah. All right then, but you must expect to clean up after him when he makes a mess.

The long grass combed and seething in the southwest wind, the dry whistle of the sand in the wind, the seagrass hissing as it bowed in green waves, and the short quick waves of green-and-white water rushing up amongst the bared brown roots of the eelgrass. The fiddler crabs hurried away, clicking, as I approached the edge of the mud flats, or farther off stood and waved their little fiddles, dancing absurdly on their hind legs, and when I trod beside the air-holes in the mud, the clams squirted water like little geysers. We hadn't had clams for a week. The clam-bake looked farther off than ever. This year I would help to build the fireplace of round stones, and fetch the driftwood myself, and lay the fire, and gather the wet seaweed, and put in the clams and sweet potatoes, the yams, the green corn. And we would take our bathing-suits and bathe in the surf, the surf that came all the way from Provincetown. And after lunch, while the others dozed in the warm hollows among the sand-dunes, Porper with his dolls and Susan with her collection of razor-shells, and Uncle Tom reading Gray's Botany. I would walk all the way to the Gurnett, see the twin lighthouse at the end of the Long Beach, come back in triumph and tell them about it. Look, Susan, I found this shell at the Gurnett. Look, Aunt Norah, I found this new kind of seaweed, one that we never got before, at the Gurnett. Mother, do you think Father will like this, it's very fine, and a lovely red, do you think it will mount well, when it's spread out.

There was a mullein wagging in the wind above my head when I lay down in the grass at the top of the beach, it was in flower, a tall one, but not as tall as the one Susan had found in the field between the McGills' and the Horse Monument. Why did she always call them Grandfather Jacksons. And niggerhead grass, why was it called niggerhead grass, and who had invented the game of niggerheads. Uncle David always won, was it because he held them with a shorter stem, was it cheating, or did he pick out the good ones. Brothers looked very much alike, Uncle David looked like Father, but with red mustaches, like a Visigoth; he was taller too, and stronger, but his face was long and funny; I didn't like it, and he looked at you with narrow blue eyes as if he didn't like you. Why did he speak so much more quickly than Father, always making jokes. Why did he have so much money, and a motorboat, and an office in Boston that he never went to. And staying here all summer, making me help him hoe the tennis-court.

I counted the flowers I could see from where I lay. Mullein. Marsh rosemary. Beach-plum. Vetch. Three kinds of goldenrod. Milk-weed. Beach pea. Hawkweed. Button bush. Dandelion. Butter-and-eggs. And when we got back to Cambridge the chicory would be in bloom, with its large stars of pale blue, or deep blue, or sometimes pink——

———the quarrelling hour after supper, the croquet hour, when we took down the soap-box sailboat, lowering the spritsail, which was made of gunny-sack, and coiling the ropes, and putting the soap-box under the porch—and the wickets and posts put into their worn holes, among the crickets and grasshoppers, and our favourite mallets chosen. The black one was cracked, I always took it because it was cracked and no one else liked it, but it was heavy, and I liked it. The handle was too long for Porper, he bumped his chin and cried.

—Oh, Porper, how many times have I told you, why don't you hold it by the end, not the middle.

—How can he, twit, he couldn't get any-where near the ball.

—He could, too.

—Here, Porper, like this.

—And don't try to hit the ball so hard.

The long sunset light lay glistening on the humped grass of the slope, golden and ruddy, and clear amber through the gap in the oak woods. The crickets chirped faster and faster. What were they doing now. What were they talking about now. Why had we been sent out right after supper, like that, and told to play croquet for half an hour. Why half an hour, exactly. And why had they all stayed in the sitting-room instead of coming out on the porch as they usually did. Did they know that Father had come, or think he was coming. The croquet balls went clop and clap and bounced over the hummocks and went along the worn familiar grooves and pathways. Mosquitoes hung in a cloud round Porper's legs. I slapped them off with my handkerchief.

—Andy, you cheated, you didn't keep your foot on the ball.

—I did too. It slipped. But I'll play it over if you like, and you'll see. It was a split shot.

—Let's play poison.

—All right, let's play poison. Porper, you can be poison. Try to hit my ball with yours. You can have two turns.

Molly and Margaret came out of the kitchen door, which slammed behind them on its spring with a double clack. It was their night out, and they were going to the village, dressed in dark blue. They looked over their shoulders at us and went quickly round the corner. I pretended to make a golfing stroke with my mallet, aiming toward the house, and let go of the handle, so that my mallet flew up on to the porch and skidded along the boards to the wall. When I went up to get it, I looked in through the long dining-room window. Mother was at the other end of the room, with her back turned, standing at the seaward window as if she were staring at the tennis-court. Aunt Norah was rocking in the wicker rocking-chair. Uncle Tom and Uncle David were walking to and fro, in opposite directions, along the long room, with their hands in their pockets. Nobody seemed to be saying anything. The lamps hadn't been lighted. I dropped my mallet to the grass, and slid down under the porch railing. The boards of the porch were still warm under my hands.

—Oh, I'm sick of playing croquet. Let's go down to the playhouse.

—But it's Porper's bedtime.

—Porper doesn't want to go to bed, do you, Porper.

—No.

—But, Andy, you know perfectly well——

—Stop arguing, will you? They're busy in there.

We sat on the doorstep of the playhouse, and made cups and saucers out of green acorns for Porper.

—Look, Porper, we're having tea, this is what Grandfather showed me how to do.

—Where is Grandfather.

—Grandfather has gone away.

—Where.

—Oh, a long way, never mind. Drink your cambric tea.

—What's cambric tea.

—Oh, you know what it is, Porper. It's hot-water-sugar-spoon.

—What's hot-water-sugar-spoon.

—It's cambric tea. Andy, what were they doing.

—Do you always want to know everything.

—If you go spying you might at least tell me.

—I wasn't spying.

—You were, too. You did that on purpose.

—Did what.

—Threw your mallet up there on the porch.

—What if I did. They weren't doing anything, if that's what you want to know, they were just talking.

—What about.

—How do I know. Nobody was saying anything when I looked in. But they looked as if they were having a quarrel.

—Is it about Father do you suppose.

—Why should it be about Father.

—Because he isn't here. Because he hasn't come to Duxbury this summer.

—Why should they quarrel about that.

—But if it isn't Father, what is it.

—Look, I can squash my cups and saucers.

—Why so you can, Porper. Would you like some more? Give him a pingpong ball, Andy.

—There aren't any. He's lost or squashed them all. Look Porper, I'll show you how I climb up into the bicycle shed. Watch me.

—I want a pingpong ball.

—But there aren't any more Porper, they're all gone. We'll get some more tomorrow.

He began to cry, and Susan took his hand and led him out again.

—Would you like to sit on top of Plymouth Rock Junior. And see the frogs and turtles.

It was getting dark when the horn blew to call us back to the house, the long sad tin horn that Uncle Tom blew from the porch to call us in for meals. But it was Mother who had blown it.

—Why, Porper, you've been crying—my poor lamb—what have you children been doing to him——

—Nothing, Mother, he's tired.

—My poor tired Porper—did you hear Mother blow the tin horn?

—Let me blow it.

—We'll take the horn up to bed with us, shall we?

—Yes.

She lifted him up and kissed him, and gave him the horn, and kissed him again, ruffling his short hair with her hand, and put her face against his cheek while he tried to blow the horn. But he only spat into the horn, as he always did, and made a whiffling sound. She opened the screen door with one hand and her foot and took him into the house.

—Andy, Mother had been crying.

—How do you know.

—She had shiny streaks in the corners of her eyes. And her eyes were red. That's always the way you can tell.

Uncle David came out, humming, he had on his gray knickerbockers and a blue shirt opened at the neck. He looked down at us with his eyes almost shut.

—Well, kids, how does your symptoms seem to segashuate?

He laughed, and went to the corner of the porch and took down his rowlocks from the hooks, and his oars, and walked off toward the Point. In a minute Uncle Tom came out, and without saying anything went down the hill toward the playhouse. We saw him disappear under the trees by the door to the bicycle shed, and saw a match flare, and another, and then he came back, with the bicycle lamp making a little yellow fan of light on the grass, bobbing up and down.

—I think, Andy and Susan, you'd both better go to bed. I know it's a little early, but we might be going on a picnic tomorrow. And don't bother your mother, she's very tired.

—Oh, Uncle Tom, do you really think——

—I don't promise—I just say we might.

—Where are you going, Uncle Tom?

—Down to the village. Now go along, and be as quiet as you can.

And it was after I was asleep, it was in a dream, that suddenly Susan was standing by my bed. I woke up with her hand on my mouth, and she was saying *shhhhh.*

—Andy, be quiet, listen.

—What.

—I think Father is downstairs.

—Are you sure.

—I think so. I thought I heard his voice.

I got out of bed, and we tiptoed to the head of the stairs. What time was it. Was it midnight. Had Molly and Margaret come back from the village, and were they in their room, listening. We stood outside their door, and for a while there wasn't a sound, and then we heard Father's voice. It sounded far away, as if he were standing by one of the outside doors, or on the porch.

—I think Doris and I had better discuss this alone.

The screen door squeaked and clacked. We listened, but heard nothing else. Susan was shivering in her nightgown.

—Andy, let me come in and sleep with you.

—No.

—Please, Andy.

—No.

—Oh, please, Andy.

—No.

————with *Calumet K* under my coat, to take back to the Library, because it was raining, though not raining very much, only a drizzle, and it might get wet. Should I say anything or not. Should I tell him I had heard him or not. All the pretending. Pretending we hadn't heard anything, or seen anything. Pretending we didn't know anything. Pretending, pretending, pretending. I was sick of pretending. First from Father, and then from Mother, and then from Susan. What was the use. My sneakers were wet with walking through the wet grass, they began to bubble, I felt the cold bubbles under the naked soles of my feet and swished them through the thick weeds and grass beside the path to fill them and refill them with cold water. They squelched and squnched as I walked. The spider-webs in the long privet hedge were heavy and bright with rain. I shook them and the spiders came out. The telephone poles were wet, the sand in the ruts was dark, the cherry trees were dripping slowly, but the sky over the village was beginning to brighten, in a little while the sun would come out again. And I ought to get *Tanglewood Tales,* to read for school. And *Ivanhoe.* But I could wait another week. I could get *The Sign of the Four. The Hound of the Baskervilles. The Black Arrow. The White Company.*

When Father stepped out of the white-sanded gap in the road, I was surprised.

—And what has he got there under his jacket? *Calumet K* again?

—Yes. I like it.

—So do I. A good story. Have you tried *Old St. Paul's* this summer?

—Oh, no, I forgot.

—Try it. But they may not have it. If they haven't got it, I'll send it to you.

He had his white raincoat on, but no hat, and his hair was standing up straight, and drops of rain sparkled on it. His hands were in his pockets. He took one of them out with an envelope in it.

—I'm sorry there was no picnic today. But we'll have it soon, I'll come down again soon, tell Susan and Porper I'll be coming back. And when you go back from the Library, give this note to Mother.

—But Father, why can't you stay——

—And tell her that I'm going up on the noon train. Will you?

—Yes, and I'll give her the note.

—Be sure. It's important.

—When you come back will you stay with us at Aunt Norah's.

—I don't think so. I'm afraid not. Not enough beds to go round, old fellow. Now run along——

—Can we take some more pictures.

—You bet we will. And now I must go and get ready. So long.

—So long, Dad.

He grinned and gave my white duck hat a tug so that it came down over my eyes, and then turned and went quickly toward the latticed porch of the Soule house. I walked along the path and then remembered the envelope in my hand. On it was written in Father's small print: For Doris. Kindness of Andrew. It was a gray envelope, speckled, and I noticed that the flap was gummed only at the tip, it would be very easy to open. What was he writing to her like this, and why was he going back so quickly. Especially if, as Uncle Tom had said, he didn't really need to for business. And why, after telling me not to say anything about his coming, had he gone to the house himself late at night. And why hadn't Mother come to see him in the morning, or said anything about him.

The mail was already sorted when I got there, and there were no letters in Box 36, only the little slip of paper that said the box was ours for three months. I saw Smiley come out of the drug store with a golden-brown cake of chewing-tobacco in his hand, a little red tin label on it. He was cutting a piece off the corner with his knife. At the bridge I stopped to watch the tide go in through the opened sluice-gates, carrying nests of green and brown eelgrass, powerful and slow and deep, eddying and clucking. Why was the letter important. What did it say—. At the Library I chose *The White Company* because it looked longer. I looked at *St. Nicholas'* to see who had won the prizes for drawings and then started home. It had stopped raining, a pale beam of sunlight flashed on the wet golden rooster at the top of the flagpole, the railings of white wood along the lagoon were beginning to sparkle. The letter was in my raincoat pocket, I kept my hand on it, and my finger went under the flap of the envelope. Before I knew it, it was open. I blushed and took it out to look at it. It would be easy enough to stick it down again. Suppose Father should pass me on the road, going to the station. I turned to the right, along King Cæsar's Road, and walked faster. I passed the cottage with the rhododendrons, and Powder Point Hall, and when I got to the pine woods I went in to the left of the road and crawled into my pine-log cabin. It was dry inside and I sat on the pine-needles. I must ask Gay if she would come down again. We might do it this afternoon, especially if it was raining. Perhaps she would come by herself, without Warren, which would be more exciting. Or with Susan. If I couldn't persuade her, Susan might.

I unfolded the letter and began to read it, and then blushed and folded it and put it back, and then took it out again. It was wrong to read it. But I wanted to know what was going on. What was going on. Why all this secrecy. If anything was hidden from us, like this, and a chance came, like this, why not take it. Why not. "Pussy dear." I had heard him call her that, and it had seemed silly. But typewritten, in a typewritten letter——

Drops of rain fell on the roof, dripped from the trees, each one a sound of threatened guilt. Who would come, no one could come, I was alone. I took out the letter again, listened, and began to read.

Pussy dear, am I mistaken in detecting a lurking trace of sympathy in thy note of apology when dealing with that evident leaning of D's towards what thee calls the racy side of life? Does thee, as thee says he does, partake in that wistful eager-yearning to snatch, before it is too late, something that perhaps solely because it is forbidden, possesses the fascination of a last untasted morsel, wanting to insure completeness in the rounding of our little life? . . . Remember, dear heart——

I got up so quickly that I bumped my head on the low roof of the cabin, then ducked and ran along the road until I was out of the belt of pine woods, and went into the field. The letter was in my pocket. It was not that I had heard any one coming. I broke a switch of wild cherry off a small tree in a broken-down stone wall, and with this began whisking the nests of tent-caterpillars out of the trees along the lane, and whipping the leaves of bayberry bushes. Take that. And that. And that. And take that, you bastard. And don't come again until you are asked. I walked slowly up the deep lane, whipping left and right, and wondered what the letter meant, and what the rest of it was. But I already knew. It was Uncle David. Did the racy side of life mean his drinking, his getting drunk, all those empty bottles, and his trying to get Mother drunk in the motor-boat. Was that it. Or was it more than that. Should I read the rest of it. Would I have time. I could stop in the playhouse and read it, or I could read it here, but here I might meet somebody, and besides I was walking. And kept on walking. It was more—of course it was—than his trying to get her drunk, and I knew what it was.

I passed the playhouse, walking fast up the slope of humped grass, kicking at the grasshoppers which skirred away from me on heavy-rattling wings, passed the grass-mat targets, which had been set up for archery practice, and let myself into the house through the screen door. It was silent, empty, and when I hallooed there was no answer. Had they all gone bathing. I went back to the porch and saw that the rowlocks had gone, and the oars, and the life preserver. And when I went in again, and looked at the stairs, my bathing-suit and towel had been put on the banisters. I took them up in my hand and felt the dry sand in them. But all the while I was thinking——

In my bedroom I began to undress, slowly, pulled my shirt over my head, drew the necktie out and hung it over the mirror, looked at the ugly, dishonest shape of my mouth in the mirror, pulled it down with two fingers and stuck out my tongue and said "yaa!" at myself, then began flexing and unflexing my right arm to watch the muscle. But this was a pretence. The letter was in my pocket on the chair. To avoid it further, I took the flytrap to the window, opened the screen, broke the trap by pressing the sides together, and let the flies go. They went slowly, as if they were dying. Would I have time to copy out the letter. Would I. Before they got back from bathing. I could say that the mail had been late. Mother, I was just coming, I had only just had time to change into my bathing-suit. And here is a note for you.

. . . *Remember dear heart, all the wisdom of the generations coined into the many world-old legends and allegories hung about this very glitter and seductive charm—trite little maxims and proverbs sure enough, but not wearing the outward marks of the pain and wretchedness, shame and filth, with which their lessons were learned, over and over again by the forgotten ones who in their own day thrilled with the excitement of adventuring and daring, of proving for themselves and filling out their own little lives! Surely, plenty have already put out forever the steady flame of their purity to follow the scintillating sparkle of gilded sin. And if thee ever fails to realize those broader, common, human warnings—if they fail to appeal to thee as too remote and cold to be real, or to touch thy heart with their warning of terror, then thee must remember that this other half of thy very self has been sent already and at thine own bidding through all the sin needed by thee and me! Treasure* thy *portion of the blessed purity at all cost, dear! It has to light my way as well as thine—and thee can never know how priceless it is in my sight! Will thee not believe me, dear, when I tell thee this is not mere jealousy or selfish temper or proprietorship on my part, but a loving yearning to protect thy soul as thee would guard one of thy babies from some dreadful disease like diphtheria? What brings this to my mind is something in my talk with Tom last night, that suggested the possibility of thy winter's loneliness, whether we decide that it should be without me, or without thy children, breeding a restlessness that might in some moment of reckless desperation cause thee to grasp at that treacherous glitter as a possible object of momentary interest and self-forgetfulness. Forgive me for entertaining for a moment such an idea, Pussy—but I must recognize it just long enough to tell thee that deep as my concern is for the needful reorganization of our home life and home relations, for the salvation of the children, I must, nevertheless, tell thee that rather than that thee should be exposed to even the remotest possibility of such a risk, I will gladly give up every consideration of them—throw up the whole plan—and act only for thy moral security. For in my heart and life, thee comes before everything else: and that one thing, thy crown of purity, is to me so precious that even the moral loss of the three children would be a small sacrifice! So that if thee needed the protection of motherly contact to keep wholesome thine own life, I would gladly turn the little ones all over to thee and give up my struggles in their behalf. Will thee promise me as thee loves thy babies to call on me to make good this statement before thee finds thy need of them too great to be safely borne? . . . This matter has had to do with depressing me, lying in my heart all day, so that tired as I am I cannot go to bed tonight until I have written it for thy reading. Again I ask thy forgiveness for assuming such a possibility, but that flaw in D's otherwise charming character, and thy persistent championing and apologizing for him, together with my rule of safety—to deem all things possible—forces it upon me. Could thee not send D away? Ask him to go? Need I* ask *thee to ask? It is because I so reverence thine own purity and so shrink into a veritable soul's death at thought of any least soil upon it that I must speak. Does thee understand, dear heart?*

THY JOHN.

2 A.M.

I copied it out on the yellow paper that I used for Latin, and folded the copy, and hid it in the wild-flower book. 2 A.M. What had they been talking about all that time. And what did this mean about the children. The salvation of the children. I looked out of the window and saw Mother and Porper coming slowly across the field by the Walker house, Porper holding her hand. I stood and watched them. Mother had on a raincoat over her bathing-suit. She was walking slowly, looking down at the ground without saying anything, and Porper was skipping on one leg. I would meet them at the porch, or by the tennis-court and give her the letter and then go on, running, towards the Point, as if to be in time to join Susan and Uncle Tom——

———the timelessness, the spacelessness, but also the wonderful and ever-renewed sense of the nearness and brightness and largeness, the vividness of small things, the extraordinary intenseness of grassblades and cloverleaves and acorns, the warmth of sand in the hand, the sound of leaves tapping against the wooden walls of the playhouse—the queer new sense of brilliant exposure to all this, each year as we came back to it, as if one had forgotten what it was to see a cloud driven with unchanging shape from west to east across the blue sky, or to try to stare at the sun until one saw purple and green blots, to lie in the warm uneven grass as if one were a part of it, the grasshoppers and crickets crawling and tickling on one's bare legs or getting into one's clothes and making spots of tobacco-juice—to come back to this, to be once more surprised by this and re-immersed in this, as if one again became a part of the wind, the sun, the earth——

—Look, Susan, if you almost close your eyes, but not quite, like this, and look at the sun, you see—wait a minute, and I'll tell you what I see——

—Oh, anybody can do that, I've done that millions of times, you only do it because you saw Gwendolyn doing it that day at the Long Beach.

—I don't either. Don't be such a nitwit. What day do you mean.

—You know perfectly well what day I mean.

—You mean that time when we went across the long bridge to see how many new planks had been put in after the winter.

—Of course, you silly.

—Well, I didn't even know what she was doing. Now it looks like a thick great jungle of hairy trees. All criss-cross and savage and with a bright light coming through them. Gosh, isn't it funny how huge they look, and they're only your eyelashes.

—That's exactly what Gwendolyn said.

—Oh, shut up, will you. You try to spoil everything.

—It was the same day we went to look at the place where we had the clam-bake last year. You know as well as I do. And we met Gwendolyn on the beach, she was with Dorothy Peters, and Dorothy took off her clothes in the sand-dunes and you said you'd seen her.

—I did not.

—Well, anyway, you said so.

—Have you tried looking through your fingers to see the red blood in them.

—And Gwendolyn was lying against the side of a dune with her eyes squeezed up, just like that, telling us what she saw. She said it was like a kaleidoscope.

—Kaleidoscope.

—Isn't that what I said.

—I said *kaleidoscope.*

—So did I.

—You think so. That's all you know.

—And you stood there looking down at Gwendolyn with that silly expression on your face——

—Will you shut up? Unless you can learn to talk a little sense once in a while.

—What else am I talking, I'd like to know.

—You're talking nonsense, of course.

—But why you can get so excited about that stuck-up prig of a Gwendolyn, I'm sure I don't know.

—Who said I was excited about her.

—Why any *idiot* could see it.

—Oh, could they.

—If you could have *seen* yourself——

—*Shut* up.

—Oh, I don't care.

—Well, then, shut *up*.

—Nice manners older brothers seem to have.

—*Will* you shut up?

I closed my eyes, and felt the sun hot on my eyelids, and thought how queer it was that the redness I could see was nothing but my own blood. Susan knew too much. She was beginning to be a nuisance. What she said about my imitating Gwendolyn was perfectly true, the nitwit. But what did it matter. I was going to keep away from Gwendolyn for all the rest of the summer, and that would make everybody think there was nothing in it. Just the same, when I thought of the box of candy——

—Well if Uncle David thinks I'll hang round here all afternoon for the pleasure of getting my feet dirty hoeing the tennis-court, he's got another guess coming. I'm going down to see if I can find Sanford. And if I find him I'll take him out for a row in the dory. You can tell Uncle David to put *that* in his pipe and smoke it.

—Good-bye, and good riddance.

—Keep the change.

Would Father really be coming back to Duxbury, and what did he mean about Mother's being alone. Was she going away somewhere. And would we stay with Father in Cambridge, unless they bought the new house in Milton. And here it was August already, and no signs of a picnic! I climbed half way up the windmill, and then came down again. The leg nearest the house was getting looser, and ought to be fixed. Uncle Tom said it would have to be bedded in concrete—they would dig a hole and pour concrete in it. In a strong wind, when the windmill was pumping, you could see the whole leg lift up a little, sometimes almost a half an inch.

—Uncle Tom, I thought I'd ask Sanford to come out for a row with me, Uncle David doesn't seem to be coming back to do the tennis-court, and I thought maybe I'd take a bucket along and get some clams for supper. Do you think it would be a good idea.

—Well, I'm afraid as a matter of fact, Andy, your Aunt Norah has already ordered some, from Gerald Soule. Still, if you want to get a few more——

—You bet I will.

—Not too many, mind you.

—Are you fixing the box-kite so we can take Porper for a ride in his cart with it. Do you remember the time when it carried him right across the tennis-court, and into the field, and upset him?

—Yes, I thought we'd get it out and fix it. All it needs is this one cross-strut—and I *believe* there are some left-over battens down in the bicycle house——

He was pulling his chin and staring at the box-kite on the grass, and humming to himself in that queer mournful way without any tune in it, the red cloth of the box-kite flickering stiffly in the wind, and I ran then down the hill past the playhouse, and jumped with a long jump over the wall covered with poison-ivy and walked through the blackberry jungle, feeling the thorns catch hold of my sneakers and try to rip them.

When I got to the Soules', Molly was swinging in the swing by herself, as usual, and said Sanford had gone to Plymouth in a motor-boat with his mother. He wouldn't be back till supper time. And not then, if they got stuck in the mud.

—Whose boat is it.

—Mr. Pigeon's.

—Pigeons for ducks.

—My mother was invited to go, but she couldn't.

—Didn't they invite you, Molly?

—No, Sanford doesn't like me. Would you like to try my swing?

—No, thanks, I've got to go. I've got to dig some clams.

—Could I come with you?

—Sure, if you like. If we have time, I might take you out in my dory.

We went across the golf-links, keeping an eye out for balls, but there weren't any, and then walked down the drive past Powder Point Hall. Molly kept wanting to hold my hand and then letting it go again. She said that her mother worked in the afternoons at Powder Point Hall, washing dishes, and wanted to stop and look in the windows to see if she could see her, but a lot of ladies were coming down the side steps and I walked quickly ahead, so that she came running after me and took hold of my hand again. We went past the Horse Monument and through the woods, where I showed her our houses, and she would have liked to stay there, but I took her down to the beach near the hunting-box and told her to wait there without moving till I fetched the bucket and spade. I told her I was responsible for her, because she was small, and made her promise. If she would promise I might take her back to the houses afterwards.

When I got back, with the spade and bucket, she was crying. She was wiping her eyes with her thin dress, and I could see her white drawers. They weren't very clean.

—What are you crying about. Do you want to go home.

—No.

—Well, then, what are you crying for.

—I won't tell you.

—All right, then you can go home. I don't want any cry-babies with me.

—It was your mother.

—What do you mean.

—Your mother, she scolded me. She came out of that little house, and she was angry with me when she saw me. She said I ought not to be here alone, and I said you were coming back, and then she went away——

I put down the spade and bucket on the sand and went to the back of the hunting-box, up above it, on the bluff, and looked down at it. Should I go and look into it, to see if there were any bottles there. No, it was like spying, or sneaking. The little door at the back was half open, and there wasn't any sound, probably there was no one inside, but I didn't like to go and look. Suppose Uncle David should be there, reading a book. Or drinking out of a bottle. And pretending that he didn't know Molly and I were right there on the beach.

I gave Molly the bucket to carry, and I took the spade, and we went down through the beds of eelgrass to the mud flats, and began walking to and fro, pressing the mud with our feet, to see where the clams squirted. I began digging, and got some clams, but we put back all the small ones.

—Which way did my mother go.

—She went straight across to the pine woods.

—And there wasn't anybody with her, Molly.

—No.

—And you're sure she came out of the hunting-box?

—Yes.

—You saw her come out of it?

—Yes.

———and it wasn't that I hadn't tried to do my Latin lesson, either, because I had sat in my room all evening, with the kerosene lamp on the table beside the wild-flower book, turning the flame down to stop it from smoking, and the mosquitoes humming on the hot window-screens as loudly as if they were in the room, and Susan thrashing about in her bed in the room across the hall, and talking in her sleep, or groaning—how could I remember. Susan, will you keep still, please. Well, how can I get to sleep with this light on my ceiling. You've done it before, you can do it again, it isn't my fault if they didn't build the partitions up to the ceiling, is it? Well, anyway. Well, anyway! And how can I study Latin if you make all that noise. Who asked you to, I don't care about your Latin, I want to go to sleep. Well, for goodness sake, go to sleep and let me learn this verb.

—I'm afraid you've got to do better than this, Andy. You've got only two weeks now till I have to examine you, you know. I think you'd better begin reviewing. And I think we'd better not do any more sailing.

He told me to tell Uncle Tom, and to ask Uncle Tom to hear me recite the verbs and nouns. I had a chocolate milkshake at the drug-store, and ate the thick brown froth off the top with a spoon. On the way home, I watched the tide spilling out over the dam, and afterwards went into the long bowling-alley, at the edge of the marsh, to watch the livery-stable men bowling. Smiley let me throw one of his balls, but I missed, and it went along the groove at the side. I didn't want to go back to Powder Point at all. I wanted to go to Boston. I walked slowly along the Point Road until I got to the Soules', and went down to the dyke, where Father had shown me how to whip-throw with apples. Then I walked all the way along the beach until I got to the Tupper landing-stage, with the canoe on it. It was wet, and the paddles beside it were wet, somebody had been out in it. Perhaps Gwendolyn. I had never been out in a canoe. Why did they never ask me to go. Was it because I had been so foolish about Gwendolyn. I took up one of the paddles, and found it was much lighter than my oars. That must be because a canoe was so much lighter than a dory. I put it down again and looked quickly up towards the Tupper lawn to see if any one was there, but there was nobody, and I climbed up the grass slope past the imitation windmill and pushed through the oak bushes on the other side of the road and went down to the little pond below the Wardman house. Had the Tuppers been up into the marshes towards Brant Rock, along my favourite channel. And at low tide, too. Where Uncle David was always taking Mother. In that deep, steep channel, with the sides of stiff, red mud and the marsh reeds growing out of it. Where the tide was so swift that you could hardly row against it. Was that where they had been. Did they go up all the way, and find that last hidden turning, the narrow one that led almost up to the Long Beach. Perhaps a canoe could go even farther up, at high tide, than a dory. And much farther than a motor-boat, of course.

I sat down under the cherry tree by Plymouth Rock Junior, and felt tired. I wanted to lie down. I wanted to stretch out as if I were in bed. I put the Latin grammar on the grass, and ground my forehead against it, as if it were a pillow, pressing my feet against the base of the rock. I wanted to be asleep. I wanted to be dead. I wanted to cry, but I couldn't. I closed my eyes and counted to five hundred by fives, and then said first the worst—second the same—third the best of all the game—the rhyme Mother always said for Porper when she blew out the light. One—two—three! Out. Goes. She. But I couldn't get to sleep, so I opened my eyes, and watched the cherry leaves moving against the sky, and the clusters of wild cherries, which would soon be ripe. And I remembered the time when Susan and I had eaten too many, and

Father made us drink a cup of mustard and water and we were both sick.

———the day of the storm, when the thunder went and came all day, moving in a great circle round the shore of the bay, crossing darkly over Kingston and Plymouth, from behind the Standish Monument, but never getting as far as South Duxbury, and then moving out to sea over the black hills at Manomet, the lightning stabbing down vividly from the belly of black cloud into the mass of white rain that hung over Plymouth and the sea, the thunder almost continuous. Before lunch, the wind rose to a steady scream, but on Powder Point the sun still shone brightly, and we tried to have archery practice. The wind blew the arrows every which way, blew our words back into our mouths, and Porper was always being flung down on the grass, and saying that he couldn't breathe.

—Porper, you silly, stand here behind the corner of the porch, it's nice and quiet here, you can watch the lightning just as well from here.

—What lightning.

—*You* see, the lightning, over there, over Plymouth. And just listen to the thunder it sounds like lions.

—Where are the lions.

—At the zoo, don't you remember?

—I want to see the lions.

Uncle David went in and got the box-kite with the two enormous reels of twine, and Uncle Tom said we ought not to try it, the wind was too strong, and it might break away, but Uncle David laughed and said no, it was all right, he would hang on to it, and hitch it to the cart and give Porper a ride across the tennis-court, or even down to the end of the Point. The wind almost blew it out of his hands when he took it out to the tennis-court, and then he lifted it up over his head, staggering, and let go of it, while Uncle Tom ran past the porch with the cord, and the red kite gave a swoop to one side and then began to go up so fast that Uncle Tom just let the cord whizz through his glove, while the reel danced up and down on the ground at his feet.

—Andy. Susan. Go and get the cart. Where is the cart.

I pulled the cart from under the porch, but as soon as we tied the cord to the handle and tried to let it go the kite dragged it over on its side and yanked it in leaps and bounds over the tennis-court, so that we had to sit on it and stop it. Uncle Tom and Uncle David both had hold of the cord, but it kept on pulling them step by step towards the Walker house, while Mother untied the cart again. It was hard to hear what people were saying in the wind.

—We'll never be able to get it down.

—Of course we can.

—Everybody take hold, come on Doris, and you, Andy, and we'll see if we can pull it back and make it fast to the porch.

We all pulled, but we couldn't budge it. We stood there, holding it and watching it. It was high up, and seemed almost half way to the end of the Point.

—Can we send up some messengers, Uncle Tom.

—No, I don't think we'd better—we've got our hands full as it is——

—Susan could cut them out.

—We might manage to make it fast to the Walkers' barn——

Susan was just running in to cut out the paper messengers, the little rings of paper to send up the cord, when suddenly there was a twang, the cord had snapped, and we all took a step backwards, so that Uncle Tom almost had to sit down.

—It's gone. As I thought.

We stood there, all of us, in the wind, and watched it go. It got smaller and smaller and in a few minutes we couldn't see it at all. It was going straight out towards Provincetown, across Massachusetts Bay.

In the afternoon the wind dropped almost as suddenly as it had begun, but the clouds were gathering again behind the Standish monument, getting blacker and blacker. Everything became silent. The trees and bushes were as still as if they were listening. We played bean-bag in the sitting-room with Porper, until Porper got silly and wanted to throw the pine-needle cushion at the board instead of the bean-bag, so then we played the battleship card game, but Porper always wanted to have the *Amphitrite* and the *Vesuvius,* so he and Susan played croquinole, while I went down to the playhouse to study Latin. When I went out, Mother and Uncle David were standing on the porch, looking across the bay with the telescope.

—Are you going to the playhouse, Andy?

—Yes.

—Ten to one you'll get wet on the way back.

—I don't care.

In the playhouse it was almost too dark to read, so I left the door open; and I could watch the lightning behind the monument, and see the oak leaves beginning to stir again in an icy-cold draught of air that seemed to come very low over the ground. This was going to be a humdinger, and no mistake. What Aunt Norah always called a shingle-ripper, because it sounded as if the shingles were being ripped off the roof when the lightning and thunder came so close. *Utor, fruor, fungor, potior,* and *vescor*. The ablative absolute. Who wanted to know about ablatives. And what silly names they had for them, anyway. I went through the fourth declension three times, reciting it aloud while I bounced a cracked pingpong ball against the partition of the bicycle shed. That. And that. And that. And that. And then suddenly the wind came, and whirled half the pages in the book, and the window-screen whistled, and when I went to the door I saw that the water in front of the Standish Hotel had gone completely white. I was afraid, but excited. Perhaps I'd better go back to the house, and be with the others. Before the storm actually got to us across the bay.

I closed the window and door and ran up the slope. By the time I got to the house the wind was so strong that it almost took me off my feet. I saw Uncle Tom standing at the base of the windmill, looking first upwards at the top of it, with his eyes shaded by his hand, and then down at the foot. When I joined him he pointed to the leg of the windmill nearest to the house and then put his mouth close to my cheek and shouted.

—I'm afraid it will go over. We'll have to lash it. Do you think you could climb—I'll get the clothes line.

He went into the kitchen, while I stood and watched the windmill. The slender steel leg was heaving out of the ground and then settling again, four inches at a time. The mill was shut off, but spinning just the same, and pumping slowly; the wind was so irregular that whenever it caught the wheel broadside on, it whirled it and at the same time pushed it so violently that the whole frame of steel seemed to tug out of the ground. The diagonal struts were singing like telephone wires. I stood on the lowest strut and the leg lifted me right up with it.

Uncle Tom came back with the coil of clothes line.

Do you think you could climb up. You're nimbler than I am. Are you afraid.

—No.

—All right, then, take this, and climb up to the third crosspiece and make it fast to this leg, above and below the crosspiece, and then carry the rope round the next leg, that one, and then back again round this one. Do you see what I mean.

I took the coil of rope and climbed up the little galvanized iron steps, one at a time, with my khaki trousers flattened against my legs like boards, hardly able to breathe, and stepped out on the crosspiece. The whole windmill was rocking like the mast of a boat. I lowered myself to straddle the gray crosspiece and dropped the coil over the corner of it and brought it up, twice, and made three square-knots, the way Mr. Dearing had showed me, and then slid along to the other leg and looped the rope twice over and under the crosspiece there.

—Now the same thing with the first one again.

I slid back and did it.

—Now drop me the rope. And come down. Before you get blown down.

He yelled this up at me, grinning, and I dropped the coil to him, and he went towards the kitchen porch with it. When I got there he had taken half a dozen turns round a post with it and was knotting it.

—That ought to hold. What do you think.

—If the post will hold, Uncle Tom.

—Oh, the post will hold all right. I'm not so sure about the rope.

We went back to the windmill and watched it. The leg was still lifting, but not so much, the rope was holding it down. The first rain was beginning, coming in large fierce drops, almost horizontally, separate and stinging, and smacking against the side of the house as loudly as hailstones. Aunt Norah came round the corner to the edge of the porch and shouted something.

—What did you say?

She put her hands to her mouth.

—If it's all right——

—Yes, it's all right.

—You'd better come in—Doris and David——

—What?

—Come in.

—All right, we're coming.

It got dark very suddenly, and as we ran along the side porch I saw a lightning-flash crawl quite slowly down behind the statue of Miles Standish, a pale lilac color, very bright, and almost as slow as if it were being drawn down with a pen. I remembered what Father said about counting the seconds between the flash and the thunder, a second to a mile, and started to count, but the crash came between the first count and the second, a terrific shingle-ripper, and so low and close that it seemed to go right over my hair. As I dived round the corner to the sheltered part of the porch at the front the rain made me shut my eyes, but I could still see the little black figure of Miles Standish with the sword-stroke of light behind him. What was this about Doris and David. Uncle Tom was holding the screen door for me, but it got away from him just as I went in, and clapped back against the wall. Then he pulled it shut by main force, against the wind, which sang through it, and closed the inside door, and we were in the dining-room-and-sitting-room, where everything seemed quiet by contrast, and the lamps were lit, one of them hanging on chains over the dining-table, the other over the table at the other end of the room, with a bowl of bayberry leaves. I could hear Porper shouting to Susan upstairs. Aunt Norah was holding her spectacles in her hand and wiping the rain off her cheek.

—They've gone out to the boat——

—What do you mean.

—Doris and David. I tried to stop them——

—You mean in the *Osprey*——?

—It was David's idea, he thought it would be nice to go out in a storm—do you think you could stop them. It isn't safe. It's crazy.

—When did they go.

—Five minutes ago. If you ran straight down to the Point——

—Can I go, Uncle Tom, I can run fast——

—No, Andy, you stay here.

—I'll go down and see.

He took his raincoat from the cupboard under the stairs and went out. I wondered if he would be struck by lightning. And whether the *Osprey* would be struck, because of the little mast at the front. What a silly thing to do, it was just like Uncle David, he was probably drunk. I went upstairs to Susan's room, where Susan and Porper were building a fortress in the middle of the floor with blocks and books and tin soldiers and the rocking-horse and the elephant, and the waste-basket for a tower, and helped them with it, now and then going to the front window to watch the storm, which got worse and worse. Every time the lightning came Porper shut his eyes, but he didn't cry. The whole bay was dancing with lightning, and now and then we could see all of it, every single detail, even the white houses on Clark's Island, in a green flash, but we couldn't see any boats, only the water, which seemed to be nothing but white-caps. Uncle Tom must be down at the Point now, but what could he do. How could they see him or hear him, even if they were still there. But where would they go.

It was after supper, Susan was putting

Porper to bed, when he came back, soaked to the skin, and tired, and said he hadn't been able to find them. They had gone off in the *Osprey,* and taken the tender with them, he could make out the mooring, but that was all. He had walked out on the long bridge as far as the draw without seeing anything, there were no lights in either direction. If they had gone out into the bay, and got caught, they might be safe enough by this time if they had got into the lagoon, by the village. Or they might have gone up through the bridge into the cove, and perhaps anchored there in the lee of the bluffs, or perhaps even beached the *Osprey.* In any case, he didn't think anything more could be done. They were probably all right. What could you do, in this rain that came in sheets, and this wind like a hurricane. Though he thought the thunderstorm itself was about over, was moving out to sea.

—Do you think we ought to telephone the police.

—What could the police do. And probably they've cut off the telephone service.

—If they aren't back by ten I think we ought to tell them.

—You mean send out a search party. But what could a search party do. Nobody would go out in a boat, not if he could help it. You can't see as far as your hand.

It was after I had been sent up to bed that I heard the telephone ringing. The thunder had stopped, and the wind had gone down, but it was still raining hard. And a little later I heard voices downstairs, and the doors opening and shutting, and when I got out of bed and went to the window I saw Uncle Tom and two other men going off towards the Point with lanterns, the three lanterns nodding up and down over the drenched grass, and showing the bright yellow edges of sou'-westers. I got back into bed and listened to the hard rain on the roof, but I couldn't go to sleep. It seemed to me that I was awake all night.

———and in the playhouse that afternoon, alone, it was hot and steamy there, and quiet, and Uncle Tom came in, and looked at me, tapping on the Gonko table with his fingers, and I could see that he was wondering if I had been crying. But I hadn't been crying. And then he said that Sergeant Homer was at the house and wanted to ask me a few questions. Just a few questions. About how I had found them. About how I had found the *Osprey* in the marsh channel that morning.

—Don't be worried, Andy. It's just official. Just tell him what he wants to know, it won't be long. It's all right.

The Sergeant was sitting at the dining-room table, with his hat upside down on the floor beside him. Aunt Norah was standing by the window, she had just said something when we came in, and the Sergeant was writing it down with a pencil. She was blowing her nose.

—And your name, young man, is Andrew Cather, isn't it?

—Yes, sir.

—You went out in your dory this morning at about five o'clock, that's right isn't it, and rowed up the marsh channel towards Brant Rock?

—Yes, sir.

—And you saw the tender of your uncle's boat there, in the channel, and that led to your discovery that the *Osprey* had been sunk there. How much under water was the *Osprey* when you saw it, would you say.

—I should think about two feet.

—So that you could see everything quite clearly?

—Yes, sir.

—Was she on her side?

—A little on her port side.

—You could see quite clearly into the cockpit, you could even have got into it—but you didn't get into it, did you, Andrew, or interfere with it in any way?

—No, sir.

—Was the door to the cabin open or shut.

—It was shut.

—You are sure of that. Did you notice whether the boat had been anchored?

—Yes, sir, the anchor had been dropped.

—Could you see anything through the portholes?

—I could see some brown cloth quite close to one of the portholes, and I knew it was my mother's dress, the one she had on yesterday.

—You didn't touch the doors of the cabin, did you?

—No, sir.

—Thank you, Andrew—that will be all.

I went out by myself to the tennis-court, and met Juniper there, and he swished his tail against my bare leg and made the sound that Porper always called *puttenyarruk,* which meant that he wanted grasshoppers. I caught him a flying one, and he ate it. The tennis-court was almost dry again, but the rain had made deltas in it, it would need rolling, and the lines were completely gone. It was August the 11th. I wished they hadn't put Mother and Uncle David in the same room. And would Father come down to Duxbury now——

)

III

—PERHAPS, after all, I'd better go. I'm afraid you were busy, old man. And I think it's stopped snowing.

—No—I don't think it has. What about a drink.

—Well—well——

—It'll do you good. Release the inhibitions, et cetera. Remove your consciousness from one plane to another, you know.

—Oh, yes?

—Yes. . . . Here. . . . Say when. . . .

—When. Thanks. . . . Thanks. . . .

—And come to think of it, why don't you spend the night. You might talk it all out, between drinks. Plenty of whisky here—some Rhine wine, if you prefer—quiet as the tomb—you can sleep on the couch if you get sleepy— What do you say.

—Well, maybe—if you don't mind—after all—good God, I feel like crying.

—Why not sit down.

—No, thanks, I'd rather stand—walk—touch things and hold on to things—do you mind if I put my hand flat on that picture of Michelangelo and feel the glass——

—Why should I?

—He, too. I wonder if he ever went as deep. Did he ever talk to a psychoanalyst and weep? Did he ever pace about a room, at midnight, with a glass in his hand, a glass that might have been his heart, and drink his own bitter blood? Christ, what am I chattering about.

—Don't we all do it, sooner or later?

—Before I came here, half an hour ago, do you know what I was doing? I was walking in the snow, hardly knowing what I was doing. Oh, yes, I did know, too, for God's sake let's be honest. I was crying as I walked, and I enjoyed crying—I felt the tears at the corners of my mouth, tears mixed with melting snow, and I deliberately opened my coat and shirt, so that I could feel the snowflakes on my chest and throat. My feet were getting wet, and I didn't care, I stepped into the puddles and slush, thinking what a good thing it would be if I got pneumonia. Isn't it amazing how even at such a moment, when one is absolutely broken, dissolved, a mere whirlwind of unhappiness, when one walks without knowing or caring where one is going, nevertheless one still has to dramatize oneself, one sees oneself as a pitiful figure under an arclight in the snow, one lifts a deliberately tormented face to the storm, and despite the profound actuality of one's grief, there is also something false in it too. Suddenly the snow is paper snow, one almost expects to hear an accompaniment of sob-music on nicely ordered violins, or the whole world breaking into applause! Good God. Let's laugh.

—Ha, ha. I'm laughing.

—Where is honesty then? I don't believe we've got an honest fibre in our souls. We're all colossal fakes—the more power we have, the more ingeniously and powerfully we fake. Michelangelo—what the hell. Did he ever tell the truth? Or Shakspere? No, by God, they went lying into their graves, nothing said, their dirty little mouths twisted with deceit, their damned hearts packed full of filthy lies and blasphemies. Their whole lives wasted. One long fake, a pitiful and shameful glozing and glazing of the truth, slime upon slime and prettification on prettification, each new resolve to tell the truth coming to nothing, somehow turning to a neatly turned verse, a fine purple flight of rhetoric, a bloody little tune, an effective action, or a figure of which the very secret of power is artifact. Christ, Christ, what an agony—poor devils, they knew it too, and still they went on surrendering to the lies inherent in language and marble. Why? And why, even when I want to kill myself, do I have to cast myself as little orphan Annie with a rag doll clutched to her shawled bosom? I'm ashamed. No, I'm not either. Yes, I am too. I went into the Waldorf and cried into a cup of pale coffee. I could hardly swallow. I wanted to be dead. That damned dado of college banners made me sick. Old Turgenev, the cashier, was having trouble with a couple of drunks, they started to fight, and I got up with my coffee-cup in my hand and went to talk to them—I persuaded them to go out to the sidewalk, and I went with them, holding my coffee-cup. One of them, a tough guy from town, got the other down, the other was a mere kid, and when he got up his eye was cut open. I stopped the fight, with plausible words, feeling like a damned little pewter Galahad—Come on, now, I said, that's enough, the kid's had enough, leave him alone, what's the idea, and I smiled a God-damned sickly smile at them both as if I were a paltry little Messiah, and they quit. I think it was the sight of the coffee-cup out there in my hand in the snow that did it. One of them went down Holyoke Street and the other into the Yard, and I went back into the Waldorf feeling important and sat down with my coffee-cup, and began to remember that I had wanted to cry, to die, to lie down on the mosaic floor with my coffee-cup, just to stretch out like a dead Jesus on the dirty floor of this dirty and stinking world. But of course I didn't do it. I merely thought about it, luxuriated disgustingly in the idea, imagined myself lying there among dead matches and wet sawdust, poor pitiful little Andrew Cather, him that was betrayed by the everlasting Judas tree. What is unhappiness, Bill?

—Defeated pride. A highball without ice. Ignorance.

—Ignorance be damned, and damn your eyes anyway. You and your amateur psychology. What the hell do you know about it, anyway? You sit there and goggle at the world as if you knew something—what the hell do you know? Oh, yes, I know, something hurt you irremediably when you were muscling your infant way into this cold, cold world, and you've never recovered, but you've fought your way back by superhuman intelligence to that drastic cold bath of a moment—isn't that it? So now you're wise and resigned, and smile Shaksperian wisdom on all the maimed host of mankind. You sit there and smile benignly at me, and wish to God I'd go home and leave you alone to sleep, you think I'm a fool, and you despise me because

I've been betrayed and because I make such a fuss about it. What's the use. Tea-dance today. Novelty dance tonight. There will be charming favours, and saxophones will syncopate your livers. How long is it since you've cried, Bill?

—Oh, not since I was five or six, I guess.

—Why don't you try it. It's great. I've got the habit. I cry all the time. I wake up in the middle of the night crying—I dream I'm crying, and wake up crying. Yesterday morning I cried while I was shaving— it was the funniest thing I ever saw, the tears running down into the lather. I laughed at myself and then cried again. I think I'll go insane. Deliberately—just think myself into madness. Why not?

—You're insane now. Manic.

—Manic, hell.

—You're having a hell of a good time.

—Yes, indeed. Step up, ladies and gents, and see the trained lunatic, the miching mallecho Michelangelo, the pig with wings. Here lies the winged pig, feared and befriended by many, loved and betrayed by one. Why do I always dream about pigs? Last night I hit one in the snout with a walking-stick—I thought he was attacking me, but it turned out I was mistaken. He merely wanted to attract my attention; but by that time I had fallen down in the mud, and my stick was dirty.

—It would be. Ha, ha.

—Don't make me laugh.

—Anal erotic, what.

—Scatological too. Step up and see the scatological hebephrene, watch him weep pig's tears into his snout.

—He eats them all.

—The pig with wings was a much smaller pig—a tiny pig, and such a little darling, as clean as clean could be. His wings were transparent and opalescent, lovely, and oh so tender—they were just unfurled, and scarcely dry, and imagine it, Bill, a dirty little bastard of a mongrel dog chose just that moment to attack him, biting at the wings! When I threw stones at him, he turned and attacked me.

—That dog was your best friend.

—My best friend—Christ. I mean Judas.

—You mean yourself.

—My polysyllabic soul, yes, of course I am guilty, I go about projecting my guilt like a magic lantern.

—Do you mind if I open the window a little, and let the smoke out?

—Oh, no, knock out the wall if you like.

Einstein is waiting just outside with the fourth dimension on his forehead.

—I'll ask him in.

—Do.

—Meanwhile, have you called up Bertha today.

—No, I went to see the Dingbats. The Dingbat sisters. I met them in the elevator, and one of them was carrying a bottle of gin, and I was already tight and so were they a little, and what with one thing and another, though I'd never spoken to them before, we smiled at each other and they invited me to come in and have a drink. So I did. The mystery women of Shepard Hall. They're always getting telephone calls from the Navy Yard, and it amuses me to hear them at the public phone trying to answer indiscreet proposals in discreet words of one syllable. The older one took me into her bedroom to show me photographs of her two kids in Montreal. I hadn't known she was married, and that put me off a little—I understood then why her breasts were so—ahem—mature and maternal. She leaned one of them against me, Bill, but I didn't budge or feel a tremor. Not a tremor. Then they gave me six cocktails in rapid succession, in the dining-room, a horrible room with red walls and fumed-oak furniture with an umbrella-stand in one corner and such jolly coloured prints of John Peel singing at the hunt breakfast. Why had I never been to see them, they said. They were always glad to see the people they liked, and if I just rang their bell six times, any time of the day or night, they would know it was me, and get out of bed even, if necessary. Very obliging. I asked them if they ever cried, and they were amused. I told them that I had a peculiar passion for crying, and would be glad to come in from time to time and have a good noisy cry with them while punishing the gin bottle. They laughed their heads off, and thought I was a hell of a wag. Then I said I must be going. The younger one, who is not so pretty, but who has no children, she is tall and has a gentler face, not quite so tough, you know, perhaps a trace of what you fellows call the anima type, she pleaded softly and cajolingly with me at the dining-room door, standing so close to me that I couldn't get past her without embracing her, and she followed me to the front door and there, what do you think, just round the corner from Alice, we had a ten-minute non-stop kiss, you know the kind. Alice after a few minutes of the silence, said, Hey, there, what are you kids doing out there, and laughed, and then I went back for another cocktail. Oh, it was great fun, you have no idea. And when I finally came away I kissed her again at the door, a long, long kiss, not forgetting the tongue, and so went to the University Theatre, where I suddenly and inexplicably felt very drunk. An undergraduate in front of me said, I smell boooooooze, and looked round. I smiled at him, very amiably.

—Well, and what was it all about? Do you understand it?

—Don't be simple-minded. Of course I do.

—And what about Bertha.

—That's what it was about, you idiot. That's what I'm talking about all the time.

—So I see.

—Well, then, don't interrupt. This was my little attempt at a counterblast.

—Not the first, either.

—What do you know about it?

—Oh, I've been here and there myself, and in and out, and up and down, and heard a thing or two, some from your own lips, before this.

—Too true, too true. I've always been your best case, Bill, your richest specimen. What on earth would you have done without me. I'm one of those talented fellows who combine all the madnesses in one—paranoia, dementia præcox, manic depressive, hysteria—name another. And so I watched faces on the screen—large weeping faces, eight feet high and five feet wide, with tears the size of cannon-balls on the common and teeth like gravestones in the snow. Eyes—! You never saw such eyes. Like glassless windows in a ruined church. I think bats were coming and going out of them and into them. And the hair was like high-tension wires, and I saw a louse the size of a sparrow being electrocuted. It was great. Did I ever tell you of the time I stole a girl's hat at the University Theatre?

—No.

—Then I won't. Now don't tell me what Freud thinks a hat means.

—What do you think a hat means.

—If I were a Martian, strayed to earth, long after the death of the last man, I could reconstruct the whole of human civilization from one female hat. Preferably one of those early specimens with a lot of ostrich plumes. But this is a hypothetical question and I won't go into it. The truth is, I want to cry.

—Go ahead and cry.

—No, I can't. You've become my alter ego for the moment, the sceptical and analytic part of myself, and you disapprove of crying. So do I. Did you ever cry at a prize-fight?

No? Why, Bill, I'm surprised at you. I don't think you can have been to any prize-fights. Everybody cries at a prize-fight. The tears of Christ. You can buy them at the soda fountain, if you can get near enough to buy *anything,* which you seldom can, between bouts. And on Vesuvius once—but that was long ago, far away, and besides it was in the spring.

—You're a riot. I wish to God I could take this down. But I don't doubt *you'll* remember it.

—Why should I. It's my business to forget.

—So you think.

—So it is.

—The ostrich puts its head in the sand.

—I'm an ostrich, one of the best. An Arabian sparrow. Hiding my head in the desert of memory.

—I don't think you'd better drink any more. You're pretty well advanced.

—Not at all. How easily whisky comes out of a bottle—did you ever notice? Just like that. I think I'll sit down. I think I'll lie down. I think I'll put this nice cold silk cushion on my face. Oh, that's grand. Mmmmmmmmmmmmmmmm. And so I came back from New York, in response to a note from Fred (nice fellow, Fred) and found a hat, a man's hat, a dirty felt hat, just as he predicted, on the chair in the front hall. What a melodrama. I had foreseen, in the train, every detail—that's my way, Bill, I always foresee. So the hat wasn't really a surprise at all. I was so sure it was there that I let myself in very quietly, like a cat, and banged the door behind me, and went up to the hat. It occurred to me to address the hat in Elizabethan style. O thou, most treasonable shape o' the human head, cornuting horror . . . but there were gloves also, and a stick—and what do you think of this—this is the dirtiest touch of all—a pair of humble muddy galoshes. Side by side, so meek and subservient, waiting for their exhausted master.

—For God's sake, Andy.

—Yes, for God's sake. You shrink from the horror, the plain physical horror, just as much as I did. Isn't it wonderful? What a symbol, what a symbol. The hat, the stick, the gloves, the galoshes—a little constellation in the front hall, of which the meaning was plain even to me, who am no astronomer. I saw the whole life which they signified: Thomas Crapo, idealist, scientist, professor of biology, my friend, excellent tennis-player, frequenter of wrestling-matches, lover of

Beethoven, but also the lover of my wife. And the apartment was so quiet, Bill! I could have heard a pin drop—and perhaps I did. A hairpin. Ting! And then silence.

—I'll shut the window. It's getting cold.

—I hear a snowplow.

—It's one o'clock.

—Where?

—Here. One hour past midnight in the human soul.

—Then we're getting on. If I were a dead leaf I would swallow myself.

—Why wait to be a dead leaf.

—Ah, I see, you're bored, and quite rightly, with this harangue. Poor fellow, that's the unfortunate duty of analysts, isn't it? They only sit. I forget my Milton. But, seriously, have you ever found Christ's hat in your front hall? And his gloves and stick and galoshes? You wonder what to do. You feel—as you should—like an intruder. How can you most tactfully announce your inconsiderate arrival. It would be tactless to go to the bedroom door—don't you think—and say, Are you there, darling? Or perhaps darlings. It might be better simply to go to the bathroom and pull the chain, which would give them a cheerful warning that father was come home again. But there is this murderous impulse, too—have you ever killed a fly, or thrown a baby out of a window? I have, from time to time. Oh, my God. Look—I see my pulse on the radial side of my wrist, at the joint. I'm a doomed man, thank heaven. This is that blood that brought me where I am. You can throw the hat out of the window, of course—and perhaps that's the best solution, though not the easiest. Hat equals *schadenfreude*. Bi-lingual pun, Bill, which does you credit. But why not open the bedroom door dramatically, and stand there frozen for a moment, eyeless in Gaza at the mill with slaves? I don't like the smell of this cushion—I believe you've been entertaining young women here, Bill, and I think I recognize—do I recognize—yes, I've certainly come across that before. Now where was it?

—It doesn't matter—go ahead.

—Yes, go ahead. Forward into the untrodden—but that's an unfortunate suggestion. Do angels fear to tread? Not by a damned sight. And he was such an angel, such a white man, so gentle, so good, so shy—his little mustache is so neatly clipped with his nail-scissors, on Tuesdays and Fridays always, and he always blows his nose before going to bed, and every penny he spends he puts down meticulously in his little notebook.

Cup of coffee at Liggett's—five cents. Carfare to Boston and back—twenty cents. *Boston Evening Transcript*—three cents. But I'm forgetting about Michelangelo. Do you suppose Michelangelo ever saw the sea?

—The sea?

—Yes, the sea. You know, the ocean, the bounding main. That thing that has waves, and bears ships, and laughs unarithmetically at the moon. Did he ever see it? I wonder. I wonder if he wanted to get back to it. What do you think. Don't sit there and grin at me!

—Go on, let's get back to it. A little free association, please! While I have a drink and try to catch up with you.

—Oh, my God, I'm a fool, a bloody, bloody fool. Why am I always in such a damned panic, in such a hurry to make decisions, why do I run round in mad circles like a beheaded hen?

—You know pretty well why.

—For six months I've been doing it—I've done no work—I've drunk like a fish and gone from one wild party to another. An unreasoning terror, a terror that had no particular shape—nightmares one after another too, I'd wake up sweating, my heart beating like hell—dreams of falling, dreams of climbing and falling, desperate efforts to carry monstrous loads up broken and rotten ladders, fantastic scaffoldings which fell away beneath me as I climbed—night after night.

—You saw it all coming. You were already aware of the insecurity of your position—perhaps you even wanted all this to happen. Perhaps you were precipitating it. God knows your way of living can't have made Bertha like you any better, can it. I'm surprised she hasn't rebelled or broken out before.

—Now be fair about this, Bill, be fair. I admit it wasn't too good. But I think you go a little too far when you suggest that I wanted this to happen. Does a man deliberately want to cut himself in two? Jesus. Does he deliberately seek to be abandoned? Jesus. Does he carve out his own heart and throw it to the dogs? Jesus. No, I decline the gambit, thank you. Just because I vaguely foresaw and feared the thing doesn't mean I wanted it. I know I've been a damned fool. Why did I get into that rotten affair with Molly? God knows. But even that might not have done any harm if it hadn't been for the party in Prescott Street, when we all got drunk and took our clothes off and did a Russian ballet, and so on and so on, and that damned fool little Mary Thurston running all over town telling about it, just because some idiot of a

Ph.D. student, a philosopher, thought he was a satyr and tore her shirt off. Those are the damned trifles that ruin our lives. Precarious, precarious. But nothing to the precariousness of the mind. I still believe I shall go insane. All of a sudden, my mind stops—goes blank—I can't either think or feel. I forget the simplest things, names, events—things I've known all my life. I carry my laundry into the Western Union Telegraph Office. Wild fits of shyness come over me, the kind I used to have when I was a kid, and I stand foolish and speechless, leering like an idiot, forgetting where I am and what I'm there for. The other day at the bank I found I couldn't write—my hand began to shake—God knows why—and I couldn't even sign my own name. The cashier looked at me in astonishment. I really thought I'd gone mad. I looked out of the window, trying to think of something, saw the sunlight, saw the window of my old room in Gray's Hall, with my initials still carved on the window-sill after all these fifteen years, and the pen shook in my hand, and then I tried again, pretending for the cashier's benefit that I'd merely been doing a little calculation. Calculation! Good God, I was calculating for my very life. Then I managed by making a series of separate feverish little tremulous strokes to get a few quivering marks on to the paper, which bore no resemblance to my signature at all. Mr. Howe looked at it in surprise, but made no comment. I suspect he thought I was trying deliberately to disguise my handwriting so that the check wouldn't be charged to my own account. Now what the hell was that all about. I walked out shaking like the well-known aspen leaf, or a stricken doe, or something, and went straight to Molly's apartment, without even knowing what I was doing. Her door was unlocked and I walked in. She was taking a bath, and yelled at me in alarm from the tub, not knowing who it was. I opened the door and looked at her. She threw a sponge at me. Then I went back to the sitting-room and stared at the cactus on the window-sill, which had just given birth to a purple blossom. It was very beautiful. She came in and said she was surprised at me. She was obviously rather pleased. We sat down on the couch, she in her kimono, and she expected me to make love to her. Instead, I cried, and she was the most astonished woman you ever saw in your life. When that was over, she gave me a gin and ginger ale, and I told her my dream about the sea. I'm always dreaming about the sea. We all know what that means, don't we? I'm going to be born again one of these days. Oh, yes, we rise again. Back to the womb, and forth once more we swim, like the mighty hero of the *Kalevala,* after nine months in submarine caves. We all crowded to the railing on the port side, where the captain was pointing to the masthead of a sunken ship, a masthead from which a pennant still fluttered. It was a sunken galleon. I knew that, even before the tide went out and revealed it to us all—the tide went out in no time, and there, behold, was a little island, submerged at all but low tide, and on its shore was the little galleon. We got out of the ship and walked up the shingle beach to the galleon, and I climbed up on to its deck and it was very strange, it was a little museum of seashells and pearls and precious stones, the decks were lined with glass cases, and all of them filled with beautiful—indescribably beautiful—cowry shells and razor shells and wentletraps and corals and ambergris and black pearls and God knows what. I was enthralled. And to think—I reflected—that these poor fellows, four hundred years ago, after collecting these rare and lovely things from parts of the world and all the oceans, should at last have been overtaken by fate and their marvellous collection buried here with them and forgotten. I examined great scarlet shells like butterflies, and blue shells like dragonflies, and red sponges, and flying fishes with wings of opal and gold. Never have I seen such concentrated beauty. It was all my childhood dream of treasure-trove come true. All those dreams of finding nests of buried gold coins, marbles made of moonstone, jackstones of silver—you know what I mean. I climbed down again to the beach and walked round to the stern of the ship—and there, what do you think? was a skeleton standing with his hands folded on a rusted musket, standing upright as if to guard the ship with its treasure, and staring with empty sockets at the name of the ship, which I saw, when I looked up, was *Everest*. Ever rest. Now what do you make of that, Watson. But I had no time to loiter—the tide was rising swiftly again, the captain called us, and back we went to our own ship, and no sooner were we on the decks once more than the tide had risen, the little galleon, with its melancholy guard, was engulfed, and all that remained was the fluttering pennant. And so we sailed away. I told this dream to Molly—oh, yes, I know what it means, I daresay the old fellow is my father—and before she could comment on it I told her we were going to the Greek's for lunch, and so I helped her to dress, handing her odds and ends of clothing, and I picked the damned little cactus flower, which made her really furious—she stamped her foot and I thought she was going to have a cry herself—but she recovered and we went to town in a yellow taxi. And that was that. And, oh, yes, we went afterwards to a hockey game at the Garden, and she was bored to death, though I gave her a hot dog and a bag of peanuts to keep her happy. I think she thought I'd gone crazy.

—You wanted her to think so.

—Of course I did. But also I didn't. Now just how do we dissect *that* out. But I'd prefer to have a drink. I'll have a drink. This is to Michelangelo, Shakspere, and Melville, bisexual wonders of the transient world, magicians of the epicene, bastards of heaven and hell. Here's to you, Mike, old boy. May your shadow never grow less, nor your fifth leg shorter. And so they went to hell all three to learn the fraud of Calvary. Good old Mike—I know all about him. His best friend was a homosexual, a minor artist who is now forgotten, and none of whose works survive, one of the lesser Florentines, a small man with a beard, a courageous coward, an exquisite, with a taste for scarlet in dress and a passion for perfumes and silks. A gentle fellow, he carried himself well, square-shouldered and erect, and his sword he managed with a grace, though he never put it to use. He had red lips and green eyes and a thick Florentine cad's curl swept away from the fine feminine forehead, and his nose was proud and of good breeding, and his accent in the reading aloud of poetry was of the very subtlest and finest. He was older than Michelangelo and richer, and his purse was open to his friend, for he could be, though a miser by nature, generous with those he loved. But this fellow betrayed him. Yes, he betrayed him. He left his hat in the hall, and his sword too, and his scarlet-lined cloak. So Michelangelo studied Plato, and modelled the titubant Bacchus, which is commonly considered his most ignoble work. And why was all this? Ah, Bill, you may well ask. Unable to draw Michelangelo to himself as he wanted to do, he took the next best course—viz., to wit., i.e., he took Michelangelo's mistress. Surely you understand that? And so we have a rare kind of incest, we have—and a sort most painful to the heart. Now if you had a brother, Bill, and you had also a sweetheart, and this brother, behind your back, slept with your sweetheart—would you be unhappy? But I'm tired.

—I'm not surprised. Why don't you lie down again.

—What about you, Bill? I feel damned guilty about you. Have you got lots to do to-morrow.

—Nothing that counts. This is much better. I've got a patient at twelve and nothing before that. So don't worry.

—Why do I talk such tripe.

—I think there's method in your madness.

—Madness in my method. It's all the same. You must forgive me. I'd do the same for you, Bill. I've got to talk, and talk frantically. This is what I've been unconsciously looking for for a week. Something is broken. What is it. I don't now. Suddenly I'm becoming, or trying to become, a child again. Now why is that—do I see it? I half see it. But, my God, Bill, how sick it makes me to mix so much that's fraudulent with all this—at one moment what I say to you is genuine, at the next it's almost deliberately a fake. I daresay you see through the fake with your fierce analytic eye, and so it's all the same. A calculated fantasy or lie is as good as a dream, for your purpose.

—Just about. Your fantasies are pretty transparent. Which I perceive you're quite aware of.

—Oh, am I, b'gosh.

—Anyway, you fit them in pretty well.

—In the pattern, you mean, the preconceived pattern.

—The preconceived rôle.

—Oh, Christ, yes. Isn't it disgusting.

—Not at all. I sympathize with you. You're all right, Andy. Why not get really drunk, and let yourself go. It won't do you any harm.

—I've been drunk too much, and it does me no good.

—It's all the path to regression. Healthy enough, too. There's nothing wrong with regression, so long as you don't stick in it. It's really, in such a case as yours, a sign of creative growth. You'll eventually come out of it with something new.

—To be sure. You mean I'll get rid of that damned little winged pig, that revolting little symbol of disguised sensuality, that little pretence of idealism, that sweet little romance as to the facts of life.

—I didn't say that. You said it.

—You might just as well have said it. Don't be so niggardly. What the hell is it, Bill, that gives you such a sedentary kind of composure? I believe at bottom you're afraid of life, and your calm is the calm of the abnegationist.

—Perhaps.

—Now you choose to be Buddhistic.

—You choose to think me so.

—I believe you're a coward.

—Thou sayest.

—Now you're playing at Christ.

—Well, spit on me, and become the wandering Jew.

—I hate you extraordinarily, Bill. You're simply revolting, when you put on this superior manner, this know-it-all air, as if you were God. You think you can look right through me, don't you. Oh, yes, you see every little shred of dirt and rot in my festering soul. And you have an unfair advantage in having known me for fifteen years or so. And in having known Bertha, too.

—Why didn't you call up Bertha today.

—Very simple—I didn't want to.

—Why not.

—Why the hell should I.

—But why not.

—Oh, for God's sake, Bill—what do you think I am.

—I don't know what you are—I merely want to know why you didn't call up Bertha.

—I didn't want to hear her voice.

—Oh, yes, you did.

—Well, all right, I did.

—So that's that.

—Very clever of you. The professor is right every time. He wanted to hear his little wife's voice, he did, but he didn't want to either, and so he didn't call her up. He knew she was there at the other end of any telephone, just waiting, just dying to be called up by her little husband, not daring to leave the apartment for fear he would call up in her absence, and call once only. But it suited him not to call her up. So he didn't. He enjoyed thinking of her there, pacing restlessly from the bedroom to the hall, from the hall to the stinking, cockroach-ridden kitchenette, crying, with a wet crumpled handkerchief on the chest of drawers, another in her left hand, a third on the mantelpiece by the lacquered candlestick, a fourth on the top of the ice-chest, a fifth on the edge of the gas-stove, a sixth——

—Go on and be really funny, why don't you.

—I will. Go on and be really nasty, why don't you.

—You ought to be spanked.

—Oh, no, papa, please.

—In some respects, you're behaving like a child—and a damned cruel spoiled one at that. I thought you knew better than to give in blindly and stupidly to a mere primitive possessiveness. It doesn't seem to occur to you that Bertha is going through a tragic experience too—does it.

—Oh, doesn't it, Professor. I may be a child, but I wasn't born yesterday. What does that mean, yesterday? It means tomorrow. I shall be born tomorrow, and this time it's going to be an immaculate contraception, by God.

—You said a mouthful when you spoke of dramatizing yourself. You're deliberately trying to frighten Bertha with the idea that you're going to kill yourself. She's been ringing up every one in town to find out where you are and what you're doing.

—Don't I know it?

—Of course you know it. Why don't you do something about it. Don't be so damned selfish. Just because your pride is hurt you haven't got to be criminally selfish and mean.

—Straight from the shoulder. . . . Why don't I do something about it. For God's sake, Andy, do something about it. Take your heart out and tie it up with baby ribbon and send it to poor little Bertha as a Berthaday present. Pretty hot, that one. . . . Oh, Christ, Bill. I know you're right. You know I know all that. But it isn't so damned easy, and it can't be done offhand like that—you ought to see that. It isn't only that I'm dramatizing, either. Some of it, maybe—but much more is a need for time. I want time. Good God, it would be easy enough to rush back there and cry on her perjured breast—where else do I want to go, in God's name? To Molly? Not by a damned sight. To the Dingbat sisters, or old Mary's? Well, as a matter of fact, I've been to all of them, and last night I slept with old Mary and all her lousy little pomeranians, not because I really wanted to indulge in the flesh, but simply to avoid going to Shepard Hall. Just as the three previous nights I slept in the bombproof at the Harvard Club. . . . Give me time. Let me suffer in my own way. I've got to eat the ashes and bones in my own way. If I want to die, let me want to die. I want to die.

—That's all right—sure. Go ahead. But in the meantime it isn't going to hurt you to say a word or two to Bertha.

—What sort of word or two would I say to Bertha.

—Anything to calm her a little. If you propose to go on staying away from her, just tell her everything is O. K., but that you just want a little time by yourself to think things over. Why not.

—I did call at Tom's last night.

—The hell you did.

—He was out.

—Well, thank God for that.

—Oh, I don't know.

—What did you want to do.

—I wasn't going to kill him, or even beat him up. I couldn't if I wanted to; he'd knock hell out of me. Bertha always did have an eye for athletes—the hairy-ape stuff. Now she's got her refined cave-man, let her keep him. Now she's made my bed for him, let him lie in it. All I want to do is tell him what I think he is—a merd. That's all. And I shall smile as I say it to him. Hello, Tom. I just came to tell you that you're a merd.

—You still believe in magic, don't you.

—I still believe in the right of the individual to do what suits him, so long as he doesn't break the God-damned laws of this idiot society. If Bertha chooses to do what she's done, I choose to absent myself without a word. And Christ knows we had words enough—I've got to laugh.

—Laugh.

—I'm laughing. I can't think of it without laughing. Ha, ha, ha.

—That's the funniest sounding laugh I ever heard, if you'll excuse my saying so.

—Step up, ladies and gents, and listen to

the laughing embryo. He laughs through his primordial gills, like a lizard. He applauds himself with tiny dorsal fins, and his eyes, now shut with tears, are when opened much too large and all-seeing. He sees bang to the end of the world. The grave has no secrets from him, the tomb no horrors; when he is born tomorrow he will have a bone in his mouth, and this he will present on his birthday to his loving mother, who is none other than our old friend the worm. All his days he will walk attended by an orchestra of Elizabethan worms. The death-watch beetle will precede him in his march to the frontiers of consciousness; and arrived there on the final morning, it is he himself who, by thumbing his nose at God, will give the signal for the trump of doom. Which, in the circumstances, will be a great disappointment.

—You bet it will.

—Old Mary is a brick. You never met old Mary, did you. You ought to meet her—a grand old dame. Getting too fat, you know, and past middle age, too, but she's a good sport. And it's a liberal education to spend a night with her. What she doesn't know about this town you could write on a two-cent stamp. She knows the college inside out—you'd be surprised, Bill, you'd be really surprised. More than one member of the faculty has wept on Mary's ample scented bosom, and told her the secrets of Cambridge. Good God, did you ever go to Sanders Theatre, to a Thursday night symphony, and see the wives of the professors? Of course you have. It's a joke. If it weren't for Mary and a few others, those poor fellows would be dead, that's what. Why, they aren't female at all. They're a kind of lichen. Have you ever talked with one at a dinner party, or a Brattle Street tea? Of course you have. Oh, God, they're so refined and intelligent—what a lot they think they know—and their estimable husbands have to sneak off to old Mary just to be reminded that they're alive. What a joke, what a joke. Mary knows the names of their children, and how old they are, and where they go to school, and when they have measles, and when they die, or are born, and what Professor X's bank balance is, and the fact that poor old Y is going to be fobbed off with an associate professorship instead of a full professorship—why she knows as much as old Terry used to know, and that's saying a lot. And straight as a die, too. She never lets you down. I told her all about Bertha.

—What did she say.

—Just what you say, only better.

—For example.

—Forget it, she said—forget it, kid. You aren't exactly an angel yourself, are you, to be expecting miracles of yuman nature. She always calls it yuman nature. She always calls me kid, too—I suppose because she remembers me when I was twenty-one or two.

—What else did she say.

—Is this the inquisition? Or judgment day? And are you God?

—I am God the Father.

—Then Mary is the Virgin Quean. She said—what did she say. She told me not to be a fool. She gave me some damned good whisky, and massaged my head, and showed me photographs of her one and only love, some time in the last century, and told me not to be a fool. We discussed the ethics of suicide, lying in bed with a pomeranian. She complained of the street-cars in Massachusetts Avenue—they kept her awake at night. She wished she still had her apartment in Day Street—she got fired out of that because one of her visiting girls got drunk too often and was noisy. She was sentimental about the apartment in Day Street, for she had lived there twelve years. Old Foxy Smith—do you remember Foxy Smith, the gentle old dodo who used to teach us history—was one of her regular visitors for years. He used to come there straight from a faculty meeting, wearing rubbers. Can you imagine it, Bill. What an old saint and prig we used to think he was. And Mary was very fond of him, took care of him, sewed on his buttons, darned his socks, gave him advice about his health, knew he was dying of cancer long before any one else did: he told her about it more than a year before he died. When he died, she went to the service in Appleton Chapel, and saw his wife for the first time. Strange, isn't it? She knew him better than his own wife did. She sent some flowers anonymously, too. My God. Foxy used to talk about suicide with her. He thought of killing himself before his cancer got too bad. She persuaded him not to. When I asked her why, she said, well, she thought we ought to live out our lives as God intended. If death by cancer was indicated, we must die of cancer. To my suggestion that death by suicide might be indicated, she replied with a stubborn no, no, no, no—slapping my hand each time. She appealed to the pomeranian for support, his name is Yale, but Yale was discreetly silent. Now that's a queer and beautiful business, Bill—I'm having another drink, and one of these crackers. She gave the old fellow what little joy he had. Just the same, his wife wouldn't have been very grateful, would she, although I don't doubt she thought she loved him—perhaps she did love him.

—You amuse me. That shoe seems to fit you.

—Not at all.

—Sure it does. Look at it.

—I'm looking. But I never did think the sexes were reversible in this regard. A woman can share a man, but a man can't share a woman. And that's all there is to it.

—Oh, for the love of mud.

—Thank you, I'm not very fond of mud.

—Anyway, I'm glad to see you're calming down.

—Don't fool yourself.

—Oh, yes, you are.

—Are you trying to annoy me? Don't bully me. When I want to be calm, I'll be calm. I'm not calm. I'm quiet, but I'm not calm. I'm so full of hate you could poison New York with me. Is it hate? No, it isn't hate. Yes, it is, too. I wouldn't at all mind killing Bertha and Tom. If mere feelings could kill them, they'd be dead. The damned incestuous——

—That's the keynote, all right.

—What is.

—Incest. Don't you see what you're doing?

—Your conversational manners are very insinuating.

—Don't you?

—Well, tell me, don't badger me, tell me.

—In every one of your love affairs, you've tried to make your sweetheart your mother. That's why they've all been unsuccessful. Why do you want to do it?—that's the question. It won't work. That's why sooner or later you reject or abandon them all, or they abandon you—they have to. You force them to. Bertha is no exception.

—You make me sick. Do you mean to say I've abandoned Bertha? Don't be a fool. Or don't *try* to be a fool.

—I don't mean you left in the sense of moving from Cambridge to Reno—that's immaterial. Abandonment needn't be geographical.

—God, that's funny. Abandonment needn't be geographical! You'll be the death of me. Was Casanova geographically abandoned?

—You may not have left her board—but you left her bed. Or so you told me.

—You're damned unpleasant. Let's talk about something else.

—You mean the subject is unpleasant. I thought you wanted to talk it out.

—What a hell of a lot of books you have, Bill. How did you ever pick them all up. Aren't the Japanese a wonderful little people? And the ants too. I once thought what a good satire on man could be written with the ant as the subject. You see? Everything would reduce itself to terms of ant. In short, one would reduce everything to the anthropocentric—pretty good, that. Naturally, from the ant's point of view, all the characteristics of the ant would be considered virtues. The highest praise of an ant would be that he was, as you would expect, antly. Statues, of heroic size, would be erected to the great ant heroes—warriors, builders, or what not—inscribed with phrases like, "He was the antliest ant of all time." . . . And of course there would be an anthropomorphic god.

—Resistance.

—What the hell do you mean.

—All this is just your evasion of what is for you a painful subject—something you don't dare look in the eye. Yourself.

—Yes, indeed. There are many things I don't look in the eye, my dear Bill. Why should I. Most, if not all, aspects of existence are disagreeable. The art of living is the art of the exclusion or mitigation of the disagreeable. Why go about deliberately rubbing one's snout in the mud? Not by a damned sight. What the hell is whisky for? What the hell is music for, or painting, or poetry, or psychoanalysis? All of them escapes. Don't tell me analysis is an abstract pure science—good God no. It's an anodyne, both for the analyst and the patient, and they both enjoy it thoroughly. It's a debauch at one remove. You can't fool me. No. There you are, in your God-damned Morris chair—I hate that chair—goggling at me and leering and having a hell of a good time ferreting out my secrets—why? Disinterested service to mankind? Not by a hell of a way. You're a paltry little *voyeur*. Afraid to live yourself, you take it out by digging into other peoples' little filths and disasters. Yes, by God. That's what it is. Vicarious sexperience! What a dirty little thrill you get in reminding me that I stopped sleeping with Bertha! And in suspecting all sorts of dirty little reasons for it! I drink to you, Bill, old boy—you have a swell time, don't you. You wrap yourself in all the dirty sheets of the world. The world is your soiled-clothes basket. What's them spots on the sheet, Miranda? Oh, them's the maculate conception, them is.

—Ha, ha. There's a hell of a lot in what you say.

—Of course there is. Have a drink.

—Why do you hate this chair.

—Oh, pitiful little Bill.

—You're fond of the word *little,* and the word *dirty,* aren't you.

—Dirty little.

—Equals fæcal infantine.

—Look at the snow, Bill—it must be six inches deep.

—No, I think it's seven.

—We are seven. Against Thebes. Did you ever read the Anabasis? Do you remember the Arabian sparrows?

—You mentioned them before. Why do you mention them again.

—Damned if I know. Rather funny.

—Why don't you sit down, instead of pacing round the room. That's the second time you've knocked over that ash-stand. Give it a rest.

—Perhaps I'd better. Whoooof.

—Do you feel sick.

—No. I'm all right. A little bewildered all of a sudden, that's all.

—Eat some crackers.

—No, I'm all right. I'm all right. But what a whirl. I thought I was unhappy. What a whirl, what a joke. You know the feeling. Delirious, delicious. Clutching the inevitable.

The postage-stamp going for a ride on the back of the ant. What did I say to her? *Ma non è vero. Voi credete che si muove—ma non è vero.* And she laughed like hell. . . . Christ, what a breeze.

—Yes, indeed. I suppose you see it.

—Why shouldn't I—pigs see the wind, and it's pink. But, my God, how I hurt her feelings. *Ma non è vero.* She said she saw me in the Piazza, drinking a cup of *café nero* at one of those iron tables, and that I was thinking. I denied it. I never think. And she laughed like hell.

—What the hell are you talking about.

—From Venice as far as Belmont.

—Why don't you try to take a nap.

—Good God, man, what am I? Don't be insulting. Take a nap yourself if you feel like it. Go on, you take it. Take the couch. Wrap your feet in snow, it's pure. Puzzle record number two is now ready, on sale at the nearest dealer. Contains two tunes. Can you find them. I think I'll be an advertising man. There's no money in private tutoring. None. Never. But puzzle record number two is now ready, that's the thing to remember. That ought to interest any analyst. Analist. How do you pronounce the anal? Christ, what a breeze.

—I'm laughing.

—That's good of you. Presently I'll laugh too, I'll join you. Take a seat, madam, and I'll join you presently.

—What's this about Venice.

—As far as Belmont. Shakspere said that. He was always saying things like that. He said everything, the damned bastard, except the truth. But, my God, how I hurt her. I think she was in love with me. She was teaching me Italian at the Berlitz—excuse me—school. And I ran away from her. I paid off and left without even saying good-bye to her. She saw me. She came out into the hall just as I was paying the bill, and saw me. And even then, I didn't say anything to her. I just smiled. What kind of a smile, Bill? There are many kinds of a smile. You know. This was a guilty smile, a Judas smile, a cut-throat smile, a tombstone smile. *È divieto il nuoto. Il nuoto è vietato.* As if anybody would want to swim in their foul canals anyway. Did you ever see them? Jesus. It's a lot of liquid garbage. But at the Lido, those German fräuleins, with their one-piece bathing-suits and their delirious, upstanding breasts—Christ, what a breeze. And strawberries, too, *con panna.* She admired Tiepolo. One afternoon we took a gondola and saw them all. Putty cupids. Wings everywhere. Angels ascending and descending and all diaphanous—such pinks and blues, Bill, such pallors of pink and blue. But that was far away. And then there was—hell, I can't even remember her name. At Interlaken. I ran all the way from Venice to Interlaken, and the hotel was only just opened for the season, and I was the only person there, and the maid who waited on the table—I've forgotten her name. Elsa! When I paid my bill after a week, the manageress looked hard at me and said, "Elsa will be sorry you go. She will miss you." I went back into the dining-room and gave Elsa a good tip, I don't remember how much it was. She was crying. I told her the number of my room, but she never came. I told her I would take her for a walk, on her afternoon off, but I never did. I said she ought to marry and have six children, all of them with blue eyes and golden hair, and she laughed, she giggled, she simpered, she went to the other side of the room and stood up on a chair, pretending to rearrange dishes on a shelf, so that I could have a good look at her legs. My God, I was excited about her. But when I saw she was excited too, I got frightened. I ran away again, this time to Paris. What I really wanted was to get back to the Atlantic Ocean, to salt water, freedom. Something I knew. I wanted to leave behind me my wife, Elsa, and my six blue-eyed golden-haired children, by gum. Elsa, with her lovely teeth, false every one of them. That's what Alan said. I met him later in London, and told him about her, and he said he would go there, in Interlaken, and give her my love. He did, and she cried again. And he said, on a postcard, I love her false teeth, every one of them. Just the same, she was damned pretty, damned nice. I'm sorry about it. At this very minute I might be living in a Swiss châlet with Elsa and the six children and the cow. And an Alp-horn, Bill!

—What the hell.

—Where else. Cambridge, Mass. Harvard Central Kendal Park, through the subway in the dark. But this was later, much later. And now Alan is dead, and all the others are dead, everybody I loved is dead, whenever I pick up a newspaper somebody is dead. Anyway, Elsa's skull will have detachable teeth. What a rush there must be on the escalator to hell. Among the lost people. *Per me si va nella città dolente.* Have your tickets ready, with your passport, please—have your tickets ready, with your passport, please. Brattle Street is, as you might say, one of the main arteries of hell. Cambridge is a flourishing suburb. What swarms of hypocrites there be mounting the slopes of Calvary.

—Why Calvary again.

—Ah, but my dear chap, I've changed it this time. That's my cunning. You thought you'd caught me, didn't you. Why, here's some Rhine wine, some *echt* love-lady milk, as I live and breathe.

—I wouldn't begin mixing drinks, if I were you.

—But you aren't me, Bill. *Quod erat demonstrandum.* Why not hang yourself on the wall like a bat beside that rusty harpoon. Upside down, like Dracula on the turret. Jesus! What a turn that gave me, in Paris, on Christmas Eve! It was snowing, too, just like tonight. Snowbroth. . . . Oh, sorry, damn that ash-stand anyway. Why do you have it. It's ugly.

—Why don't you sit down.

—I will. There's nothing I like better. Whoooof. My God, that went fast. But I saw it going, just the same.

—What.

—I think it was the *nasturtium quid.*

—What did it look like.

—Excuse me. I'm not really drunk, Bill. I'm not as much of a fool as you think. I can see pretty straight. I am thinking clearly, too. Very clearly. I see you distinctly, there, you with your three eyes, and an extra one in your ear. Oh, I know what you have them for, it's all right, I understand it perfectly, every man to his taste, as the farmer said when he kissed the pig. There's the pig again. But this death business. This dying business. These coffins. These funeral parlours. These greasy undertakers, and the ribbons on doors. Do you know what, Bill? We're dying piecemeal. Every time some one you know dies, you die too, a little piece of you. Now a finger-nail, now an eyelash. A hair today, a corpuscle tomorrow. Slowly, slowly. The liver, then the lights. And the worst of it is that what's dead isn't buried: it rots in you. There's Alan, dead in my side. Elsa, dead in my prostate gland. Uncle David, dead in my right hand. My father, dead in my memory of geometry, turned to a putrid phosphorescent rhomboid. I'm a walking graveyard, a meditative dance of death. So are you. A bone orchard. Why if I were to investigate you, Bill—good God, how I widen my eyes at the mere thought! I'd probably know why you're an amateur analyst. I'd know why you're afraid to speak out. Why you sit there and wait for your poor fool of a patient to do the speaking for you. Who died on you, Bill? Who lies dead on your heart? Oh, Jesus. I feel sick. But that eye in your ear. What's that, synæsthesia? Dislocation? *Per auram wollen sie? Und das hat mit ihrem singen. Per auram.* I suppose it was your little sister, who died when you were twelve. I'm sorry—I shouldn't have said that. Perhaps it was only a cat. But this death business—aren't you really dead, Bill? And if not, why not? I'm dead. Any further death for me would be merely, as it were, a publication. No essential addition. Just take the bones out, Felix, and spread them on the grass. Burn them, and spread them on the grass. I feel sick.

—I don't wonder. Why don't you try the Roman feather.

—Don't be simple-minded, you idiot. I don't feel sick in any sense so God-damned easy.

—No?

—No.

—Then where's your mother.

—Ah, ha! The cloven hoof. I knew I'd get you down to that at last.

—Down to what.

—The mother.

—Speak for yourself, Andy. I'm only trying to help you.

—Yes yes yes yes. So you are. Good old Bill. Top hole. But this death business. This dying, this piecemeal dying. This death that creeps in from the extremities, slowly, slowly —and up from the unconscious, too, darkly —these dreams of death, corruption, rot— it's all been said, I know, I'm tiresome. But it's real, just the same. To lie in massed corruption, and to stink. To walk through cold corruption, and to speak. To think through foul abstractions, and to live. You know what I mean. I hate you, but I'll tell you. Shall I tell you? Yes, I'll tell you. You don't deserve it. You understand nothing, you have no perceptions, you're a fool, a well-meaning fool, a failure, but I'll tell you. What is it gives you such a power over the subtle, Bill? Your pseudonymous calm? No doubt. Your rare combination of muscle and breadth of brow. Brawn and brains. But the brains, not so hot. Not so hot. Why, with your stupidity and my brains, Bill, we'd rock the world. Let me see —I was going to tell you something. What was it. Oh, yes, it was my dream last night. This will be easy for you, and I make you a present of it, gratis. How did it begin? I was asleep with Bertha, that was it—and she woke me. She said we must go upstairs. So I got up and followed her upstairs, taking my pillow with me. It seemed to be a strange house, and yet somehow familiar. At the top of the stairs we went into a dark bedroom, and there, in a wide double bed, with a single bed beyond, were my mother and father. My father was in the single bed, and Bertha walked round to it. Meanwhile, I myself—tee-hee—crept softly into the wide bed with my mother, who was asleep. Isn't this a beauty? Could consciousness go further in deliberate self-torture? I lay on my side, facing my sleeping mother, drew up my knees, and by accident touched her flank with one of my hands. I felt very small, my head and hands were small, my hair was close-cropped and thick (you see how young I was)—and also, suddenly, I was filled with horror. I got up hastily, and spoke to Bertha, who was somewhere in the dark. Told her I was going. She answered from the dark: "Do you call this a MARRIAGE?" I ran out into the hall, and darted down the stairs, which were dark, and there I discovered a strange thing—the stairs were strewn with the family silver—forks and knives and spoons were scattered all up and down, some of them still sliding slowly and heavily, as if only just launched downwards by the burglar, who, I assumed, must be still in the house—a nameless ghost-like horror came over me, and I woke up. I woke up. Sweating.

—Jupiter and Semele.

—I don't get you, but we needn't go into it. Every man to his own interpretation, all of them correct. Œdipus complex, castration complex, anything you like.

—What about that silver.

—My family silver, that's all.

—You recognized it.

—You bet. Acanthus pattern and everything.

—I suppose you have it?

—Of course I have it. It came down to me from my mother! . . . Hot dog.

—Pretty good. I don't seem to know much about your mother. You've never spoken much about her, have you.

—Why should I.

—How did she die.

—She was drowned.

—How old were you.

—Twelve. Anything else? I'd got all my second teeth. I knew how to read and write. My favourite book was *Jackanapes.* After that, *Twenty Thousand Leagues Under the Sea.* As you might expect.

—You said it, Andy! You're hopeless. None so blind as those who see and doubt it.

You know all this, but you won't let it do you any good. Isn't that it? Think it over.

—Oh, for God's sake, Bill.

—Anything you like. That's a swell dream.

—Isn't it, though? By God, yes. I knew you'd like it. But wait till I tell you the one about the bones.

—Why not go into this one a little more, first.

—Oh, no, what's the use. It's all as plain as a codpiece.

—It is to me. I'm not so sure it is to you.

—Take my word for it. I know what you mean—don't be stupid! Sure, I'll have a cracker and a drink. Why, hello, Michael, old fellow! Are you still there? My God, if I could only sculp—is that the word?—I'd twist the whole damned college yard into a single group of agonized gods that would send the northstar west. What a chance, what a chance. I'd squeeze Appleton Chapel with one squeeze into such a shape of hypocrisy and cold slow sweat as even Cambridge would recognize. . . . Take it from *me,* kid, take it from me.

—So you're resisting again, eh.

—Why not. I believe in resistance. Why acquiesce.

—There's a lot to be said for acquiescence, Andy—and you know it. Don't you.

—Oh, have it your own way. You want every one to be a yes-man. A pitiful dirty little yea-sayer. No ironies, no doubts. Everything for the best. God is good, the snail's on the heart. And all that kind of honeycomb tripe. If you feel sick, why, yes, that's good, that is, and all the swarm of sick lights in the brain that go with it, now to port and now to starboard. I see them now. Maggots. What the hell. Put your head down. No, I'll open the window. . . . Thanks. . . . That's better. . . . How they drift, Bill, how they drift, did you ever notice? In little slow streams, and then hot swarms, and then little slow streams again and then all swooping upward like a lost meal. Woops, my dear. I'll put my lunch out into Massachusetts Avenue, shall I? A nice warm waffle for some nocturnal policeman to study. If he were really intelligent, he'd know what I'd been thinking, wouldn't he.

—Go on, try the feather.

—Get the hell out of here.

—Just as you like.

—Of course it is. This is just what I like. A cold band of air on my pituitary body. That interstellar current of the soul. Birdwings, too, and the albatross, and the arctic sponge of nescience. . . . This is free association.

—So I see.

—See something else for a change. Go fry yourself.

—Go kill yourself. Jump out, why don't you.

—I would for a nickel.

—Here's the nickel.

—Let me see it. Why it's actually a nickel.

—Why not cut out the melodrama for a change and settle down to a little hard thinking?

—You mean hard drinking, Bill. I've thought too much.

—You've behaved like a spanked child.

—Well, why not, that's what I am.

—You needn't be. And you needn't think only of yourself.

—So you're going to preach again.

—I'm just telling you the truth.

—Keep the truth for yourself. What I want is darkness. I want to sleep. I want the sea and the moon. Above all, the sea. Did you ever think of it. Did it ever really terrify you and delight you. You know, at midnight, under a brown wild moon, with a warm south wind, and a surf running. So that the surf is all of sinister curled bronze, and the sound fills the whole damned night, and the beach looks like a parchment on which nothing has been written. Nothing. Wide silver. Smooth. I know just where it is, too. North of the Gurnett. Not far from Clark's Island. The seals are on it, and I rowed there in the dark. I had a tin can to bail with. Did you ever row a dory, Bill. I had one, it was named Doris, and a little four-pronged anchor, which I buried in the beach. I love the feeling of a sea-soaked rope, a salt-water painter. And the slow sluggish slushy grind of the flat bottom as it slides up the sand and pebbles and swings to one side. . . . What was I saying.

—You were talking about your childhood.

—So I was.

—It made me homesick.

—You don't mean to say you had a childhood, Bill.

—You'd be astonished.

—Why have you never mentioned it.

—Why should I.

—Well, anyway, it's still snowing, isn't it.

—I note the interrogative touch, and congratulate you.

—Yes. . . . Mum's the word. . . . This snow on the wrist feels good. Try it.

—Do you remember——

—What.

—No.

—Christ. I see disasters, and I bring them

back. The whole world fills with fæcal madness. I am a—I am here, in Cambridge, Mass. You offered me a nickel to jump out of the window. I didn't jump, because you showed me up. So I'm quite properly ashamed. Evidently I don't want to die, which is what you wanted to prove, isn't it? If I want to live; what do I want to live for. What. Rhetorical question. For hot dogs and western sandwiches. The feel of walking, which is a matter of always keeping the left foot going. The sound of the clock. Step up, ladies and gents, and see the fellow who lives with his left eye on the almighty clock. It's all a matter of keeping the hand going. Har har.

—The right hand.

—*Voi credete che si muove, ma non è vero.*

—From Venice as far as Belmont.

—Farther, if you like. I'll ask no questions, and I'll tell no lies.

—For God's sake, Andy, settle down. This gets us nowhere.

—Don't I know it?

—Well, it's late.

—Where? Lateness is relative.

—For one thing, it's late in Shepard Hall. I mean, to be brutually frank, it's late for Bertha.

—Too damned late, if you ask me! But I'm

sorry, Bill. You know how it is. How can I say it. I can't. There's all this—there's all that. The heres, the theres, the unders, the overs. The pasts, the futures. The dirty stockings, and the dirty sinks. Peeled potatoes. Beds, here and there. One after another. The clipped finger-nails on the floor. Coffee grounds, Brattle Hall dances, lemon peels, the Dramatic Club, muddy galoshes in the front hall, and bills from the cleaner. Just ordinary human dirt and effluvia, you know. One night after another. Sweat under the arms, gouts of pink toothpaste clotted on the toothbrush that hangs on the wall. The little crinkled hairs left in the bathtub, too—so telltale. Intimacy! Why the hell do we want it? . . . Don't tell me.

—That's the question to begin with, perhaps.

—Or end with. . . . I'll close the window. The snow seems to be coming in.

—Thanks.

—That's the question to begin with. It can't be done. Not permanently. Everything against it. So beautiful, too, so beautiful, so bloody beautiful—but is it possible? No, I don't think it is.

—Not for you, perhaps. Why not.

—Why not. . . . The exquisite beginning, in mystery always—the subtleties of the approach—the sunrise wonder—Alpen-glow on the Jungfrau—joke, Bill, joke. But when you've spent a night on the Jungfrau, that's another matter, by God. A different kettle of fish, a nightmare of another colour. Now don't open your mouth with that super-cilious arch—I know what you're going to say—you're going to quote Stekel about Don Juan and Casanova, or something like that. Oh, yes, indeed. Step up, ladies and gents, and see the juvenile don Giovanni. Why, the poor fellow's lost his mother, he has, and that's why he smokes and drinks. But old Mary's as good a mother as you could want. You ought to see her in her bath. Marvellous, the aplomb with which she sponges that enor-mous pink and white area, and the candour of it, the absence of shame—she's a good child of nature, and clean as a sea-cloud. Yes. Yale always barks beside the tub, and Mary scatters water at him and laughs. And the equipment of that bathroom, Bill! . . . What the hell am I talking about.

—Intimacy, I believe!

—So I was. . . . Intimacy. . . . That's where marriages break down. That's just where they break down. That's why Shak-spere left home, and Michelangelo never had one, or Beethoven either. That's why Melville tried to wring his wife's neck. Good jumping Jehosaphat, isn't it plain as day? Do I need to say another word? Why don't you go to bed.

—I'm wide awake. I may close my eyes, to rest them, but I'll be awake, you can go on talking. . . . So you've got the horrors.

—The horrors, yes. And don't misunderstand me. But what the hell do I mean, I wonder. What horrors. Why the horrors. What's wrong with it. Why can't it last. There are the obsessions, as when one is gardening. You kill aphids, millions of them, day after day—squashing them against the rose-stalks between your thumb and finger, green juices, green pulp, tiny clots, one rosebud after another, and finally you get an obsession—at all times of the day or night you see the swarms of little green insects, feel them thickly under your fingers, you even begin dreaming about them, a foul clotting of them occurs in your dreams, you have them under your fingernails, they fall in solid green coagulations from behind your ears, they are in your hair—that's the way it is. That's the way it is with sex, I mean. I must have a small drink. Do you see what I mean. It's the endless repetition of what should very seldom be repeated. Is that it? I don't know. I've thought about this a lot. It's very baffling. By god, no matter how much you love a woman, the time comes when you don't want to sleep with her. For a while, anyway. Or at any rate one wants holidays. But how are you going to manage it. You can't say to your wife, Darling, I'm fed up with you—I know your body too well—the toes, the knees, the flanks, the moles, the hollows under the clavicles, the median line, the asymmetrical arrangement of your breasts, the pelvis, the pink patch of eczema on your side, your perfumes and undergarments and brushes and combs, your toilet habits, every one, the faint bubble of caught breath with which you fall asleep—but just the same I love you, will always love you. If only you'll be tactful and not too exacting about this. Don't ask questions, darling, whatever you do. Don't say a word. Sing cheerfully as you go about the house, greet me with the happiness of the lark when I come home, be busy, have lots of things to do, put no pressure upon me, don't betray by so much as the flicker of an eyelash that you're aware of the fact that I've abandoned you (but not geographically)—and who knows, one fine night, or one night when it's raining cats and dogs, or snowing like this, or we're both a little tight after a party—who knows, who knows? Everything might suddenly become beautiful and strange once more. You would be a stranger to me, and I to you; we would commit a joyful infidelity with each other; each of us would be new. Hell's delight, that's only the beginning of it. The fringe.

—You've said it.

—What do you know about it, you're not married.

—I don't need to be.

—How many times have you told me that if you hadn't been analyzed, you couldn't know anything about analysis. Woops, my dear. I've been hit with a hammer. My head's ringing.

—Go on with this idea—this might be helpful.

—Ask me an easier one, old chap. Would you like to see my spleen? It's a nice little spleen, never yet broken, either. Bertha never understood that. No. Nor cleanliness either. The strange things she did. I read a short story once about this. Yes. Very good. A husband who had left his wife and his best friend fell in love with her. You see. They were quite amiable about it, they were still good friends, and the other fellow decided to marry her. You see. But he was damned inquisitive about the husband's reasons, and one night when they'd dined together, he asked him, point blank, why it was. The husband merely said that it was something absolutely unmentionable, that it would be a terrible injustice to his wife to speak of it. Result —can you guess it? The friend went off by himself to Bermuda, and the wife was left high and dry. . . . Zingoids! I've got rings like Saturn. Can you see them.

—Not from here.

—Oh, yes, that lovely story of the idiot. What, from here? Ha, ha, ha.

—But those things can always be managed with a little understanding and patience. No need to get excited about them. And what about the pot and the kettle? Are you so damned immaculate yourself? I'll bet dollars to doughnuts you sometimes don't change your socks often enough, or let your toe nails grow too long, or forget to shave, or smell of good honest male sweat. What about it. And Bertha probably never said a word of it, did she.

—Of course not. Why the hell should she. Women don't feel the same way about the physical aspect of a man as he does about the woman. No. No. You know that, what's the use arguing about it.

—The hell she doesn't.

—The hell she does. She even likes a little uncouthness—a rough chin, a careless shirt or tie—dirty fingernails—you know damned well she does, Bill, so there's no use trying to kid me. But Bertha is careless. She is unfeminine. Good Lord, you ought to see some of the underclothes she wears. They look as if they were made of cardboard, or sheet-iron or something. Or cut out of circus tents. What the hell. Doesn't a woman know any better than that?

—I suspect this is just a cover.

—Cover! . . . What next. You make me laugh. I don't say there aren't other things, too, but that isn't saying that this business didn't hit me pretty hard. It would have hit any one. You wait! Tom will get it. I'll bet he's got a surprise already. . . . Jesus. Jesus! I see disasters and I bring them back. Fæcal madness. I didn't want to think of it. I didn't want to think of it. It's like a sword, a red hot sword. When I think of it I go mad—I see it in every detail. What time did he get there. Did they have dinner together. When was the first time. Where. In what order did they go to the bedroom. She first? Both together? Oh, God, Bill. Isn't it funny how, when a thought is too painful, you give way to definite physical impulses—find yourself actually averting your face, looking out of a window, making a gesture of erasure with your hand, as if at a child's blackboard—making speeches too to yourself, words that have no sense in them, just to divert the current of your madness. The moon, Andrew, what price the raucous moon. Third alive, third rail alive. Why did you speak to me like that you pimply pimpernel. Or you address a picture on the wall, or a candlestick on the mantel, you pace up and down and fling words at it over your shoulder, madder and madder words, you swear at it, you call it a merd, a pimp, a slut, a whore, you take the candlestick and wring its neck, shouting, then smash it on the floor—and then you turn away from it ashamed, as if it were watching you, for you know that if you don't turn away you're going to cry abominably, you already feel the contraction in the throat, a rigidity in your eyes, a stare of blindness that begets tears. No. I won't look at it. I won't remember it. I won't think of their going along the hall together, or to the bathroom. O God, O God, O God. Why did she do it. Why did she do it. Why the hell did she do it, Bill, how *could* she do it. If she'd come to me and confessed that she was falling in love with him, that would have been bad enough, would almost have killed me, but to wait like this till I was in New York——

—How do you know she did? What makes you think there was anything planned or deliberate in it? My impression, as a matter of fact, is that the whole thing was accident, an impulse.

—Don't fool yourself. Fred says he's suspected it for a week, and that Tom's been going there every night during that time.

—That's got nothing to do with it. I think it came by accident.

—I don't believe you.

—You wouldn't.

—Resistance, I suppose. Oh, damn you amateur analysts and all your pitiful dirty abstract jargon. Why can't you say what you mean. Why can't you call a spade a spade. What the hell's the difference between the soul and the subconscious and the unconscious and the will. Or between castration complex and inferiority complex and Œdipus complex. Words. Evasions. Vanities, on the part of the respective respectable analysts. *Nicht wahr*. For the love of mud, define any one of them for me, so that I'll know absolutely what they mean. Or tell me where they reside in the brain. Have you ever looked at a map of the brain? It's like those imaginary maps of Mars. Full of Arabia Desertas. Canals, seas, mountains, glaciers, extinct volcanos, or ulcers. The pockmarked moonface of the mind. And all that strange congregation of scars, that record of wounds and fissures, is what speaks and acts. I speak with it, you listen with it. What the hell. What have I got to do with it? Nothing. Something hurts me, and I act. Something else hurts me, and I speak. If I could act, I wouldn't speak. *Voilà.* All your bloody psychology in a nutshell. For which reason, Bill, Cambridge, Mass., is the city of free speech. The women talk freely, the men sometimes act, but more often die. Isn't it funny? The colossal humbug of it. But it's changing, just the same, it's changing. And that's funnier still. All the gentle dodos going down Brattle Street in their rubbers to lecture on Grimm's law or the finals in syphilis or the abrogation of the electron, and their fiendish hatchet-faced wives going to mothers' meetings, where they discuss the psychology of the child, without knowing to begin with what the devil a human animal is, and meanwhile their adolescent sons and daughters are dancing naked on Belmont Hill or going on moonlit bathing parties *au naturel* at Gloucester, or simply getting quietly and lubriciously drunk together in Prescott Street or where have you. And the secret little affairs that go on. Good God! How the old dodos would faint if they knew about it. Just cast your eye over the list of our acquaintances. How many happy married couples? Eh? You could count them on your nostrils. X flirting openly with the wife of Y, while his wife, talking about it frankly everywhere, sets her cap at Z, and tells you at tea about the roses he sent her. If he does it, she said to me, why shouldn't I? Where do the children come in. Then look at Ann. Did I tell you about my little flurry with Ann. No. It didn't amount to much, but it was significant. Is that the word. . . . I feel funny. Rarefied. Is there any oxygen in here.

—Help yourself.

—I thought you'd gone.

—Oh, no. I'm waiting for Ann. Who is Ann. I never heard of her.

—Ah, Ann. Neither had I. That's part of the joke. A total stranger, but not teetotal.

—Yes, yes.

—Yes. It was when I went once, a month ago, to call on Tom, you know, in Montrose Hall. I was a little tight, as usual. Just a little. Vague. You know, I have a key to Tom's apartment—I used to use it to work in, or play the piano. Oh, yes, many's the time I've played the "Liebestod" there. But that's not the point. What's the point . . . I feel floooey.

—Ann.

—Ann. Yes. Was I talking about Ann? But I never told you about Ann, did I. No.

—No. Go ahead.

—Well, it was funny about Ann. . . . Hell, I feel drunk. Wait a minute. I'll eat some crackers again. Perhaps if I stand up. Can I put some water on the fire. It's much too hot in here. Much too hot. Can I.

—Sure, go ahead.

—Look at the steam.

—This amuses me.

—What's this mean. A symbol. Symbolical Bill the sailor.

—All right, it's out. Don't pour any more in, it will make a mess.

—Ha, ha, you're afraid of messes, aren't you? Why is that?

—Why are you afraid of fires. I've seen you do this before.

—The hell you have. You know too much. Anybody'd think you spent your time shadowing me. Good God, Bill, a fire in a steam-heated apartment is an affectation anyway. But to go back to the key——

—Yes, the key. You've been stalling long enough.

—Oh, go crawl up a gum tree. The key—yes, the key. Let me see. Just how did it happen. I can't seem to remember. Oh, yes, oh, yes. Now I remember. You see, I was a little tight, just a little vague, you know, and I got out of the elevator at the wrong floor. The floor above. And they all look just alike. And so I went to the door of Tom's flat and opened it and walked in: and what do you think. It wasn't Tom's flat at all. No. It was a different one, or else everything in it had been changed. Very puzzling. I stood there and stared at it, there was a picture of a clipper ship right opposite the door, where it had never been before, and a banjo clock beside it and an umbrella stand with a red umbrella in it. You can imagine my surprise. I stood and goggled at them. Funny—I thought—what the hell has Tom been doing. Then I walked into the sitting-room, and the piano was gone, everything else was changed, and where the table ought to be was a terrible green plush sofa, under the window, and on the green plush sofa was Ann. And I stood there with the key in my hand—you see, the key had fitted the lock—and stared at Ann, and Ann stared at me. You can imagine my surprise. And Ann said, "Well, who let *you* in." And I said, "My little key let me in.

Isn't it funny? What floor *is* this, anyway?" And Ann said, the sixth, and began to laugh at me. So I laughed too, just to be agreeable, and we laughed together, and then she said that as I was already in, I might as well stay, so I stayed. In no time at all we were talking about God and life and death and love and marriage and babies and birth-control and the morals of the new generation and the difference between the East and the West and the difference between the sexes and whether pure friendship is possible between them and what a young girl should do in a big city if she's a stranger there and what drinks we liked and whether it was better to marry or not and at what age and if one didn't marry whether one should remain a virgin (you see, she meant herself) and if you didn't remain a virgin whether you should tell your husband when you *did* marry. Just like that. Bang, bang, bang. Everything opened with a zipper. We had some drinks, and then we made some coffee, and she played the phonograph, a lot of jazz, and we had some more drinks, and we told the stories of our lives, every damned detail, and she cried and said she was terribly lonely in Cambridge, where she didn't know a soul, and she was bored with the art school and hated everybody there, they were all so cold and superior and so unlike the Westerners and she couldn't make friends of them. It was terribly sad, terribly. You have no idea. I was overcome. I told her I would give her a good time, take her to dances, dinners, shows, prize-fights, introduce her to lots of people, and she cried some more and kissed me very, very nicely. About three o'clock, when I suggested that we go to bed, why not, she looked archly at me and said, "Be yourself!" That was her favourite remark: be yourself. She must have learned it from Socrates. So we talked some more, and kissed some more. Now and then she would draw back very coyly and bat her long golden eyelashes at me and tidy her beyootiful curls and say, "Too much kissing spoils a friendship!" Isn't that wonderful? By gosh, Bill, isn't it wonderful? Too much kissing spoils a friendship. A whole new philosophy of life, presumably from the Middle West. What a light it sheds. What a light. I gather that in the Middle West, where the heart beats warmer and there aren't all these God damned eastern superiorities and conventions, everybody kisses everybody. I could hear Ann saying it to countless men, old and young, in back seats, at movies, at dances, in canoes, on beaches, at Sunday School picnics and

Bean Suppers and burgoos and corn-huskings—No, too much kissing spoils a friendship. Be yourself! . . . I learned a lot.

—Well, and what was the upshot.

—The voice of the scoptophile. Aren't you ashamed? You want to know whether I slept with her.

—Of course I do! Don't be an idiot.

—Well, I did. Innocently.

—Says you?

—Says me. At five o'clock we went to bed, worn out, and slept side by side with our clothes on, like babes in the wood. Pretty as a picture. When I came to, I didn't know where the hell I was. There was Ann's little white face, close beside me, one hand under her cheek, with the damp golden curls beside the temple, and her little poached knees drawn up and protruding charmingly from under her dress. The most innocent-looking thing you ever saw in your life. Yes. . . . But why did I start to tell you all this.

—I believe it was supposed to be significant of changing morals.

—Oh, was it? Well, I guess it is.

—Have you seen her since?

—Oh, sure, several times. I like her. She's a nice kid. Lots of fun. Absolutely direct and honest—no hesitations or ridiculous modesties—if she decided to make an affair of it—which she hasn't yet done—she'd say so. Very generous, very simple. Absolutely lost here. Why don't you go and see her. She'd do you good. She has a nice skin, too. When you put your hand under her dress, she smiles and says, "Why, no! That's my naked skin!" and giggles, and waits for you to take the hand away, which you do. . . . Was that a pistol-shot?

—Backfire.

—Backfire. In this street once. I ran up behind a taxi and put my chin over the back of it, it was an open one, and screamed. The two old ladies in it nearly died. It was after my initiation—Good God.

—What.

—How can you bear to sit there, Bill, and watch my entrails being wound out of me on a winch.

—Oh, it's lots of fun.

—It *would* be. Damn all you intellectuals anyway, you cold fellows who—who——

—Who what.

—Live in your brains. I'm sick of it. I want to die.

—Need for punishment.

—Oh, sure. Nirvana principle and everything. I'm all for it. Step up, ladies and gents——

—Why not try a different formula, in dramatizing yourself, for a change.

—Are you trying to be nasty?

—I am nasty.

—So you are. And may you fry in hell for it. A lot of help you are! Why don't you go to bed.

—I'm seriously thinking of it. You seem to have come to a kind of stop. Unless you really want to get down to something——

—Of course I do, dammit! I'm trying to. I want to. I stand here, perfectly still, don't I, except that I rock a little—I stand here before you perfectly still—but inside I'm rushing from one end of the world to the other. Speed. I'm everywhere at once. There and back. Torrents of things rushing with me. All the dead men. All the living women. What stopping place is there—where can I rest for a moment and pick up one bright single detail and begin? I'm afraid, precisely because I can't stop, because there's no one thing that I want to hold on to more than anything else. Can I hold on to you? No. The truth is, there's not a damned thing or person or idea in the world you can trust, not one. You're alone. You run about falling in love with people, with things, with flowers, with surfaces, with weather, with *ids* and *quods* and *quids,* and what the blazes do you get in return? Nothing: or only a fleeting reflection of your own putrid little face flung back at you crookedly from a broken mirror. Isn't that it? Have I lost my self-love? Has it been devoured by the totem-animal? I think I'll be a pansexualist, and become a child again.

—You *are* one now.

—Of course. To be sure. I'm clinging to my mother's skirts again. I'm crying at the encroachment of the dark. I hear my father going to bed with my mother, hear them talking together tenderly, and in the horror of night I become once more a crawling little inspectionist. I creep to and fro, whimpering. What are they doing. What are they saying. Why have they hidden. Have I a right to know what they are doing or saying? Is it a real need or an imaginary one? But why do I want to know at all? Is it worth knowing? Or would knowing be any less painful than imagining? How can you decide not to know, or not to imagine? It can't be done. If you don't know, you imagine; and once you've imagined, you want to know. One of the penalties of consciousness.

—Now you're getting pretty close to home, aren't you.

—Oh, am I. You think so. I'm discussing

general principles, Bill, general principles. Nothing homelike about it. To be aware is to suffer. One of the cornerstones of existence, you can't dodge it, you know you can't. It's all very well to say to the child, crawling there in the dark, listening and spying, don't whimper, don't listen, don't spy—it's all very well to say to him you don't need your mother any longer, she doesn't belong only to you, nothing belongs only to you—or to say the same thing to him when he's grown up—but the fact remains he can never get over that suffering. Never. All he can do is translate it into other terms, pretend it's something else, give it a lot of fool names, or comfort himself with the discovery that every one else is suffering in the same way. The right to suffer in our own way—that's what we demand, by God. And we won't be deprived of it. No.

—Who the hell is stopping you?

—Not you, anyway, you damned fool!

—Of course. You're projecting. You set me up in order to knock me down. I grant you your little necessity to suffer—you're not unique in that. Go ahead and suffer. Howl your head off. And if it will do you any good, abuse me for appearing to stand in your way. It's all part of the same picture, isn't it?

—Yes. You're right. I'm sorry. I seem to

have missed my step somewhere. Tell me what to do, Bill. Hit me with an axe and sober me.

—You'll sober yourself when you're ready. Meanwhile go on howling. I'll lie down if you don't mind.

—You're tired.

—Kind of. But it doesn't matter—go ahead—I'm listening.

—Now you make me feel ashamed, selfish.

—Oh, for God's sake don't worry about that. You'd do the same for me, wouldn't you? Or I hope so.

—Of course I would, Bill. Of course I would. We're interchangeable. But where was I.

—You were suffering, I believe.

—So I was. I was demanding the right to suffer in my own way. In my own terms. And not to have some one come along in a purple airplane, a kind of bloody little *deus ex machina* of psychology, and tell me that my little suffering—which we'll call *x*—wasn't really *x* at all but *y*—as if to call it by another name made it any the less suffering. That's what makes me sore with you fellows—you seem to think that merely by driving us back from one set of phrases to another, by a series of historical substitutions, you've settled everything. Childish, by God. Childish. I say sweetheart to you, and you reply, brightly, mother. I say drawers, and you say diapers. I say whisky, and you say breast. All wrong. All completely wrong. Mere jugglery. Granted that the child's suffering is the exact equivalent of the man's—for the sake of argument—you're left just where you started. You've still got on your hands the initial quantum of suffering, unanalyzable, the burden which we pick up in the act of birth and carry until we damned well die. Perhaps you'll argue that my suffering in the present case, my loss of balance, is excessive, and that to force me to revalue it in terms of my childhood experiences will bring me back to my senses. But will it? I wonder.

—Try it and see, why not. Isn't it at least useful to observe that it's all relative? And that it's all determined? If you'll take the trouble to know a little about the aetiology of behaviour, and of emotions and feelings, then you can't take yourself so damned seriously. You can laugh at yourself.

—I don't want to laugh at myself—not yet. I want to indulge in a good primitive yell. Good God, Bill, do you mean to say we aren't to be allowed to know pain? What's the good of being conscious, then? Of being a man? Hell's delight, it's something, isn't it, to know what crucifixion is, in a complicated modern form, and to make an outcry about it! If we find ourselves here, on the surface of this little planet, and feel like shaking our fists at God, and cursing Him for giving us the thing we call life, is some paltry little society for the prevention of unkindness to gods going to rush up and say No, no, you can't do that, you aren't really suffering at all, and even if you were you have no right to say so, you only misunderstand things, everything is for the best, come along now and see the sunrise? I like to think that this existence here is hell. That's what, *hell.* We ourselves are the doomed, and our pitiful little ideals and hopes are precisely our torment.

—Very ingenious. Our little pewter Christ is now ready for the great betrayal.

—Gosh, yes. It's all arranged. Did I arrange it? Months ago? Did I will it? Zingoids. What depths there are in the hell of human nature. What a theme for a play that would be—think of it, Bill. Myself willing my own betrayal: myself my own Galeoto: sowing the seeds of my own dishonour. Did I do it? How can I prove I didn't. I see them coming together—watch them approaching each other—encourage them subtly to see more and more of each other—to go to concerts, dances, parties—I stay away myself, get drunk night after night, confess my delinquencies with Molly—seize every occasion to discuss the necessity for complete freedom in such matters, so as to accustom them to the idea—and then when the situation is ripe I go away to New York and leave the coast clear for them, thus providing the final temptation. Clear as a nutshell. It isn't their fault at all, is it? No. Step up, ladies and gents, and see the man who cuckolded himself. See the man who grew his own horn in a windowbox, watering it with his tears. But if I did it, why did I do it? What does it mean. Could I prove, psychologicallly, that I didn't want to do it? Doubtful. You're asleep. You aren't listening. Why should you.

—Saint Pandarus.

—Yes, fry, lechery, fry. Isn't it wonderful. Along the banks of the Styx on the obscenic railway. In that room once, in that bed once. But it's imposisble that I should have willed it, Bill, impossible. Why should I want to do such a thing? Or half want to do it. Am I in love with Bertha? The angels are coming to tell me what love is. I can hear them: they are galloping along Massachusetts Avenue in a fleet of—. What. They are giving tongue. The snowflakes are their voices: innumerable: I hear them calling me. I shall attend the convention of angels in the ballroom of the Statler Hotel, and make an inaugural address on the nature of love. Love is cruelty. Love is hate. Love is a desire to revenge yourself. It's a bloody great butcher's cleaver, that's what it is. It has eyes of a ferocity known only to comets, its hands are red, its feet are claws, its wings are scythes of jealousy. Its will is destruction: it tears out the heart of the beloved, in order that its own heart may break. Love is murder. It's a suicide pact, and all for what? All for death.

—The little boy has been reading Latin poetry again. *Odi et amo.* Ah, yes, the cruel ambivalence of life, poor Andy. Where have I heard all this before. Who bit you.

—I bit myself, in the cradle, when I first puked my mother's milk.

—I thought so. Little Andrew Suck-a-Thumb.

—So this is love: we reach a new conception of love, Bill, and one that does us credit. I see it exactly—exactly. It's nothing on earth but a domestication of death. Our little domestic death. It's a ballet. See them go to bed together—listen to them murmuring adoration—hear them whisper and kiss—O God, all that silken sinuosity and hypocrisy and ecstasy—the beautiful painful dance—which twinkles starlike, moves so swift and fine—and all of it a thin masque to cover the raw red tomb-face of primordial hatred. Skull purring at skull, death's-head kissing death's-head, the caress a strangle, consummation a swordthrust. It's killed me: I'm dead. I've eaten my father's skeleton and I'm dead. I shall never love again, any more than I'll ever be able to stop loving. Christ, what a fix we're in. Helpless. Burn off our hands. Drink ourselves into permanent unconsciousness. Love—don't make us laugh. It's automatic—no virtue in it—might as well praise the grass-blade for being a grassblade—the weather-vane for turning in the wind—the blood for pouring from a wound. In the spring the young libido lightly turns to thoughts of lust. Pressure of the seminal vesicles, and Tom falls in love with my wife. And meanwhile what am I doing? What indeed: the answer is nothing. I stand still like a whirlwind that hangs in one spot, uncertain where to go. Enormous concentration of energy, aimless, like an undischarged lightning-flash. What in the name of God shall I do—where shall I go—tell me.

—Go back to Bertha. And hurry up about

it. Try to be civilized. Or pretend to be, if you can't. Give the poor girl a break, why don't you. She probably hasn't slept a wink for a week.

—Doesn't deserve to, either. No. Plenty of time for sleeping later on. Let her lie awake for a while and think: she's put it off too long. She ought to have done her thinking beforehand. Now it's a battle of wits. And do you know what I think I'll do? Gosh, I've got an idea. Yes, I see it all of a sudden, and it's going to be good. This bottle's empty. I'll have to go back to whisky.

—Well, what's the bright idea.

—I'm going to surround them.

—What do you mean.

—Just exactly that. I'm going to surround them. That's my one great advantage, don't you see? I know more about it than they do. I know more about Berty than Tom does, and more about Tom than Berty does. And there I am, and there by God I'll stay, like a third consciousness, present at every damned thing they think or do. I'll haunt them like a ghost. I'll go to bed with them and get up with them. I'll make them so selfconscious that they'll go crazy. I'll be everywhere—they'll find me in the bath-tub, at the piano, on the pillow, in the kitchen sink. My whole history constantly before them. How can they empty their memories of Andrew One-eye Cather, overnight? Can't be did. All the habits they've shared with me for hundreds of years—the jokes, the odds and ends of intimacy each of them has in common with me—how can they escape? They can't. And here's the point—they love me. Don't they? Well, that makes it all the worse. If I just stand aside with meditative irony now—if I just watch them cynically from across the street, as it were—saunter by from time to time—send them a picture postcard from Montreal or Timbuctoo—reappear before them at a Sander's Theatre concert, disguised as one of the bats that circle above the orchestra—speak to them from the forsythia bushes in the spring—eat hot dogs with them at John's—laugh at them from the comic strips at breakfast—Christ, Bill, it's going to be good. Don't you see. I'll surround them like a cloud. When Bertha kisses Tom, she'll think—this isn't Andy. This is Tom. He doesn't kiss in quite the same way. He doesn't place his arms in quite the same way. And what's the result—she's kissing two people at once. Now I ask you, Bill, can she be happy, doing that? For long? No. Nor Tom either. He'll be thinking—she has kissed Andy like this. Ten years. Night after night. He has seen her in this hat, this dress, this nightgown, these tarpaulin knickers. He is here now. And is she thinking about him when I slip my arm under her left shoulder—is she wishing, at the bottom of her heart, that it were he. Will they discuss that, I wonder. And what good would it do if they did. None. They would at once begin to tremble on the brink of the unspeakable, the unformulable, the realm of doubts and suspicions, where passionate reassurances drop dead like birds into a volcano. Isn't it wonderful? Hrrrp. Excuse me.

—You're insane. I never heard anything so disgusting and cruel in my life. You ought to be ashamed.

—Not at all. All's fair. Love and war. I think I'll do it. But come to think of it, I don't have to do it. It will do itself. I can't even help it, if I wanted to. Automatic. Guilt. Suppose I decide to be a trumpeting little angel about it, take it all with good grace and magnanimity, tell them to go ahead and make a bright little affair of it for as long as they like, Andy standing meekly and beautifully aside—all right, you fool, suppose I do. What then. It will be all the worse for them. I was just exaggerating, you see. I really have nothing to do with it. Just one of those assumptions of imaginary power. The truth is, I can't help it. Two rapid falcons in a single snare condemned to do the flittings of the bat.

—Nice. A wonderful vision. But there is something else——

—You're asleep.

—No. But there is something else——

—Well, all right, all right, go ahead, spit it out. Don't goggle at the ceiling like a pekingese.

—It's my business to goggle, you poor prune. The Freudian technique of the colorless and dispassionate auditor.

—Dispassionate hell.

—But just the same, I'll give you an idea.

—Oh, very kind of you, darling little Bill. How much will I owe you.

—Your life, very likely.

—Keep the change. Do you think we'll have an early spring? Will the Bruins win the Stanley Cup? Or what have you.

—If you'll shut up and stand still for a minute, instead of running up and down the room like a——

—Pterodactyl.

—I'll tell you. That is, if I can get hold of it. Wait. This idea of the surrounding consciousness—there's something in it. Yes, something in it. But not as you foresee, quite—no—because you want to use it as an instrument of revenge. That wouldn't do any good—in fact, it would ultimately punish yourself most of all. But suppose you do it with real kindness—I mean, real love—for both of them. You admit you love them. Presumably, therefor, you want their happiness. Don't you?

—Well, for the love of mud.

—Don't you?

—I don't like this turn. You're disgusting.

—You know you do. That's why it hurts you so much, of course: that's simple enough.

—As simple as murder.

—If you love them, then you want to keep them. And you must choose that course of action which is most likely to keep them. And this is where magnanimity of consciousness comes in. Go ahead and be conscious—let them feel that you are constantly there with them—but let them feel that you are there in the rôle of the person who most loves them. Why not. If anything could be calculated to bring things to a happy issue, that's it. In this way, you will absorb or digest the whole situation—embrace both Bertha and Tom—and as a result of it, you will grow: you will become the wisest of the three: and the strongest. If there are latent wrongnesses in their position, this will bring it to the surface. If they are weak, or guilty, or not profoundly set on this thing—as I suspect—then this will sooner or later make them horribly aware. . . . . That's all.

—Well, for the—if somebody was to—and so saying he knocked me down with a fountain pen. Just like that. He drove up in his chariot and blew me over with a whisper, that's what he did. With bright little words of love and kindness, too, and adjurations to Christ-like mercy. You make me sick. You'd better go to sleep, if that's the best you can do, that's all I can say. Your complete lack of comprehension simply staggers me—if I weren't already staggering. Yes yes yes yes yes. I ought to do everything for them. I love them dearly. They're so kind to me, day and night, aren't they. So considerate of me. They put me first every time, don't they. Tom, that God-damned snob—what did he ever do for me. What. Oh yes, he got me into the Institute of 1770 as an honorary. I forgot that. And tried to get me into the Gas House. Helped me get the football managership. Long ago and far away. Wonderfully kind, he was—I'll never forget it as long as I live. I owe him everything. So now that he presents his bill, of course I'll pay on the nail. Yes. I'll help him in every way. I'll give him five dollars for the Sacco-Vanzetti fund, and make speeches for his parlour Reds at Ford Hall. I'll run his errands for him. I'll mix his prussic acid for him. I'll give him my rum, my Hogarth prints, my first editions of Henry James, and my collection of pressed flowers. From Duxbury, too. Why not. And all as a preliminary to the greatest gift of all, which you foresee already. Little Bertha, the Brattle Street Bovary. Let him have all he can get of her, and all he can keep. With both hands, with auricle and ventricle, with liver and lights, I give her up. And she too. The immaculate. Whom I had to teach, whom I taught, whom I made what she is today. What is she today? She is Andrew Cather, that's who she is. Saturated solution of A. One-eye Cather. What would her hair have been without me? Her hats? Her music? Her mind? Her body? A few timid Vincent Club jokes, a conversation about maids at the Sewing Circle lunch, a hundred visiting cards left in silver dishes in Brattle Street and Marlborough Street and Scott Street and Highland Avenue. I made her over in my image. Is that why I don't know whether to hate her or love her? I made her over, gave her one eye in exchange for two—ah, but what an eye, what an eye—myopic but precise—the eye of imagination—taught her the animal pleasures and with them gave her the great gift of horror—and now that she is a Cather, now that she is Andy, Tom wants her. Oh yes. He is moving in on me, closing in on me. It's the Michelangelo thing. Hello, Mike old boy—are you still there? Keep one eye on me—we're going on to bigger and better things. Dawn of the artist's consciousness, which is consciousness awaking with the last beat of the dying heart. The eye that opens in the coffin. Monsieur Valdemar—the mind that blossoms to terrific thought with the energy thrown off by the final catalysis of corruption. Christ, I must get away from here. Not geographically, but on the wings of Father Imago. Did you ever hear of him? My best friend. Myself. The one who was left—who was left—what was I about to say. I'm going too fast. Left high and dry. I must manœuvre back to the sea, that's it, I knew that all along, too, and wanted it before. Yes, I told you about it. The long, blond beach in moonlight, the bronze waves in moonlight, the dory whose name was Doris, named of course after my mother, the dry curled waves of seaweed, the blackened stones left from clam-bake fires, the Indian arrowheads of white quartz—there it all is, spread out, miles long, world-long, on the way to the Gurnett. I shall go to the Gurnett. Along that frightful beach. At midnight, in mournful moonlight, alone, or with a whore.

—Take Bertha with you.

—That's rather witty of you, my boy. I might do worse. I could point out the exact spot where we always had the picnic, the annual picnic, the clam-bake. On clear days, the mirage of Provincetown, and the smoke of the Provincetown steamer streaked along the horizon. Yes. And the Plymouth boat too, closer in, white and glittering. And all the dead fish on the sand, stinking in the sun. Shall we take off our clothes and bathe? Have we brought our bathing-suits? Shall we divel-licate? You're snoring, Bill. Go to bed.

—Sorry. Go ahead. I'll just put this paper over my eyes.

—It's funny—I get soberer and soberer, the more I drink. What's that—tolerance? Clear as a bell. And all the agonies in rows, as separate and distinct as sea-shells in a glass case. Were we talking about that before somewhere? Seems to me we were. Where was it. Let me think. Those wet ashes remind me of something—there's a puddle on the hearth, too—what is it they remind me of. Not Bertha, no. Not that camp in Maine, no. Not Jaffrey, or Jackson Falls, no. But what. Was it the Madison Hut at sunrise—no. But it was Bertha somewhere, yes it was Bertha, much younger, before she'd got such a belly, and begun to shave her legs with pumice. Yes. Did she shave—did you know she shaved her legs with pumice so that the hairs wouldn't come sparkling through her stockings, Bill. Did you know that. Must be painful, I wonder. Before the bath or in the bath. Did you know there was a barber in Washington Street where women used to go and get shaved all over, or depiled, or whatever the word is. Can't be *depiled,* can it. Did you know that. You don't know anything. You're snoring again. But this has been a wonderful non-stop talk, hasn't it, you didn't know I had it in me, did you. And now as you see, I'm all at peace with myself—like hell I am—with all the little separate agonies in rows like sea-shells, the ones I was telling you about.

—Oh, sure.

—Yes. Did you know that.

—Oh, sure.

—If you can't say anything but Oh, sure, go to sleep. You're no use to me.

—I think I will if you don't mind. Here.

And when you get tired of addressing yourself you can have my bed.

—Greater love hath no man than this. But I would feel guilty. But you're already snoring again. But I'm alone again, alone as always, alone as you are in your subterranean world of sleep, you with your middle-aged and far too fat hands crossed on your breathing and automatic belly. Good god what a thing it is—and the snow too—all night a night of snow—covering the college yard so innocently, so that all the sad traces are obliterated—even the President's footsteps gone, and the little privet bushes mantled, and the neat little vomit by Appleton Chapel covered over, and the little trefoil bird-tracks filled in, and the dog-stale and cat-stale gone. How many times have we crossed it? How many times our footsteps lie there, Bill, immortal but invisible, on the way from Heeney's Palace of Pleasure to Seaver, from the Union to University 4, from the Bursar's Office to the Coop, from *x* to *y*. Do you see them all, sleeping Bill. That network. Do you see them all, Mike old boy. You with your Homeric curls. Shall I tell you a dream while I walk up and down with this drink in my hand. Shall I. Yes I will, thank you. I will start with the simple premise of the actual and delicious dream, that one, the one of the crucified pig, my old friend the bleeding pig, Andrew Pigsnout Cather, the winged pig, whose wings were bitten off in childhood. It was like this, or like that, but you won't mind if I just change it a little as I go along, will you, and touch it up like a photographer; you know, just to make it brighter. Shall I do that. Oh, Christ. I don't care. It comes out like a ribbon and lies flat on the brush. Listen Bill, listen you prostrate and sleeping guts—it was like this. I was in the Swiss Navy at the time. I was in Gibraltar, with my Spanish grammar in my hand. I was on my way to my castle in Spain, the ideal, the everlasting, the infinite, the beautiful. Do you hear—all those lovely words, all the evanescent ones, the pale plasma of sublimation. Alloplastic, autoplastic. Have you ever ridden in an autoplastic? Bores me. And it was in the spring, it was when birds fly north, and I too was flying north, and I sent Tom a wire to say that I would meet him and the two other fellows at that little place in the mountains, way off there, at that high altitude, in that remote village, and in that familiar and dearly-loved little inn, where we knew all the people, and had gone so many times—you know the place. I wired him, and took a train and rode all night. Who were the other fellows. I didn't know, but one of them was a Spaniard. I rode all night in the train, and got to the mountain village before sunrise. And walked in the twilight up the muddy road, for it had been raining in the night, and I knew my way perfectly to the little inn, with its yellow plaster walls and the purple clematis growing on the trellis, and I went in and turned to the left, into the little breakfast room where I knew they would all be sitting and having their morning tea, and sure enough there they were —Tom, burly and athletic, damn his athletic eyes, in his rough tweed jacket with shapeless pockets full of books and his English pipe stinking the room out, already in possession, and the Spanish fellow, and the other fellow, whose name I never knew—there they all were, their breakfast finished, the tea cold, the dishes dirty, the early gray light coming in on to the soiled red tablecloth, and as soon as I had come in they all got up and said they must be going. Yes, they must be going. They must be in time to see the waterfall, the famous waterfall, which was the show piece of the village, by sunrise: for that, ladies and gentlemen, was the Thing to Do. Oh, yes. You always had to go and see the waterfall in the glen by sunrise. And would they wait for Andrew? No, indeed. Out they went, taking alpenstocks with them, just like God-damned mountaineers, and Tom rang the bell to tell the landlady that Mr. Cather would now have his tea, and they would go ahead, and Mr. Cather having had his tea would follow them to the waterfall. Do you hear me in your sleep, Bill. Do I influence your dreams. Do you hear the waterfall, is it rushing down in a shapeless pour past your subconscious ear. Do you feel in your pancreas the sunrise light that never was on land or sea. Do you feel the cold peaks of the Cantabrigian mountains, the sunrise clouds, towering above you there on your putrid sleep-ridden couch, you with your hands on your belly, which is full of Liebfraumilch. Do I draw you forth into that realm. Are you climbing goatlike among those wet crags of slate and gravel. Are you stumbling or slipping there, your feet wet and cold. Oh, Christ. So I had my tea and followed them, but they were already out of sight, they had gone down into the glen. And as I went down the muddy road to the village I knew that I didn't quite remember where the path was, the little field-path, that led from the road across the fields to the glen. And I stood there by a stone wall and wondered, and a peasant with a bicycle stopped and pointed out the path to me, but said that it was almost impassable with mud, as I could see. We leaned over the wall, and I saw that what he said was true. The mud was knee-deep. It was like soup. But he added that if I walked further down the road to the next farm I would come to a barn, and if I went into the barn, and through it, and out at the back, I would find another and better path which would lead me safely down to the glen, from which I would easily enough find my way to the waterfall. So I did it. I went to the barn, which was on the right hand side of the road. But this was the appalling thing, Bill, you must dream vividly about this. I'm telling you about it. This was the appalling thing, for as I entered the gloom of the barn, in the morning twilight, I heard, from somewhere near me, the most dreadful and heart-rending screams, animal screams, animal agony, and I stopped, terrified, and looked about me to see where the screams came from. And in a dark corner, then, under some cobwebbed stairs, in a sort of pen, so dark that at first I could hardly make it out——

Christ, Bill, it was the pig, the crucified pig. You won't believe it when I tell you about it. Nor you, Mike, you won't believe it. It was the huge naked pig—supported upright, with arms outspread, as on a cross, by a devilish machine, an affair of slowly revolving wheels and pullies, with an endless belt which was attached by steel claws to the flesh of the pig. But my God there was practically no flesh left on the pig; none, except on the breast over the heart; the belt had torn the rest away, and as I went a little closer, appalled by the screams of the pig—whose head was flung back in a final ecstasy of anguish, turned to one side, the mouth wide open—as I went a little closer, and watched the endless belt slowly moving down the red breast of the carcass, between the ribs of which I could see the entrails, the steel claws fetched away the last strip of flesh, the pig was automatically released, and with a final scream of pain rushed out of the pen. It was nothing but a skeleton full of guts, but it was alive and sentient. Sentient. It whirled madly about the floor of the barn, driven by such a demon of suffering as compelled it to translate the consciousness of pain into the wildest energy—and this was only last night, are you listening, Bill—and I was frightened of what it might do, and ran out into the street again and climbed with incredible speed up a waterpipe on the wall of the house opposite, and managed to hang there, out of reach. And sure enough the pig came rushing out, as if it were going to destroy the whole world. But at this very minute the miracle happened, Bill. I saw in the road a little scaffold hung with gay cloths, like the ones mountebanks use at country fairs, and on this a monk, in a gray gown, with a rope tied round his middle, stood and rang a brass bell. And he began announcing, as the pig galloped up the stairs and stood upright beside him—Ladies and gentlemen, you will now witness the farewell performance of the dying pig. The pig will first give you an example of his acrobatic prowess, on the parallel bars, the trapeze, and also without the use of any implements whatever.

Before he had finished speaking, the pig began performing at lightning speed—standing somersaults, running and double somersaults, Catherine wheels, handsprings, chinned himself rapidly innumerable times on the trapeze, whirled to and fro over the parallel bars, and finished with a series of giant swings so swift that I could hardly follow them. Ladies and gentlemen, ladies and gentlemen, ladies and gentlemen, the dying pig will now play the Chinese whole-tone scale on an arrangement of coins, with his hoof. And instantly on a table, where the monk had flung down a haphazard handful of gold and silver coins, the pig tapped out rapidly with his hoof the Chinese whole-tone scale. I could see that the pig was dying. But the monk rang the bell again and said—ladies and gentlemen, the dying pig will now give you a demonstration of the fact that the death-agony can be transmuted into pure genius of consciousness. Without previous knowledge of Sanskrit, Hebrew, or Greek he will translate passages from those languages as I read them aloud. He will first translate a passage from the Sanskrit Upanishads, which, as you know, represent the earliest attempt of the Hindu mind to understand the nature and reality of existence. The monk read aloud, and the pig translated. The bell clanged again, the pig translated a passage from the Hebrew version of the Book of Genesis, at the end of which the monk said that the pig had corrected several inaccuracies in the King James Version. The bell rang again, the pig was about to translate from the Greek, but suddenly——

Are you dreaming about this, Bill. Am I making you suffer. Are you and Michelangelo listening to this. As you should by God. But at this minute I couldn't stand it any longer. I didn't want to see the pig die—perhaps not unnaturally, for I know as well as you do—damn you—that the pig was myself. Oh, yes indeed. Step up, ladies and gents—so I slid down from my waterpipe and went hurrying up the road again toward the path that led to the waterfall, leaving that scene behind me to finish itself as it would. I went toward the path, and I thought—Tom is there by this time, he and the others, they have seen the beautiful waterfall in the sunrise. Christ yes—they've seen the ideal, which I have missed. While they have been looking at the ideal, I've been seeing the real. Shall I go and join them—is it too late—will I be in time to see the ideal. Do I want to see the ideal. Or is it—tell me Bill—is it enough to have seen the real. Is it enough? Can you tell me that, you with your outer eyes shut. You with your two eyes. Can you tell me that. Does it tell you everything or doesn't it. And don't feel that you must wake up like Lazarus and explain it to me. Oh, no. You go on sleeping, you go on rotting there in that deep mulch of the underworld, where good and evil meet. While I drink and walk up and down here on this dirty carpet and spit into your dirty fireplace. Yes, you go on. While I unwarrantably despise you merely because I'm more conscious than you are. Or am I. And put my hand on your arm to see if you react. And you don't do a thing or say a thing, you're to all intents dead. Christ, what a dream. Did he die, will he die. Performing. Turning his very death into an entertainment. Turning his pain into perception. Christ, what a dream. And where do we go from here. Is this the turning-point, do we turn back from the underworld, do we move to the bloody little sunrise now—the little Christmas card sunrise—is that where we've got to go. Do we go back to the sea from here, Michelangelo, as we said before—is it there—is what we want there—shall we burrow back to the sea, while Bill sleeps with his hand over his eyes to keep out the light—instinct again—do we feel sorry for Bill—have we been mean to Bill—must we give Bill a present to make it up to him—what shall we give him. A dozen bottles of Liebfraumilch. An Australian wimpus. A fountain-pen filler. An old shoe. Shall we cry on the floor beside him, lie down and cry, so quietly that he won't wake. Shall we walk out into the storm with the glass in our hand, walk all the way to Fresh Pond, meet the ghost of Bertha, salute her among the algæ, how-do-you-do, madam, and have you slept well. Or else. What. What else. Fatigue again, the feet are slow and uncertain. The feet are reluctant. They do not miss the legs of chairs or stems of ash-trays. No. The feet and hands are detached. But shall we continue to say all this aloud or merely think it. It is becoming—a little—false. Unconvincing. Parepractical. Without a listener, why does one become dramatic. Or so much more dramatic. Alloplastic and autoplastic. And all these books here, these masses of words—must we swallow them only to spit them out. Bill, there is a fly walking on the back of your hand, and you don't know it. You don't even hear me tell you about it. He doesn't know that I am thinking about the Gurnett again, walking along the beach again. Brant Rock. He doesn't know how heavy the sand is, how it pulls at your feet, as if you were falling asleep. How it seems, as you drag slow footsteps, even to come up over your eyes, over your brain. He doesn't know that. He doesn't hear the nymphæ singing as we slowly divellicate the waves of sluggish foam. How could he know that. Have we translated the book of nosogenesis, or done our dreamwork. Can we unravel the perception-material on our feet, walking slowly, walking slowly, from one bipolarity to another. Have we devoured the id, or seen the dead ids lying on the beach and stinking in the east wind. Am I going toward the bedroom or first to the bathroom. Bedroom. Put the glass down you fool. Are we inclining towards, swooping towards, the streaming horizontal. Christ, to sleep—to sleep now—and without a single dream—not even those lumps, those clots, those whirls—not even those sickly lights—that fringe of lanterns under the eyelid, that fringe of slatterns—nor the mounting of lattices—textures of bedspread under the hand—the threads, the thralls, the threshes—must the leaning of the chin lead us into the southwest inevitably—into the dull darkness of whiteness with the room in the other light still on—forgot it—or this edge under the cheek—this cold edge of sheet—must we go downwards there, leaning downwards, and all for a last long slow deluding and terrible curve O God—is it there we go with a last little spinal effort——

IV

——one thing and then another one thing and then another the fresh wind the thickness the fine webs tender about the extended fingertips the dust sifting on the point of the shoe the cart track the car track the long glong trail into the sunset west of mountains purple gashes and the sun gone gloom and walking there walking westward with the solitary ghost above my head is this the bad sort is this the good sort where are you going and what do you mean why do you float there flow there just above my head to the right of my face avoiding the edge of my felt hat what is your precise shape old fellow and are you harmful I will turn away down this little muddy path look those trees there I will go down there swiftly I will run am running but the solitary ghost is still there this must be a bad one a ghost a ghost one of the white kind the cold kind the penetrating kind the thin and snowy kind o god shall I wake up in time will he enfold me chill me kill me SCREAM

one thing slower and then another thing slower it is a bulge a block a bulkhead a buttress of rock a wall there is a light there above it and a tree hanging over the light there was a face there but it is gone and I knew that face it was that girl no it was Susan no it was Doris no it was a negress with gold hair no it was gold teeth grinning in the lamplight it is gone the wind comes evenly warmly slowly caressingly hums under the edge of my felt hat burns my left cheek and I am climbing among the sun-warmed rocks my hand is no warmer than these rocks is there a volcano under them will steam come out of the fissures will it all crumble and sink in it is crumbling and sinking crumbling and sinking and shaking my foot goes in my other foot I sink to my knees among warm disrupted rocks they are all falling apart and inward downward SCREAM

first second third fifth first second third fifth it is the fifth of forth the forth the forth and in the bed on the wall in the bed on the edge of the wall beside the lilac hedge beside the path between the two strange houses in this strange place and evening too or is it early morning in the bed ill or half awake I am lying here at a loss I should not be here and look there are people coming out of the other house three people three women no a mother and her two daughters and the path brings them close to my exposed bed shall I pretend to be asleep

But we don't know the way to the beach
Shall we ask someone mother
But there is no one to ask
We might enquire at that strange house
Yes at that strange house what a queer house
Did you ever see such a house it's a ruin
It has no wall on this side
And how dirty it is
Do you see how dirty it is
out of my bed then and running across the lawn and then slowing down so as to pass them not running and veering off from them toward the porch while they approach the side door they have not seen me I am safe I can get in without being seen I can get into this strange house where Bertha lives and all our children and all our relatives and the stove and the icebox and then they will come in and ask the way to the beach which is the way to the beach can you direct us to the beach

You must go through the village the little wooden village of a winding two-storied road and flagpoles and shingles and the white church I know the way well I have often been there it has a flat and washed look slightly crazy the houses are flimsy the beach is small the sea is cold

Can you tell us the way to the beach
Yes you follow this road to the beach
they didn't see me in my bed on the wall beside the hedge although they came so close to me no they didn't but here is sand on the floor filth and mud on the sittingroom floor and under the diningroom table the blood comes into my hands and face I am angry hit something it is all one room but there too is a door to the pantry and there is Magma standing
This room is dirty you must sweep it out Magma
Sweep it out yourself
Give me a broom
piles of sand under the table under the chairs along the walls on the sills heaped against the screen doors shavings too blocks dolls paper soldiers with wooden props toy-cannons rags dirty clothes
This room is filthy you must clean it at once Magma
Clean it out
with the broom I am in the pantry and rush towards Magma the freckle-faced sister where is Bertha and where are the children but now we are in the corner of the sittingroom again blood is in my hands and face and neck I am angry

I will not be made a Christian slave by the Berthas

What did you say

with the broom hitting the saucepan on her head crash have I killed her but she is moving away and the brothers and cousins lean silently closer to me press closer and lean closer on all sides five six seven evil faces hard faces American army faces tough mouths menacing

What was that you said

I will not be made a slave to the Berthas

Squads right

Give him the bootsit

Is it

Squads left

Out with him

It's the wibbots what

this is that ghost again under the rim of my hat this is a dream is it the bad kind or the good kind shall I wake or not what will it be this squads right and bootsit tar and feathers hanging a beating and merciless men shall I keep still fight now or later SCREAM

peace on the left ear left hand peace

one shape and then another the little turmoils lead to big turmoils turmoils turmoils who said turmoils what is a turmoils this is the way to the this is the way and it is a clear landscape a clear cold landscape such as you saw in ice but far off cold and small the tiny splinters come out of it against my face look there are splinters of ice stars fragments glass bright landscape against my face against my eye and now the glare must be a fire and in the mirror I see the reflexion the little red bead from the unseeing eye it was those glass eyes on the little plush carpet all looking in different directions watchful and quiet how often do you wash them how often do you take them out can I do it myself must I use a lotion an eyewash and I am walking along the beach alone the little lonely beach is it Nantucket is it Plymouth is it Nantasket no it is somewhere else it is Melville it is Shakspere it is the edge-beach the wild beach the beach where I shall see the octopus it is the end and far Bohemian sea-coast

Go ahead and wait for me
I will go ahead and wait for you
I have something
Is it the what is it where
It is crying

alone I see it I step over the long black thick tentacles of a quivering celluloid jelly I am among them what if they should move seize me but it is really dead here on the sand it is quite dead I am sure it is dead o the poor thing it is dead shall I touch the tentacles with my stick shall I turn back and look at the body the corpse the crystal globe the bell-shaped body motionless on the wet hard sand with the tide going out it was left here by the tide and is dying look it is still alive look the eyes are watching me and what is that it is but don't SCREAM it is a it is a quite the largest octopus I ever heard of vast enormous the enemy of Moby Dick WHITE too but look

Go ahead and wait for me

I will

o christ it has a man's head inside the transparent jelly a man's face a fine man's head a magnificent face a face in aspic a head in aspic it is Michelangelo's head in aspic and o god it is still alive the life is ebbing backward along the long lucid tentacles the tentacles which are drying on the sand and this face is watching them dry watching them die feeling them die watching the tide go out and see the agony on that face the lips contorted in hatred and scorn the eyes that watch you with malevolent godhead that watch the receding waves with horror and hatred it is conscious it sees you and despises you even in its death it does not want your pity or your help how can you help it what can you do it hates you anyway if you saved it even if you could save it even if you could cast it back in the sea it would want to kill you for it is more intelligent than you and knows it but what is it thinking now that it is dying what terrific thought is it thinking for the face is wonderful it is intelligence meeting death with a vast thought

and walking away walking away

now the man with mustaches is showing us the new house the peculiar house with glass walls we follow him up the stairs all four of us follow him the three others ahead of me I am last going up the glass stairs the glass curtains too and the cupboards of glass it is all very bright and clear and artificial it is an artifact where have the others gone I hear their voices but I do not see them they have gone round the corner or into another room and here is a w. c. and I am determined yes I will have time will I have time yes there is plenty of time but the voices suddenly come nearer they are all looking in what a nice bathroom too O isn't it a nice bathroom but the stairs we go down are narrower and darker than before and who are these people these three people and the man who has gone ahead somewhere with mustaches into the street and along towards the factory alone the waterfall is pouring out of the side of the factory across the sidewalk how can I get past is it safe shall I cross to the other side of the street no I will stay on this side but it is poisonous water it is acid it is yellow I can feel the spray burning my cheek and hands it spouts out in innumerable jets and splashes upward from the sidewalk yellow and acid

Is that you Andy is that you Bertha Andy and Bertha

and this medical student whom I knew at Harvard too walking beside me and looking at me in a peculiar way over the tip of his mustache

No I don't live there any more do you live there still

I am married

I am now a gynecologist

I will walk with you as far as that little Catholic church

We played tennis once on Soldiers' Field the ball hit you in the face is that why you are blind or was it because you were looking through a peephole I can see that you don't like me

he grins at me as if he knew that I am afraid of him he is tall and takes a longer step wears tweeds brown shoes and an A.D. hat band or is it the Gas House we separate in silence before the church and I am going in beside an old woman it smells of incense and is full of images chasubles crucibles chrysms chrysoprases columns and columns and columns of white plaster the cheap painted stations of the cross gaunt yellow jaundiced marble crucifix and all the old women kneeling among the images I stand behind them and look at all the bright brasses and silvers and hanging lamps the rows of little candles and the priest is coming down the aisle toward me as I go out again his crooked mouth

My dear friends I would like to tell you that although this is the house of god you need not only think of it as a house of images it is not only a collection of images and objects and simulacra it is a place of friendship here you can speak to a friend of that which is nearest and dearest to your heart lay down your burdens before embodied kindness I am your friend

the voice dies down behind me dies away here are the fields and the trees there with sunlight on their bark and leaves and the stone wall beside the road here under the tree I am sitting in the grass on a little knoll and looking into a green wood and in the secret grass what is this a thimble a crushed thimble Bertha's thimble and also the rouge compact but

I open it and there is no rouge in it no powder only three old corroded pennies and I walk with them to the corner of the park opposite the tall apartment house where the negress is standing watching me by the door it is Clara the cook does she know what I am coming for yes she knows and is watching me Bertha has told her to watch me

Good morning Mister Cather

I am not coming in I am going down there where the children are playing in the meadow beside the marsh picking flowers the little boy and the little girl picking flowers spring flowers too wild columbine and crowfoot violet look children there is another flower over there do you see it in the marsh how is it you have forgotten to get that one too it is an orchid you can see it is some kind of green-and-white speckled tall orchid perhaps it wasn't there a moment ago but now it is there you can see it but can you reach it or is there too much water in the marsh yes it is very wet but wait by the wall don't go back to the city yet and it is I who will nobly go to the edge of the marsh stepping now on the spongy moss the water bubbles my hand out body stooping can I reach it yes the rare orchid for the two strange children

the shape of my left foot made of hollows

built like a crystal a bone of slow dark crystals off there too curving downward as if a pain of accretions items but this is a walk I am walking this is Harvard Street Arrow Street Bow Street the College Yard and there is Fred walking ahead of me turns his head a package under his arm looks away from me the buildings have changed moved away where is Gore Hall the path strange too yellow sand no trees but a wideness

Widener

Are you going to the poolroom

pays no attention goes to the left walks ahead of me looking back is on wheels in a little car cart an old Ford is it Rodman saying the Spanish Grammar has been read and is a deep sleep yes a deep sleep I am rolling a large hoop ribbons tied round the rim he watches me it leans always to one side the wind blowing the ribbons it careens why

Why don't you hit it on the other side keep it straight and here is the Fair will you go round or through it if you go through it you may lose your hoop and once we played ping-pong in Concord Avenue or was it Shepard and the Fair here

Good by I am going in I will get through diagonally the narrow crowded path of children drums horns the squealing merry-go-

round calliope steam spouting an enclosure of wire a long alley for pingpong the Japanese hits the ball to the other end of the wire enclosure look it explodes when the other hits it it opens becomes a go-cart rolling quickly back to us on wheels with a child in it no a doll a puppet nodding and another ball hit another explosion flash bang a little balloon going up diagonally then I am turning to the right and cross the street something my foot lifting the two feet together hopping see I am walking slowly queerly like an animal what animal is it a penguin can I get across doing it without being hit by that car yes it is all right and Shepard Hall there but changed redder brighter smaller and a restaurant in the hall no letter boxes what has happened but I was living here where is the janitor where is Mister O'Connor where is Jack a strange janitor with a mop on the wet marble floor this is now a dormitory for students

Can you tell me Jack's address

No he is gone perhaps I could find it

Send it to Widener

Yes

obras obras obras that book is out Mister Cather for another week but here is the key with the large wooden handle and on the han-

dle is Jack's address Waxage Street somewhere in Somerville carved on the handle and his name too carved the last thing he did before he went away Uncle David is of course dead Uncle Tom has gone off for the day not back in time the house he lives in now too far away take a Belmont bus walk through Craigie Street and find the house with open walls go upstairs Aunt Norah is very old and small bending down to the floor her white head wants to go downstairs you will have to carry her how small light white she is as I go down the carpeted stairs her arm is round my neck

I am your child now

the saucy face impish smiles detachedly looks at me indifferently wide-eyed like an infant at the breast but on my shoulder the small head I have been kind am being kind will give her a conch-shell a house by the sea in that village leave her here and call Bertha

Bertha Berty

lifting from the dark the open suitcase the nightgown holding it up laughing but it is spotted dirty a large spot she is laughing can't be helped you don't mind do you what can I say nothing say nothing but turn away sadly in the hotel room no it's all right perfectly all right but sad I am going up the hill on the grass behind juniper trees birches the road dusty she is coming up the other side yes there she is look it is who is it not Berty no Molly no a girl with red hair comes through the oak trees beautiful loves me puts out her hand kisses me we are kissing become one face floating in air with wings one fused face with wings Turner sunset and this and this and this and this and this WING-beat and WINGbeat where whirled and well where whirled and well where whirled and well——

To come upward from the dark world, through the mild shafts of light, as a swimmer in long and curved periphery from a dive; from the whirled and atomic or the swift and sparkling through the slower and more sleekly globed; effortless, but with a drag at the heels of consciousness—to float upward, not perpendicularly, but at an angle, arms at sides, turning slightly on one's axis, like a Blake angel, through the long pale transverse of light—with the sounds, too, the bell-sounds, the widening rings of impalpable but deep meaning, as if someone far off with spheral mouth said, Time—and the goldfish-mouth released its bubble, and closed, and then again opened to say, Time—to come upward thus slowly revolving, thus slowly twisting, the eye scarcely opened and almost indifferent to light, but opening more widely as the light with obscure and delicate changes teased at the eyelid, teased at the sleepy curiosity—and the textures too, the warm or soft, the wrinkled or knotted, those that caressed whitely and obliquely, and those also that withdrew, or focussed slowly in a single sharp point and pressed—to float upward like this, from plane to plane, sound to sound, meaning to meaning—the attitudes changing one into another as the hands shifted, the feet shifted, the breathing altered or the hearing cleared—from turbulent to troubled, from troubled to serene—but with the bell-sound nearer and nearer, as if the head were emerging into a glistening ring, and as if over the edges of this ring came the words like bubbles, at first meaningless, and then with half-meanings, and at last—not with meanings precisely but with gleams, as of fins that turned away in a flash and vanished——

To move upward like this, surrounded by one's own speech, and continuously more closely surrounded by one's own body, the hand heavy on the heart, the heart beating insistently in the ear, that which a moment ago was the chime of a dream become the rhythm of the pulse, the distorted faces and filaments of the dream becoming only the fluttering defence of the eyelashes against the square of light from the window—all the somatic disturbances, as of cramped elbow and bent knee and cold hand and stifled nostril, which were a moment since so marvellously translated into wastes of snow or ugly corners of rock or difficult escapes from social awkwardness, now again assuming the simple physical reality, against which the dream had fought, as it were, a rear-guard action—to say again, after all this obscure welter of images and spaces, this kaleidoscope of times, "here," "now," "time," "I"—I that was there, twisted, twisted into that strange shape, am here again, but with a queer difference——

The confusion fell slowly away, in ebbing rings of sound, he looked more firmly at the window, putting one hand up to touch the brass knob at the head of the bed above him, he looked and listened, and knew that the sound was the bell of Memorial Hall. How many strokes he had missed, or heard only in his sleep, he couldn't know, but he counted four. Four. Not in the morning, it was almost that when he had fallen asleep. It must be five or six in the afternoon. The light from the square of window at the foot of the bed was that of winter twilight, and lamplight, mixed—cold natural gray tinged with artificial orange: and something in it, too, suggested the pale reflections of snow. Thursday. Another day gone, soundlessly gone, an agony got through without pain, as if he had been anæsthetized. What a good thing. And to wake up, or come to, comparatively refreshed, comparatively calm! But *how* refreshed? He explored dry lips with his tongue, tasted the salt, opened and shut his mouth experimentally, and found himself thirsty. Turning his head from side to side on the pillow, he felt no headache, or only a very slight one, at the base of the skull. He looked at his watch. Seven o'clock.

But it was difficult to get up, if one didn't know what one got up for. Or at such an hour, so dislocated, in such a place, after such a series of nights, with so much of oneself gone, so much of one's secret gone. Idiot! You have confessed: your virtue is lost. Only the reticent man retains his virtue. But was virtue precisely the word? Or if not, what was it? He tried to remember the details: Michelangelo, the sea, Melville, the Gurnett, the secret of intimacy—intimate secrets. Sleep was better, or perhaps laughter.

He laughed lightly, almost gaily, but as if without meaning, and turned his head toward the door that led to Bill's study; then cut the laugh short and said "Bill." There was no answer. He heard the study clock ticking. He said it again, and listened again, and still getting no answer clasped his hands under his head. So it all came to this. After all the agony, all the confusion, all the death, one came to this. One awoke on a strange bed, at twilight, and found that suddenly everything was—peace. No longer a need to run, to hurry, to evade, to escape. No problems to solve. No people to avoid. No single person to hate. Except perhaps oneself. And why bother to hate oneself? Why bother? This curious amiable little collocation of wishes and repugances—but more amiable than hateful—decidedly more amiable—with his hands clasped under his head and a fixed small smile—and the sounds of the Memorial Hall bell agreeably in his ear—why hate him? Or had it been the Unitarian Church. No, it was Memorial Hall. But was it still snowing?

He groaned, and heaved himself off the bed, and went to the window, which was six inches open at the bottom—that must have been done by Bill. A soft current of rain-washed air flowed in coolly over the sill, it was raining a little, and when he looked down at the street-lamps and the College Yard he saw that most of the snow was gone. The slope of the hill towards the Union was white, but a white soddened and darkened; the street was cleared; only at the sides were the piled and hardened drifts. And the sound of the snow-shovels, scraping the rain-loosened snow—the raucous scraping and chopping, the ringing of steel on stone——

The face that looked back at him, from the lamplit bathroom mirror, was pale, the cheeks pale and a little sunken, but it faced him steadily and calmly, and the eye was not as bloodshot as he might have expected. Nor did the hands, which supported him on the cold marble, tremble, though he felt weak. You, Andrew Cather—old One-eye Cather. You in the flesh again, redivivus; you emaciated and with a hangover; but with that soft-clear sort of hangover which a fried egg and a stiff whisky would put right. Clear-headed, amused, detached—and with a queer deep historical sense. Wash your face in cold water. Dip your face in the cold green basin of water. Your hair too. The time-worn temples. And the three-days' growth of brown stubble, so long as to be getting soft. And shave, with Bill's dirty little brush and rusty safety-razor. The little ridged clots of soaped hair, floating testimonially in the water, the dirt-streaked water. And a borrowed collar from Bill's bureau.

But where was it all gone, where was all the tumult gone? Into what remote sunset sound, what slow and distant and delicious thunder of crumbling, as of a world lost in entire peacefulness?

He switched on the light in the silent study, and found that the chaos had been once more reduced to order; the empty bottles had been removed; a new fire of white birch-logs had been laid neatly in the brown brick fireplace; the cigarette ends were gone from the ashes and the ash-stand. A fresh bottle of whisky stood on the brass tray, and on the table was a folded note, over which lay a small key and a pink ticket. Sanders Theatre. Of course, the symphony concert tonight. From Bill. And the small bright key. "Andy. Going to Portland for a few days. Use the ticket if you like. Also my car, at the Church Street garage. Why not go off and think it over quietly, if you can—first telling Bertha, please! Not a bad idea. I suggest Duxbury. Were you saying something about a pig when I fell asleep. Bill."

The crucified pig, of course! He touched

his smoothed chin and smiled, recollecting; feeling again the drunken glass in his hand, the precise torrent of eloquence in his mouth, the spate of ideas and images. Had it been absurd. Had it been as logical as it had seemed. Had he been as wonderfully in control of it as he had thought. He went to the window and looked across at the lights in the Widener Library and Boylston Hall, watched the dark figures going and coming through the gate to the Yard, figures in raincoats, figures hurrying in the soft rain. All the Smiths and Joneses of the world, accumulating knowledge, the ransackers of others' words, the compilers and digesters. Those who knew nothing, and those who knew a little, and those to whom life would painfully teach more. Were they jealous. Did they betray, or had they been betrayed. Were they sex-ridden, was sex a monster for them, a nightmare, was all this busy come-and-go a mere flight, a disguise, a pretence, a raincoat surface which concealed——

Concealed what.

The slow pang, recapitulative, rose in the darkness of his thought, lazily, languidly, as with the perishing last little energy of an exploding rocket, undecided at the last whether it should be propelled further or fall in a broken and slow dishevelment of fire-streaked pain. Bertha. Bertha and Tom. Yes. This deep violation, which was now past, this blood which was now shed and lost. This wound which was now beginning to be a scar. The inevitable, and God-to-be-thanked-for, cicatrix; the acceptance—but was it cowardly or was it merely wisdom—the acceptance of all of life as a scar. The pig, not crucified, perhaps, after all, but merely cicatrized. Circumscribed. But we mustn't be misunderstood —! Like that unfortunate fellow in the hospital; who said—"*circumcised—that's* what I meant!"

He poured himself a whisky, smiling, measuring the quantity idly by the deepening of the colour in the green glass, held it, looking at the picture of Michelangelo, and walked to and fro slowly, before the hearth, as if for the pleasure of repeating, or reenacting, a lost attitude. Here's to you, Mike, old boy. The insufferable vanity of the human being, who identifies himself with everything that's greater than himself! I identified myself with Michelangelo. With Shakspere. With Melville. I was their grandchild. And why not, after all. I inherit them. They produced me, I couldn't escape them. They taught me how to suffer. They taught me how to know, how to realize, gave me the words by which I could speak my pain. They gave me the pain by giving me the words. Gave my pain its precise shape, as they gave me their consciousness. As I shall give my pain, my consciousness, to others. Did I say this to Bill.

He drank the whisky at a gulp, shuddered, set down the glass. The warmth in his belly crawled slowly about, like a crimson-rambler, and he smiled, putting a cool hand against his forehead. It had been a good show, it had been funny; and it was strange, it was disconcerting, to think that an agony could take such a shape—it made one distrust the nature of agony—was it possible, as this suggested, that all sincerities, even the sincerity of agony, were only sincerities of the moment? Only true in the instant? Relative? And for the rest insincere and unreal? Had it all been a fake? And had Bill seen through it? Absurd. In that case, the present calm was just as unreal, just as insincere, just as much an affair of the precise point in the sequence of cause and effect. How do you know your calmness is real, old crab. Do you really dare to think back, to feel back, into the yesterday which has now made itself into today? Are you really calm, or is it a mask which you have put on in your sleep. Have you changed—have you, have you, have you. Shall we look at the face in the mirror again, to see if it is calm. Look at the hand, to see if it shakes. Take the Binet test, to see if you are intelligent. Could you cry, now, although you think you feel like laughing. And how much part in all this has been played by alcohol. At what point in your spirited dramatization of yourself did the drama become drama for the sake of drama, and cease to be even so justifiable as a dramatic "projection" can be? Ah—ah—and is it true—can it *possibly* be true—that sudden and terrible idea——

He returned to the window, to gaze downward at the dark wetness of Massachusetts Avenue; emphasized, by the arclights, between the piled snow; and found himself staring at the idea. Could it be true—and if it was, what a relief! what an escape!—that consciousness itself was a kind of dishonesty? A false simplification of animal existence? A voluntary-involuntary distortion, precisely analogous to the falsification that occurs when consciousness, in turn, tries to express itself in speech? As the animate, then, must be a natural distortion of the inanimate. Each step a new kind of dishonesty; a dishonesty inherent in evolution. Each translation involving a shedding, a partial shedding or abandonment, and an invention of a something new which was only disguisedly true to its origins, only obviously true to itself. But in that case, what was truth. Was truth the suffering, or the calm that succeeds the suffering. Or the comprehensive awareness of both, the embracing concept. Was suffering, as it were, merely an unsuccessful attempt at translation, in this progress from one state to another? An inability to feel what one is, to say what one feels, to do what one wills? A failure, simply, to know? A failure of the historical sense?

He lost himself in the succession of half-thoughts, a genial dissipation of ideas, of which he troubled only to feel the weights and vague directions; feeling that he could, had he wished, have followed each divergent and vanishing fin-gleam or tail-gleam to its psychological or physiological or metaphysical covert; but that to do so would add nothing to what already he deeply and animally and usefully knew. Bores me, the sum. If it was a fake, all that dramatized and projected agony, it was a genuine fake: suffering, even if it is only a transition, is genuine. Speech, even if it must be only incompletely loyal to its subject, incapable of saying all, is genuine.

The fluidity of life, as long as it is life, can never have the immobile integrity of the rock from which it came. It will only be honest rock again when it is dead. And in the meantime, if it suffers, if it is aware that it suffers, if it says that it is aware that it suffers, and if it is aware that it cannot say completely *why* it suffers, or in severance from what, that's all you can ask of it. In sum—idiot!—it is only unhappy because it is no longer, for the moment, rock.

He put his hand out of the window to feel the soft rain, as if in demonstration of the smaller uses of feeling; the minor advantages of the temporary emancipation from rock; the pleasures of dishonesty, or treason, to which evolution has led us. Item: rock suffering rain. Rock enduring infidelity. Rock conceiving a philosophical synthesis which explains, if it does not actually diminish, the pain involved in being not-rock. And assures the not-rock that it has, in a sense, a kind of reality. Andrew Cather has really suffered, but his suffering has no importance, except to himself, and only to himself insofar as he fails to realize—what? That rock, sundered from rock, does not cry.

The clock on the mantel struck the half-hour, with a single surprising stroke, and he was interested to notice that the clock itself went on ticking, as if in no astonishment at that sudden comment on division of time. Half-past seven! The clock was fast. The concert would be at eight. If a little walk, to the river and back, perhaps along Memorial Drive, and then a newspaper and quick supper at the Waldorf, the stock market and sports column surveyed over the fried eggs —if this interval, in which to accept more rationally what in fact he had already accepted, the idea of meeting Bertha at the concert—and perhaps Tom as well—the idea which had been fully formed as soon as he had seen the pink ticket on the table, and so exactly as Bill had foreseen——

And the little key. Duxbury. Had Bill foreseen that too.

When he emerged into the street, and drew a long breath of rain-soft air, abruptly throwing back his shoulders in the gesture he had learnt from Tom, he stared at the dull piles of snow and said aloud—Duxbury. Of course. What could be simpler. All that wild magnificent farrago of nonsense had been leading back to Duxbury—or had it been Bill who had been leading back to it. And all the drunken fantasies and fandangos—it was too absurd. It was too obvious. All this mother-fixation business, as if everything in the soul could be charted like a sea! No, Andy, no. Be honest, on this rainy night in February. Walk honestly down Linden Street. Cross Mount Auburn Street honestly; and proceed as honestly toward the Charles River as you would proceed to death. It is not Bill who has given you this idea—not, Bill, not Tom, not Bertha, nor any combination of these, nor any disaster to you, any accident; it is yourself; it is your own little worm-curve; the twist that is your own life; the small spiral of light that answers to the name of Andrew Cather; the little rock-pain which chooses this particular fashion of saying that it is tired of being not-rock and would like again to be rock. Touch your hand against the wet wall beside you, the dripping icicle on the wall, which breaks away so softly and falls soundlessly into the snow—feel the wet coldness, the moist surface which will again soon be glazed with ice—know these things, as you know the wet and slippery bricks beneath your feet—the river toward which you walk—they are not more real, more solid, more permanent, than the past Andrew Cather, who has now suddenly and painfully told the present Andrew that there is also a future Andrew. Murder him, if you like, but he is yours.

Would Tom be there; or would Bertha be alone.

He ran quickly across the lamp-reflecting river of Memorial Drive, dodged the twin headlamps of an approaching car, which funnelled bright swarms of raindrops out of the night, and on arrival at the other side, suddenly slipped and sat down hard on the half-frozen gravel path, striking his left knee. The pain sickened him, he hugged the lifted knee derisively, sat still for a moment, laughing silently, then rose and limped forward, looking over his shoulder to see if he had been observed. And what sort of pain was this, was this not-rock too. Was it real or unreal. Less real, or more, than the pain of separation. Ridiculous! Tuberculosis, intervening, will arrest the progress of dementia præcox. Good God. If everything was as relative as this—if a sudden physical pain could thus completely shut off a psychological pain, and make the return to it seem forced and deliberate and false—a mere self-indulgence——

Boylston Street, a lighted garage, another garage, the bookshop-sign swinging and dripping in the narrow dark street, Erasmus, the lights in the gymnasium. Rodman had said that he must have the completed text in two weeks; and here a week was almost gone—

twenty more translation exercises to be compiled and written out—but that would be easy. That Ronda poem. That absurd guide-book. Correct the errors in the following. And at least two of the exercises devoted to the *corrida*—a novel idea to introduce the bullfight into Spanish grammar. With perhaps a spirited photo or two. *Sol y sombra.* And what about a quotation from the Spanish translation of "The Waste Land," *Tierra Baldia,* by Angel Flores. *Abril es el mes màs cruel; engendra—Lilas de la tierra muerta, mezcla—* And the guide-book, *Guia de Ronda.* "Ronda is an intricated old Moorish town. Being highly salubrious the longevity of the place is proverbial." And the "polite youngs." Translate these passages into what you think might have been the Spanish original. Or something from *Toreros y Toros.*

At the bright door to the Waldorf, beside the subway entrance, three cents for *The Boston Evening Transcript;* and then the ticket, accepted from the ticket-machine, with a slow clink; and the fried eggs, fresh country eggs, and bacon. Old Turgenev at the desk, with his beautiful white tobacco-stained beard. Eddie, the negro taxi-driver, sprawling in his usual chair beside the door, reading a paper, his taxi drawn up at the curb outside, in readiness for undergraduates bent on pleasure. And the marble clock with black hands.

Was suffering one's nearest approach to an acute realization of life? Of existence? And therefore desirable?

—All I can say is, he's a stinker. It ought to have been a D.

—Why don't you go and see him.

—The squash courts——

—Sure. Five o'clock.

—And a side order of bacon. Three to come. Blue plate.

—Oh, gosh, it was good. It was the cat's pyjamas. It was the bee's knees.

—No, it was Crab that seconded him. Not me.

Complete Wall Street And Boston Stocks Closing Prices Heiress Fights to Keep Her Baby Child Flogged Boy Is Black and Blue Boston Stage Star Dead Famous Singer Began Career With Medicine Show at Age of Ten Years.

But where was it all gone, where was all the tumult gone, into what remote and dwindling sunset sound? And as Bill had said, Bertha must be suffering too. Walking to and fro with a soaked handkerchief in her hand. Unable to sit down, to rest, to think. Unable to sleep. Telephoning to all her friends. What had she said. Had she told them that he had left her. Or what. How had she explained it. Had she told them that she and Tom——

He crumpled the paper napkin, as if to crush once again the recapitulative pang, pushed back his chair. What dress would she be wearing—as if it mattered, by God. The blue velvet opera cloak. And all their friends, all the wives of faculty members, to see them when they met. Look, there is Andrew Cather, he's talking with Bertha, do you see them, in the back row, you know what they say about them don't you, they say—and do you suppose Tom Crapo is here tonight—can you imagine——

In Bill's room again, without turning on the light, he poured himself a whisky, drank it straight, resumed the automatic buzz of phrases. Was there no way to stop it. Was it wise to go to the concert at all. Should he go to see Molly, invite her to come to Duxbury with him, simply to have some one to talk to. The light from Massachusetts Avenue filled the room with imitation moonlight, sharply angled, ghostly; Michelangelo gazed down sombrely through a diagonal shadow. Telephone to Molly now, or later perhaps. Go to Shepard Hall while Bertha was still at the concert, to have a look around, get the mail, put on a clean shirt. And telephone to Molly from there. Hello Molly, this is your old friend Andy, I wondered if you would like —I wondered if we might—what do you say to a little elopement—expedition—would you like to drive me down to Duxbury tonight—all expenses paid—what ho, Molly, how about a little spree to Montreal. Dance at the Lido first if you like. Or stay in your flat and drive down early in the morning. It's all over but the laughing.

He chose a book at random from the shelf by the fireplace, turned on the light and began to read, standing with his back to the hearth.

"Man is pre-eminently distinguished from the lower animals by the enormous development of his libido . . . he loves a great deal more than is necessary."

He loves a great deal more than is necessary. Christ!

The impulse to fling the book down violently was translated quietly into a precise reinsertion of it in its place on the shelf. These psychologists. These fellows who become psychologists because they understand neither themselves nor any one else. These phrase-makers—man with his enormous libido, man with his persistent libido, man pre-eminently distinguished from the lower animals because his love is not confined to the rutting season! Pre-eminently distinguished from the birds by his lack of wings. Look at the poor devil, staggering through the world under his enormous burden of libido. I forgive you, Bertha, for now I realize that the burden of libido which you carry everywhere with you is far too much for you. Yes. Let us share it with you. Hand it about to the audience at Sanders Theatre—God knows *they* could stand a little more. And if they and Tom don't want it all—if there is something left over—a quantum, a surd, one tiny flame-plume—one eyelash-flicker of a loving look——

But no. Not that. My dear Bertha—Bertha my dear—need I explain to you the so very simple fact that after what has happened it will be impossible for us to resume—I mean, impossible for us to live—we must wave away the notion of a shared bedroom. You understand that. Old-fashioned of me, I daresay, but honest. Honest Andrew. What arrangement shall we make. Can we discuss it now quite calmly and sensibly. Shall I take a separate apartment next door. Shall we separate, or is it possible that now—now that this action has freed us—we can come together more usefully on another and perhaps more realistic plane. But not exactly—need I say—the planes of Abraham. No. And strange too that it is still with such a pang, though partly retrospective, and therefore sentimental——

And why was it with excitement, with quickened heartbeat, with unseeing eye, the familiar sensation of the face lowered so as to avoid the impalpable psychological problem, precisely as if it were a thing physically visible, that he approached Memorial Hall in the rain, slowing his steps as he passed Appleton Chapel, and even tempted, as long ago, to make a deliberate circuit of a block or two, for the mere gaining of time? Dismay? fear? doubt? animal distrust of the unknown? Pull yourself together. Enter. Climb the stairs. Ten minutes to eight. Take your seat and look about you.

The brown programme in his hand, he climbed the steps to the balcony, found the seat near the parapet, which overlooked the absurd brightly lighted little auditorium of wooden Gothic, which Tom called late Visigothic or early Swiss Châlet, and watched the musicians filing on to the stage. The concertmaster, Burgin, came last, and tucked his feet backward under the rung of his chair, as if for leverage when drawing the bow. Like the bird who tightens his claws on the twig, in order to release a particularly fine burst of song. And the squeakings and squawkings and runs and trills began, the grunts of the cellos, the tappings and listenings of the kettle-drummer, all the delicious miscellany of tuning—while the audience of dodos and baldheads and wonderfully-bedizened frumps settled, and preened, and cooed at one another, or studied programmes through telescopes. But was Bertha here. Was Tom here. Dared he lean over the edge and look. Would he be seen looking.

He looked, and she was not there. Nor Tom. The two seats, in the last row, were empty. But there were still people coming in —along the back—he watched them—and not finding her there, he looked down the aisle into the audience on the floor, where here and there little groups of women stood talking. Who was it who had made a standing bet with some one that if he could find more than three men in any one row of seats—and look at them tonight. Solid phalanxes of females. Aged females. As you progressed forward, toward the stage, solid rows of white hair, with now and then one solitary gleaming baldheaded octogenarian of a professor. Music to hear, why hear'st thou music sadly? Echo answers why. What did these creatures care about music, what did it mean to them? O God, O Cambridge.

"Overture to 'The Magic Flute.' . . . Wolfgang Amadeus Mozart. Born at Salzburg, January 27, 1756; died at Vienna, December 5, 1791. Thirty-six years old."

Koussevitzky came quickly on to the stage, stepped with mathematical precision to his little dais, ascended, took up his baton, and as the applause drew him, pivoted with choreographic neatness. At precisely that moment, Bertha entered from the door at the far side and walked with quick, short steps, almost running, along the back, her hand clutching the blue velvet cloak against her breast. Alone. And as she dropped into her seat, he leaned over the edge of the parapet and felt that he drew forcibly upwards the surprised gaze that she lifted to him. She started visibly, controlled an impulse to rise again, and while still she looked at him he lifted his programme, pointed to it, raised one finger in the air, and then with the waved programme indicated the door. She nodded, and the overture began.

The Masonic chords drew themselves out, melancholy, profound, and the sad slow air followed them, the theme that later would be given to the delicious little hurdy-gurdy tune

—"Emanuel Johann Schikaneder, the author of the libretto of 'The Magic Flute,' was a wandering theatre director . . . poet . . . improvident, shrewd, a bore. . . ."

She was very white, she had on the blue velvet opera cloak, and under it the black satin. The white coral necklace. She sat stiffly, as if unseeing, but also as if aware embarrassedly that she was being looked at.

"He asked Mozart to write the music for it. Mozart, pleased with the scenario, accepted the offer and said——"

Why was the overture considered gay, happy—for an undercurrent of sadness ran all through it. Papageno. Papagenesis. The birdcatcher. She was turning her face a little away from him, with a sort of frozen precision, self-conscious and a little evasive, but firm.

"Mozart said—'I have never written magic music. . . .' . . . Goethe once wrote of the text . . . Hegel praised the libretto highly . . . symbolical meanings."

And now the break, the cessation, the almost imperceptible pause, and then the rapid chatter of the fugue, the sudden sawed-off bursts of fiddle-sound, the harsh quick downward scrapes of simultaneous bows, the brave *sforzandi* followed immediately by the swift twinkle, the delicate pattern, of the fugue, the mouse-dance of light quick sound——

"Schikaneder knew the ease with which Mozart wrote . . . knew that it was necessary to keep watch over him . . . put Mozart in a little pavilion which was in the midst of a garden near his theatre . . . inspired by the beautiful eyes of the singing woman, Gerl. . . ."

She looked ill. Her face was thinner, her eyes looked larger, were sombred, she was somehow nicer than he had thought her to be, she had been hurt. She was watching Koussevitzky intently, but the way in which her elbows were drawn in at her sides meant that she was conscious of the people who sat at left and right: who, nevertheless, were paying no attention to her.

"Velvet of itself is a natural response to the new quest of lovely ladies for a fabric, luxurious unto the demands of this exacting mode. . . ." "Schikaneder's name was in large type on the bill: Mozart's name was in small type underneath the cast. . . . Schenk gave Beethoven lessons. . . . At the end of the Overture, he went to Mozart and kissed his hand. Mozart stroked his admirer's cheek. Mozart went behind the scenes and saw Schikaneder in his costume of a bird. . . ."

And now—ah, yes, how lovely—the absurd but magnificent dialogue between god and the little hurdy-gurdy—the majestic chords, the great sweeps of sound, the laws and the prophets, the thunder from the mountain, and then the delicious and ridiculous and so humble bubble-and-squeak of the clarinets and oboes and bassoons, the birds singing in the rain—and then god again—and again the undaunted little tumbling tune—so childish——

". . . Mozart died shortly after the production of 'The Magic Flute' in deep distress . . . this opera was in his mind until the final delirium . . . he would take his watch from under his pillow and follow the performance in imagination. . . . 'Now comes the grand aria'. . . ."

Her fists doubled under her chin, she leaned forward, as if with an air of saying, look, you see I am even smiling a little, I am amused by all this, you needn't think I am afraid, or that I'm not an independent person. Nor that I won't face you bravely.

"The day before he died, he sang with his weak voice the opening measures of 'Der Vogelfanger bin ich ja' and endeavoured to beat the time with his hands. . . . Schikaneder, 'sensualist, parasite, spendthrift' . . . built the Theatre an der Wien . . . on the

roof he put his own statue, clothed in the feather costume of Papageno. His luck was not constant; in 1812 he died in poverty."

The Masonic chords again, ascending, altered, but with the same deep sadness; as of trains crying to each other across a wilderness at night; the prolonged and lost nostalgia, the sound of pain abruptly introduced into a scene of festivity, of candles, of minuets, as if coming in on a wind that blew out lights;—and then again the lovely quick fugue, the elf-dance, rising and rising to broader and bolder sweeps of sound, the intricate and algebraic pattern—this gesture coming in again, and then that other, the delicious bustle as of lights being relighted, servants hurrying with tapers, the music striking up, the dancers re-forming——

The blue velvet cloak had slipped from her left shoulder, she sat with her two hands flat on her knees, still leaning forward, but now as if at last the music alone had become real for her, had taken her away; as if she had forgotten the things which had darkened her eyes, and given the new pallor to her cheeks. She was absorbed, she was by herself, she looked young.

"Here the master, wishing, so to speak, to glance back and to give a final model of the

old Italian and German overtures with a counterpointed theme, which had served, and still served, as preface to many operas, pleased himself by exhibiting the melodic theme that he had chosen, in all its forms, adorned with the riches of harmony and instrumentation. The result of this marvellous work of the carver is one of the most perfect instrumental compositions ever produced by human genius." Oh, yes indeed.

And now again god was speaking to the hurdy-gurdy—but this time a kindlier god, less remote; the god stooping from the mountain, gentler and nearer; and the hurdy-gurdy, changed and translated, but still essentially the same, speaking in a bolder and firmer voice—and then god again—as if the two voices greeted each other—and now the beginning of the end, the slow, falling rhythm of the melancholy gayety—the last downward sweep of Koussevitzky's arms, of the bows, the held chord, another, the upward flick of the baton, the silence—and then the applause, mounting, mounting, like a storm of rain on gusts of wind——

She had risen from her seat, was looking upward at him for confirmation; he signalled with his programme, and turned to move toward the swinging door. The applause dimmed behind him as he descended the stairs and began to cross the lofty marble-paved hall to the other entrance. She emerged, and came toward him, a little self-conscious, her head tilted a little to one side, the rich copper hair gleaming, the silver buckles of her slippers alternately thrust forward, the sharp heels striking clearly on the marble. She stopped, and waited for him, holding the cloak together with her hands. He had thought she was smiling. But when he came close to her, and she made no movement to disengage her hands, he saw that her lips were pressed tight, and that in the widened and darkened pupils of her gray eyes was a curious mingling of defiance and defeat. She was as frightened as himself. He put his hand against her elbow and said——

—Let's walk up and down here.

—Do you think this was a very tactful way——

—I'm sorry. But what else——

—Everybody in Cambridge saw it——

—Good God, Berty, surely there are more important things——

—It's typical.

—Not at all. On these occasions one simply obeys one's instinct, that's all.

—Is that an excuse for bad manners, or lack of consideration?

—It seemed to me the most *neutral* way of managing it.

—Perhaps you're right. But I should have thought——

They walked to the end of the hall in silence, embarrassed, past the rows of sepulchral memorial tablets, the interminable lists of dead soldiers. Antietam. The Battle of the Wilderness. Gettysburg. Bull Run. Born, and died of wounds. Killed in action. Died in a Confederate Prison. Died in Libby Prison, of a fever. Born and Died.

—Is Tom coming.

—No.

They turned, and started slowly back. From Sanders Theatre came the sudden sound of renewed music, the beginning of the second number, a fanfare of bright trumpets and a thumping of drums. Muted by distance and the valves of doors.

—Tell me. Did Bill call you up.

—Yes.

—Did he tell you that he was giving me his ticket.

—Yes.

—I see. Just as I thought. He arranged it. You expected me. And you told Tom he'd better not come.

—I told Tom that I thought it would not be advisable.

—For *both* our sakes, I suppose!

—For *all* our sakes. I think the sarcasm is uncalled for.

—Sorry. I was only thinking aloud.

Lifting her hand from her cloak, she touched a quick finger to the corners of her eyes.

—I think you might have let me know before, what you were doing, or where you were——

—I wanted to be alone. Surely you understand *that*.

—Of course I understand it, but just the same I think you might have let me know.

For the first time she turned and looked at him, hesitating, half inhibiting her step, as if she were going to stop, or even going to touch him, as if for the first time she were meeting him. But she averted her face again.

—Andy, you don't look well.

—Neither do you, Berty, for that matter!

—Isn't it silly——

—What.

She made a downward gesture with her hand.

—Life. The way we make each other suffer.

—That's the most sensible thing you ever said.

He found himself holding her elbow quite tightly, and at the same time frowning, as if to control an excess of feeling—but what sort of feeling he could not possibly have said. Not anger, not self-pity.

—There's a lot of mail for you at the apartment.

—Yes, I thought I'd go round there now—that is, if you're staying for the concert—and get it. And a few clean shirts. I thought I'd leave before the intermission.

—What are you going to do.

—Do you mean now—or do you mean in general.

—Well—both.

He gazed downward, at the worn and dirty marble of the floor, trodden down by the hungry generations of undergraduates, among whom had been himself, and watched the parallel thrust, preposterous, of Bertha's slippers and his own mud-splashed shoes.

—I'm damned if I know yet, Berty—doesn't it really depend on *you*.

—Not necessarily.

—What I really came for was to say that I thought *time*—that I thought we ought to take plenty of *time*——

—Do you think we need any more?

—It sounds weak of me, but I don't know.

—Do you mean——

—What do *you* mean!

He stopped, and turned her towards him with his hand, and looked hard at her eyes. The look of defiance had gone, the look of defeat remained. She withdrew her arm from his hand, gently, and resumed the walk, and for a moment they listened in silence to the queer muffled and abortive sounds of the music, walking slowly, both their faces downcast.

—You ought to know. But do you want me to say it first.

—No, Berty. No. No.

—Well, then——

—I think I'll go away for a few days, if you don't mind—just to think it over quietly —by myself—I don't mean anything invidious by it——

—Where are you going.

—To Duxbury. It's absurd, but I've got a queer desire to go there. Not so queer either. It's all plain enough—I just want to go there.

—Andy——

—What.

—Take me with you. Let me come with you.

—No, Berty, I think it would be better not.

—Please.

—No, really, Berty, if you don't mind——

—Please.

—No.

There was a strained pause, they faced each other, she had tried to smile.

—And now I think I'll go—I think it's better if we don't talk about it too much yet—will it be all right if I leave you here—I suppose you can't get into the theatre again, until the intermission. But if I'm going to drive down, I ought to be starting——

—Of course, Andy. Run along. I'll sit on the top steps and listen to it through the door.

—All right. If you're sure you don't mind. . . . Good-night.

—Good-night.

He turned as he went out, and caught a last glimpse of her climbing the stairs, lifting her frock at the knees. Poor Berty—or was it poor Andy? It had stopped raining. He skirted the edge of the College Yard, crossed Massachusetts Avenue, and in the Church Street garage asked for Bill's car, producing Bill's note and the key.

—I'm a friend of his.

—Yes, sir. I guess it's all right. Can you say what kind of a car it is.

—Dodge coupé.

—O. K. I'll bring her down for you.

So it was all coming out like this—all queerly ending like this—with a humble little anticlimax like this. And what would happen now! Impossible to say. It must be thought of, felt of. And with Tom still there, but now a little farther off——

—Thank you. How is she for oil and gas.

—All set.

—Thanks.

He drove slowly up Church Street, and into Brattle, as if to go to Shepard Hall; but then, suddenly he decided against it. Why go there at all? Why not start at once; merely stopping at the Club for his bag? Yes. . . .

Turning, he swung the car through Brattle Square, down to the river and across the little arched bridge, and then accelerated as he entered the wide new boulevard. So it was all like this. Bertha was like that. He himself was like—what? A queer confusion, a queer relief, a queer delight. In two hours he would be in Duxbury, would pass the dark rain-soaked railway station, the library, the flag-pole. Find a hotel. And in the morning, at sunrise—how absurd it was—he would drive down to the Point, and cross the long bridge, over the rattling boards, and, see the beach again—or even walk to the Gurnett—unless, as was more than likely, he decided to sleep.

For already, to all intents, he had revisited that scene, in this week of so much revisiting —he knew it, every coarse or delicate detail of it—the matted waves of dried seaweed which were wet underneath, the caked salt on the pebbles, the shells, the bleached bones of fishes—the little piles of charred stones, too, on which were written the histories of clambakes—what more, now, could these things say to him? Or say usefully? But it would be good to touch earth. It would be good to touch, for the last time, that agony, and to exorcise it—to drown in it derisively, savagely, or even, at last, indifferently. No, not indifferently—at last with acceptance; as one accepts such simple things as daybreak. Such simple and shattering things as daybreak. The strange and exciting mixture of astonishment and suffering with which—at a moment of discovery—one loses oneself in order to create oneself! The end that is still conscious of its beginnings. Birth that remembers death.

He watched the swarms of raindrops coming towards the headlamps, arriving and mysteriously vanishing, the continuous vanishing swarm, and suddenly, with a sense of power, he pressed his foot on the accelerator, and laughed. Life was good—life was going to be good. Unexplored, unfathomable, marvellous and terrible. Filthy, and incalculable. Cruel, and inexhaustible. Like this unceasing swarm of bright raindrops, like the waves breaking on the beach at the Gurnett, innumerable as the atoms in the brain. The wonderful nightmare, the wonderful and acceptable nightmare! When I slap on the kalsomine I think about those gals o' mine. I'm only a Spanish grammar, but my heart is pure as mud.

MILLER, ARTHUR
Focus
Introduction by the author **$7.95**

PURDY, JAMES
In a Shallow Grave
Introduction by Jerome Charyn **$6.95**

ROUECHÉ, BERTON
Black Weather
Introduction by John Brooks **$8.95**

SCHAEFER, JACK
The Collected Stories of Jack Schaefer
Introduction by Winfield Townley Scott **$8.95**

SOUTHERN, TERRY
Flash and Filigree
Introduction by William S. Burroughs **$7.95**

WEIDMAN, JEROME
I Can Get It for You Wholesale
Introduction by Garson Kanin **$7.95**

WILSON, SLOAN
The Man in the Gray Flannel Suit
Introduction by the author **$8.50**